Blue Blooded

By Shelly Bell

BENEDICTION NOVELS

Blue Blooded

Red Handed

White Collared

Part One: Mercy

Part Two: Greed

Part Three: Revenge

Part Four: Passion

Blue Blooded

A Benediction Novel

SHELLY BELL

AVON
IMPULSE
An Imprint of HarperCollins*Publishers*

EPub Edition OCTOBER 2015 ISBN: 9780062396488

Print Edition ISBN: 9780062396495

AM 10 9 8 7 6 5 4 3 2 1

Chapter One

PUFFING ON HIS Cuban cigar, the Senator reclined in his chair, a tumbler of scotch on the rocks in front of him. He stared down the two men sitting on the other side of his desk, daring them to repeat the words that had just been uttered.

Sweating profusely, FBI Agent Seymour Fink tugged on his tie, his Adam's apple bobbing above the buttoned collar of his shirt.

For a moment, the Senator considered retrieving his gun from his desk drawer and shooting the agent in the head, but he couldn't risk getting blood or splatters of brain matter on his tuxedo. After all, he had an important dinner to attend in an hour and didn't want to disappoint his wife.

He downed the rest of his drink and then shook the ice in the glass the way he'd like to shake the mobster who was fucking with him. "Tell me what you're going to do to fix the problem," he said calmly, unwilling to allow this minor bump in the road to waylay his plans.

There were only a few problems in the world money couldn't solve, and this was not one of them. His men were loyal to him because he paid them to be loyal. They believed in his cause because he paid them to believe in his cause. The whole goddamned US of A was manipulated by money, making it possible for great men like him to become even wealthier.

But he was different because unlike most men, he cared more for this country than he did money.

"Do, sir?" Using the sleeve of his suit jacket, Agent Fink wiped the sweat from his brow, cigar smoke circling around his head like a boa constrictor. "I'm not certain we should do—"

"You listen to me, you little prick. There is nothing that will stand in my way." The Senator hurled his tumbler against the wall above the fireplace, shattering the glass into a million tiny pieces. "Do you understand me? I've got your balls in a vise underneath my blade, so let's try this again. What are you going to do to fix the problem?"

These agents had been instrumental in helping him to get the charges against Anthony Rinaldi dropped in exchange for the mobster's valuable foreign contacts. A few months ago, the FBI had arrested Rinaldi for the extortion and kidnapping of Danielle Walker and, in the process, had discovered the bodies of thirteen young women buried on his property. But thanks to Agent Richard Evans and Fink, vital evidence had disappeared from the FBI's possession, helping the judge in the case, a man all too easy to blackmail due to his expensive cocaine habit, to render his decision in dropping the charges. In exchange, Rinaldi had brokered a deal with a Congo mafia leader, and an item found exclusively in the Congo region was about to arrive in the United States. Now that the ship had sailed and all the components were successfully in place, Rinaldi's usefulness had come to an end.

Seymour swallowed convulsively. "No one was supposed to get hurt."

"Don't pull that bullshit now. You knew when I approached you that lives would be lost for the greater good," the Senator said. He handed off his cigar and nodded to the other agent, a bruiser of a man whom he'd chosen not only for his twenty years of service to this country but for his lack of empathy. Agent Richard Evans understood the risks involved in his job, the three bullets he'd taken in the chest a testament to that fact.

Evans pinched the fat cigar between his fingers and, in a flash, locked his partner's head under his arm, pinning Fink's hands to the table and singeing the top of one with the foot of the cigar. Fink screamed, his smaller body thrashing wildly as he fruitlessly tried to escape from his partner and the pain he was inflicting.

The acrid scent of burnt flesh overpowered the cigar's sweet one, a smell he would forever more attribute to power.

By the time Evans released him, Fink's skin had turned pasty white, his shirt completely drenched from his sweat. He breathed heavily, nodding. "Consider the problem solved, sir. By this time tomorrow night, Rinaldi will be dead."

The Senator leaned back in his chair and smiled.

God bless the USA.

Chapter Two

TOURING THE DUNGEON located in the basement of a private mansion, Rachel Dawson ignored the decadent sights and sounds of sex going on all around her and kept her eye on the prize. After working her ass off to gain entrance into Benediction, the prestigious sex club owned by Cole DeMarco, she was finally here.

Sure she was the only woman in the room dressed in pants…scratch that. A couple Dommes or Dominatrices or wanna-be-Matrix characters were wearing black vinyl pants and wielding whips that would make Indiana Jones proud.

Although it was early in the evening and most of the upstairs fantasy rooms were still vacant, she'd gotten to play the role of voyeur as she'd observed two different scenes. The "teacher" bending the "schoolgirl" over his desk and smacking her with a ruler had titillated her, but

Rachel had remained a removed observer, her body not engaged by the fantasy.

But the ménage in the other room had hit her every button as if someone had plucked the fantasy right out of her head. Three men grappled for control in a tangle of hands, mouths, and cocks on a bed of red silk. After two of them managed to pin the third to the bed, he surrendered with a look of erotic bliss as he opened his mouth and accepted a cock while his legs were spread and his hole breached by one of the largest cocks Rachel had ever seen.

She couldn't take her eyes off the scene, imagining herself as the one pinned to the bed. Then she remembered she wasn't at Benediction to fulfill her fantasies or to act as voyeur. She was there to do a story about BDSM, and for that, she needed to go to the dungeon.

Unlike the fantasy rooms, the dungeon was packed. In here, the sights, smells, and sounds of passion and pain seduced her senses. The potent scents of leather, musk, and sweat teased her with the promise of sex. Everywhere Rachel looked, people indulged in their kinks without judgement or recrimination. She had read all about BDSM, done plenty of research online, and spoken to her friends, but nothing could have prepared her for what it would be like live and in Technicolor.

Her mouth grew dry at the sight of a naked woman suspended from the ceiling by rope and flowing white sheets, twirling as if she was an acrobat in a circus act.

Who had bound that woman? Was *he* here tonight? She studied the space, equal parts relieved and disappointed that she didn't find him.

Some of the BDSM stereotypes were in full force and effect on this Friday night, but as she looked around, she noticed a few people dressed casually in T-shirts and jeans. Surprisingly, it wasn't as easy as she expected to determine if a person was a Dominant or submissive. Considering two of her closest friends were submissives and members of this club, she shouldn't have been surprised. Neither one of them fit the profile of what Rachel imagined when she heard the word *submissive*. That was only one of the many reasons she'd decided to do an exposé on the southeast Michigan BDSM scene.

"Where is Cole?" she asked Danielle, her escort for the evening. "I thought you said he was down here." Even though Cole had married her friend Danielle a couple of months ago, he hadn't agreed to give Rachel a full-access, no-question-barred interview until last week. Apparently, he hadn't completely trusted her.

She rolled her eyes. *Yeah, whatever.* She was a reporter. What did trust have to do with anything? Facts were facts and the story always came first. If he didn't have anything to hide, he shouldn't worry.

"I lied," Danielle said, rubbing her pregnant belly. In her second trimester, she was just starting to show. "I figured if I didn't take you down here first you'd spend the entire time in Cole's office doing the interview."

Stopping to watch as one woman had her boot kissed by the naked guy kneeling at her feet, Rachel tossed her long black hair over her shoulder and smiled. She'd look awesome dressed in leather with a whip in her hand. She sighed. Tonight wasn't about her sexual needs. It was about work. It was always about work. And that's just the way she liked it.

Never willing to show weakness, Rachel tried not to flinch at the sudden cracking sound of the whip being wielded. "I would've come down to the dungeon eventually. After all, I've been waiting a long time to see it." Ever since she'd covered the murder of submissive socialite Alyssa Deveroux more than a year ago.

Jaxon, the widower, had been the prime suspect and a longtime member of Benediction. After Rachel followed him and his attorney, Kate Martin, around for several days, she found she actually respected Kate. Somehow when it was all over, they became friends, Rachel's first since childhood. Most women were offended by Rachel's blunt and often tactless comments, but not Kate. Rachel had found a kindred soul in Kate, a tough woman who wasn't afraid to get her hands a little dirty for the sake of her career.

With Kate into the BDSM lifestyle now and a member of Benediction along with her boyfriend, Jaxon, Rachel had been waiting for the opportunity to learn what really happened here. The exposé seemed like the perfect opportunity to do some exploring of the alternative sexual lifestyle.

Danielle commandeered Rachel by the elbow and led her away from the whip scene as if she sensed Rachel's discomfort. "If you had come for the open house last winter, you would've seen it a lot sooner."

They didn't go far before a scene caught Rachel's eye. On the floor, two women wearing nothing but black collars, cat ears, and long tails licked and rubbed up against each other as a man reclined on the couch and patted them on their heads. She'd read about pony and puppy play, but kitten play was a new one. She found it odd that the man wasn't participating in the scene other than to caress the top of their heads and watch.

Ready to explore some more, she continued walking through the dungeon. "I had a bigger story to work on that night." Mobster and ex-Benediction member Anthony Rinaldi had been arrested for kidnapping Danielle and her stepmother, as well as the murders of thirteen young women. All the local reporters were following up different angles and salivating for an exclusive. If she was ever going to land a prestigious investigative reporter position in New York, Rachel had to find something to wow them and prove she was more than just a pretty face. Just because she had big breasts didn't mean she deserved any less than the men who found their way to the coveted investigative reporter spots in the New York or California television markets.

"It was your choice to forgo the chance at seeing Benediction in order to cover the Rinaldi case," Danielle said, bringing them to an area with loveseats and chairs.

"Come on, the arrest of Anthony Rinaldi was the story of the year." Rachel winced, realizing how harsh she sounded. After all, Danielle had been one of his victims. "No offense." She shrugged one shoulder. "I had to cover it. But now I've got the time to do this exposé the justice it deserves, and in order to do that, I need to know everything that goes on here."

Danielle harrumphed. "Knowing the kind of reporter you are, I doubt there's a kink or fetish out there you haven't come across in your research."

She scanned the room, checking to see if there was anything here other than the kitten play that she didn't recognize. Nope, nothing she hadn't seen on the Internet.

A petite Asian woman spanking another woman over a bench.

Another woman using a cane on the buttocks of a very large man who wore a spreader bar between his legs and a metal ball stretcher around his purplish-red scrotum. *Ouch, that looks painful.* Rachel grimaced and quickly turned away.

A beautiful redheaded woman was on her hands and knees, a fucking machine plowing her pussy with a giant dildo as a leather-clad man stood over her and watched with a stern expression.

Sprinkled throughout the space were a few different flogging scenes, but one in particular caught her eye. The man held a flogger in each hand, raining the falls in a figure-eight pattern onto the woman's reddened back. Light moans flew from her mouth as she arched up to meet the strikes, the couple completely in tune with one another.

Her gaze continued to bounce among the various scenes, until she spotted *him*.

Holding dark ash-colored rope taut between his hands as he talked to a woman wearing a latex dress that just barely covered her nipples, he appeared completely in his element. She must have said something that amused him because he threw back his head and laughed. Rather than the suit and tie she normally saw him in, he was wearing ripped jeans and a simple black Henley. Since she'd last seen him a couple of months ago, he'd grown out his light brown hair from the buzz cut. The half-naked woman raked her fingers down his shoulder, drawing Rachel's attention.

Had his arms always been that sinewy?

As she answered Danielle's question about her research, an unfamiliar flurry of butterflies whipped around in her stomach. "I like to be thorough. And since I barely sleep, I have plenty of time to do some reading at night," she said, ripping her gaze away from him. Just the sight of the damn man gave her indigestion. She sucked in a quick breath to kill those pesky insects wreaking havoc on her insides.

Her hands covering her stomach, Danielle plopped down in one of the oversized chairs. "You need to do something other than work."

Working was as vital to Rachel as breathing, but it wasn't the only thing she did. It was just the most important. "I do. I go out with you and the other freaks for drinks every Thursday night." A group that also included Gracie, Lisa, and Kate.

"Other than that. You don't have any hobbies, you never date—"

Rachel perched on the arm of Danielle's chair. "I don't need to waste my time dating when I can have sex whenever I want." Her cell phone had a list of men's names to rival any little black book, every one of them available to her at a moment's notice.

"That's probably true, but when's the last time you slept with someone just for the sake of having sex and not because you need some information for a story you're working on?"

Rachel sunk her teeth into her bottom lip as she mentally went through her sexual Rolodex. Huh, maybe Danielle had a point. "Jacob Parkman, ten years ago. His parents played bridge with my parents every Sunday, and while the rest of my family was outside playing in our yard, Jacob and I were ridding ourselves of our pesky little V-cards." Last thing she heard he was a precious-gems jeweler and had five kids with one on the way. She smiled, remembering him fondly. He was a good man, but not for her. "That was two minutes of foreplay and eighteen seconds of intercourse I'll never forget."

Danielle's jaw dropped. "You lost your virginity while your parents were at the house? Are they ultraliberal or something?"

She laughed. "No. Just oblivious."

Without looking, she felt a presence standing directly behind her, her body humming as it always did whenever he was in the same vicinity.

Danielle looked over Rachel's shoulder with a wicked twinkle in her eye. "Logan, you remember Rachel."

Rachel had met Logan a year and a half ago through their mutual friend Kate. Having just finished her report about a mother who killed her two kids and then stored their bodies in a freezer, Rachel hadn't been in the mood to socialize. But she hadn't wanted to disappoint Kate, so she'd gone out anyway.

Rachel had heard only good things about Logan and was eager to meet him. But after Kate had introduced them, he ignored her most of the evening, acknowledging her only to argue with her on every little comment she made. After an hour of it, she'd decided to keep her mouth shut, not wanting to ruin her friend's night. She'd spent the rest of the evening observing the way Logan smiled at Kate...spoke to Kate...lit up for Kate.

That night, she'd realized Logan was in love with Kate.

And that he didn't like *her.*

She stood and faced him, ready to try to play nice. She gestured to his hands. "Still playing with ropes I see."

"Still pretending you're not curious about them." His expression didn't change, but she heard the smirk in his voice.

"I'm not curious. I got over playing cops and robbers when I turned seven." She tossed her long hair over her shoulder. "And by the way, I always did the tying up."

He chuckled. "Of course you did."

"Why would you say 'of course'?"

He inched closer, the spicy musk of him reaching her nose. "Because you're a control freak."

She crossed her arms and took a step toward him, so close she had to tilt her chin up to look into his copper-colored eyes. "If the shoe fits..."

He tossed the rope onto the small end table beside Danielle's chair and wrapped his hand around the top of Rachel's arm, the heat of his fingers searing her skin. "No, there's a difference between me and you." He lowered his voice. "I find serenity in control while you wouldn't know serenity if it bit you on that finely shaped ass of yours."

He let go of her and she stumbled back into the chair. If she wasn't mistaken, there was a compliment blended in with that insult. Reminded by his comment of *how* she kept her ass finely shaped, she turned from Logan and nudged Danielle on the shoulder. "I do too have a hobby. I do Pilates five days a week. So there, I do something other than work."

Danielle rose from the chair. "It doesn't count if you're on your cell phone the whole time."

"I bet I could teach you how to relax," Logan said from behind her.

She twirled around, raising her eyebrow. "You gonna let me tie you up and gag you? Because that would definitely put a smile on my face."

Laughing, Danielle walked away, giving her a little wave. Traitor.

He chuckled, the sound of it low and deep, which for some reason created a warm, syrupy sensation throughout her body. "Not a chance. But an hour with me, your bones would turn to liquid and you'd have the best night's sleep of your life."

"All from a little rope?"

"No," he said, backing her up against the wall. He caged her in, his right hand resting above her head and the other stroking her hip. "From the heart-pumping, thigh-clenching, eye-rolling orgasms I'd give you while you were bound and gagged."

Her breath stalled in her chest as the image he suggested flashed before her eyes, threatening to steal the tightly reined control she kept on herself. Then she remembered most men were full of shit. Plenty of others had promised to rock her world in the bedroom and not one had ever succeeded. "Pretty cocky, Soldier Boy. Too bad there's no way you'll ever get to deliver."

He lowered his head, his lips hovering dangerously close to hers. "Afraid to try, Tiger?"

Afraid? She'd gone skydiving. Swum with sharks. Interviewed serial killers. "What are you, twelve? If I decide to try something, it's because it will help with the story I'm working on and not because of your not-so-subtle manipulation."

He frowned. "I take it you're still planning on doing the exposé, huh? I know Cole agreed to an interview, but he's never going to allow a news crew inside Benediction or speak on camera for you."

She didn't believe in the word *never.*

She pushed him back with her hands on his chest, allowing them to linger long enough to feel his muscles ripple under her palms. "That's because he doesn't understand how this will benefit those who engage in the BDSM lifestyle. The majority of Americans view it as a dangerous perversity, and that's because it's kept secret. Knowledge is power. If it were brought out into the open, people would see some of it already finds its way into their own bedrooms."

His jaw tensed, his lips tightening. "You may have fooled your boss into believing that angle of yours, but you're not going to fool Cole and you certainly haven't fooled me. Sex sells. You want to do this story to boost your own career, not to help the BDSM community."

What was wrong with a woman fighting to become the best in her field? She was so sick of men telling her there was something wrong with her because she didn't do relationships or seek a husband. As if the fact she was closing in on thirty years old should scare her into wanting more with a man than just a one-night stand. The men she fucked got an orgasm, and she got information. In the ten years since she'd left her parents' home, a few men had tried to tame her, but she was out the door before they could get their pants zipped. No one would ever turn her into a spineless woman like her mother.

Realizing her hands were still on his chest, she let them drop to her side. "Can't a girl do both? After all, true altruism doesn't exist. I could be like all the other reporters and uncover the true danger of the underground debauchery, but instead I'm planning on showing a positive view of it."

He grabbed her wrists and brought them over her head. "How can you do that without experiencing it firsthand?"

Chapter Three

RACHEL'S HEART BEGAN to race, excitement thrumming through her veins. "I'm here, aren't I?"

"Just walking the floors of Benediction doesn't make you a part of it. Until you surrender, you'll never understand the truth of the lifestyle."

"You're making quite the assumption, Soldier Boy." She brought her knee up to the level of his crotch and pressed it against him as a threat. "Maybe I'm the one who likes to be in control."

He glanced down at her knee before smiling and shaking his head disbelievingly. "I'm sure you tell yourself that, *Tiger*, but that's only because you're not strong enough to surrender."

"What's wrong with being the Dominant?"

His smile disappeared, his expression growing serious. "Nothing if that's what fulfills you." He released his grip on her wrists, and in an odd display of what she would believe was tenderness coming from a different man, tucked a strand of her hair behind her ear. "But don't you want to know what it's like on the other side? I promise, I'll keep you safe. You can even keep your clothes on."

She could count on one hand the people she trusted completely, but since Logan would never jeopardize his friendship with Kate, she at least trusted him not to harm her.

Besides, wasn't that why she was here? She wanted to know what it was like to be a part of this world, what drew her friends to this lifestyle. She didn't get off on pain, and she couldn't imagine enjoying submission, but bondage fascinated her. Some of the photos she'd seen of Japanese rope bondage were absolutely beautiful, more artistic than sexual.

And if she was honest with herself, she wanted to know what Logan did to earn him a bondage bunny fan club.

Rachel eased her knee off his dick and lowered her leg to the floor. "Fine. I'll try it. For the story. Will you talk me through it? Explain what you're doing?"

He blinked a few times as if he wasn't sure he'd heard her correctly. "Will I be explaining it to Rachel the woman or Rachel the reporter?"

How could she answer when she didn't know herself? She took a step back, needing some distance from him in order to maintain a clear head. "Does it matter?"

He smiled as if he knew what she was doing. "I thought you were braver than that, Tiger."

Logan may have left the US Army, but it had left its mark on him. He stood like a soldier at attention, his spine tall and his shoulders rigid. In the heat of the moment during one of their many banters, she'd lobbed the nickname "Soldier Boy" at him, to which he'd thrown back the nickname "Tiger" at her.

"Why do you call me Tiger?" she asked.

His tongue swiped across his lower lip, leaving it glistening. "Tigers are cunning, ferocious...with cutting claws and a razor-sharp bite. They go after what they want." Taking away the precious space she so desperately required to stay in control, he inched closer.

That's how he saw her? As a dangerous predator?

She moved to push him away, but he trapped her wrists in his hands.

His gaze burned into her. "But they're also sleek and stunning creatures who are fighting to survive just like all the other animals in the wild jungle."

Although she was dressed, she felt completely exposed, as if he could see straight into the heart of her. And that terrified her. If he could scratch underneath her surface with such ease, what would happen if she ever let her guard down with him? Was her desire to feel his ropes on her worth the risk?

Yes. After all, she was apparently a tiger, and tigers were brave.

She puffed out a breath before admitting the truth as to which Rachel he'd bind tonight. "Both. I'm doing this mostly for the story, but I'm doing it for me as well."

A slight smile played at the corners of his lips. He picked the rope off the table and grabbed his duffle then, taking her by the elbow, brought her over to part of the dungeon that wasn't being used.

Her gaze fell onto the wooden spanking bench. She hoped he wasn't thinking of putting her over that thing.

He squeezed the crook of her arm lightly. "We're not going to do anything other than bondage. I just chose this area because it was empty. Sadomasochism and discipline aren't my kinks. I tie women up and give them so much pleasure, they think they'll die from it."

The idea was hot, but she knew he was full of shit. Yeah, an orgasm was nice, but it was a minute of pleasurable tension followed by a few seconds of pulsing. Nothing to write home about. She smoothed her fingers over the rope, surprised by its softness. "And what about your pleasure? Do you fuck the women when they're tied up?"

"Occasionally, but it's not about the sex. My pleasure comes from the power of having her at my mercy and from holding her trust in my hands."

It was on the tip of her tongue to ask if merely holding her trust in his hands gave him an orgasm, but when he began sliding the rope over his hands, she became distracted.

"Any health concerns I should know about? Circulation problems? Any issue with claustrophobia or anxiety?"

"No physical or mental health issues," she said, wondering if he was this invasive with all the women he played with. And according to her friend Gracie, Cole's former slave, he played with a lot.

He folded the rope into two pieces. "This is hemp rope. I'm going to do a basic breast bondage." He came up behind her and gripped her shoulders tightly. "I want you to get a sense of what it feels like."

His hands skated down to her upper back and then circled her torso, sliding around her rib cage, just under her breasts. She held her breath, the view of his large, capable hands on her body stirring up those darned butterflies in her belly again. Realizing if he moved his thumbs just a bit he could flick her nipples, a shot of arousal coursed through her, sending her pulse soaring.

His cheek whispered across her own as he leaned over her shoulder. "You okay? Your heart is racing."

"Yeah," she said, remembering to breathe. "My heart's always fast."

She felt his lips tug up in a smile against her cheek, but he didn't call her out on her lie. He also didn't touch her nipples, but instead returned to her back as he pulled the rope toward her spine. Then, before she could recover, his hands were above her breasts and she sucked in a breath, her nipples stiffening almost painfully.

This wasn't happening. She couldn't be attracted to Logan Bradford. The ex-soldier now defense attorney was the opposite of what she needed in a man. It didn't matter that he was sexy with a body that she'd like to strip and lick from head to toe. He was also arrogant, condescending, and too damn dominant. So why was she suddenly slick between her legs?

His motions stopped and she heard him take in his own ragged breath. "Do you want more?"

Her breasts felt swollen and heavy, more sensitive, the lace of her bra almost abrasive to them and her tingling nipples. She could barely manage to get her mouth working in order to answer. "Yes," she choked out, her voice sounding raspy.

Why was her body responding this way? Was it because of the rope? Would she become aroused if anyone tied her up like this?

He picked up his duffle and, with his hand splayed along her lower back, directed her toward a different part of the dungeon. Until a few minutes ago, she'd been an observer, eliciting little attention from the members, but with the ropes adorning her breasts and Logan making a silent claim over her with his hand on her, she drew plenty of interest. While some of the members looked upon her with lustful appreciation, she didn't miss the spark of jealousy in the eyes of a couple of bleach blondes whom she'd wager were part of the unofficial Logan Bradford fan club.

As a reporter, she was used to having people watch her, but the television separated her from the audience. In here, she couldn't avoid their reactions, and judging by the dampness of her panties, she liked it. What did that say about her? Did she have a kinky side?

Logan stopped her in front of a mirrored wall and turned her to it. He stood behind her, the heat of his body warming her back. "Look at yourself. You're beautiful."

In all the times she'd stared in the mirror, she'd never seen herself like this. Her skin was flushed, pink staining her cheeks, and the pupils of her brown eyes were dilated. The long strands of her dark hair draped over the rope, framing the sides of her breasts, which strained against her red blouse. Because the ropes lifted them better than any bra she'd ever worn, her jutting nipples pointed high and tight.

"Keep looking at yourself in the mirror. Watch while I bind your legs," Logan said, his eyes catching hers in the mirror. He grabbed more rope from his bag and then kneeled in front of her, his head level with her breasts.

Heat surged through her. If her hands had been free, she might have given in to the urge to lay them on his chiseled cheeks or run her fingers through his short brown hair.

A burst of panic caused Rachel's heart to race. She wouldn't become another member of his bondage bunny fan club. Allowing him to tie her up may answer her deep-seated curiosity about bondage, but it didn't mean anything more. It couldn't mean anything more. She wouldn't let it.

A look of concentration befell him, his brows pulled down and his tongue pressing against the inside of his cheek. He folded the rope in half and looped it around her waist then peered up at her. "I need you to sit for the next part."

Because she didn't have use of her hands, he helped her sit, placing one hand on her hip and one on her back, supporting her weight as she lowered herself to the floor.

Once she was settled, he slowly glided his fingers up her ankle and over her calves. Chill bumps popped up on her arms as she let out a puff of air through her parted lips.

His eyes locked on hers, and he slid his hands between her thighs, stroking his thumb back and forth. "Open your legs for me."

He crawled between and spread them wide, placing her feet flat on the floor. Without clothes, this position would've been obscene, her pussy open for anyone to see. Even dressed, she felt vulnerable. She didn't want to enjoy being out of control, but she couldn't ignore the way her body was responding to Logan and his ropes. Thank goodness he had no idea how wet she'd gotten since he'd begun touching her.

"I'm going to do an open-leg crab position on you called *Kaikyaku Kani*." He bent her legs, pushing them toward her chest. He separated the two pieces of rope and ran one down the length of each leg before wrapping it around her thigh and shin three times.

Heat snaked to her pussy every time his skin brushed across hers. Her position stretched the fabric of her panties so that it rubbed against her clit, and a slow pulse in her core had her aching for relief. She burned to touch herself to relieve that ache, but with her hands bound behind her, she was powerless to do it.

Kneeling, Logan busily and methodically worked between her thighs, only inches from her pussy. Could he smell her arousal? Was binding her arousing him?

He crossed the rope from one end to the other and tied it with a hitch. He rocked back, taking his hands away from her body. Breathing heavily and looking down at the floor, he clenched and unclenched them, over and over. Then he shot to his feet and rummaged through his bag, coming back and kneeling before her once again, this time with a long pink vibrator in his hands.

"Rachel?" His eyes locked onto hers as he swallowed hard. "Can I use this on you? I'll honor your limits and use it over your clothes."

It wouldn't work. It never did. As aroused as she was, she still wouldn't reach climax unless she rubbed her clitoris with her own fingers, and even then, there was only a fifty-fifty chance it would happen. She was a freak. Did she really want Logan and the rest of Benediction to know she couldn't orgasm?

Then again, did it really matter what anyone thought about her?

"Yes," she said, deciding she was too aroused to pass on the chance of an orgasm. "You can use it on me."

Logan didn't take his eyes off her as he flipped on the vibrator. The toy's buzzing sent a chill racing down her arms, and although she hadn't thought it was possible, her nipples beaded even tighter than before. Logan's gaze dipped to her chest. His nostrils flared as he moved closer to her and laid the tip of the vibrator on her nipple. Her pussy clenched around nothing, and a loud moan spilled from her lips.

He lazily brushed the vibrator over her nipple, back and forth, before moving to the other nipple and doing the same. She tried to close her legs, tried to pull her hands free, but she was immobile. Completely at his will unless she told him to stop.

She didn't want him to stop.

Their gazes locked and his lips inched closer to hers. He dragged the vibrator down her belly toward her waiting pussy, and she cried out when it rolled over her clit. He teased her, running it all the way down her spread slit before sliding it up again. With each pass of the toy across her clit, she felt herself edge closer and closer toward climax. The muscles inside her pussy tightened, her legs trembling.

Teasing her, he hovered his lips over hers, his warm breath mingling with her own. She wanted his mouth on hers. Wanted to know if he tasted as good as he looked. What would it take for him to kiss her?

"Please," she whispered, pleading with her eyes.

His own hooded eyes darkened, his irises swallowed by his pupils. He cupped her cheek in his hand, skimming his thumb over her desperate lips. His mouth inched closer to hers, and she closed her eyes, ready for him.

"Sir Logan?" A voice she instantly recognized as her friend Gracie's broke the tension and popped the odd spell she was under.

Rachel's arousal slid away, taking any chance of orgasm with it. What had she been thinking? Thank goodness Gracie had interrupted.

Logan's lips tightened into a straight line, and before he turned toward Gracie, he gave her a look that told her they weren't finished. "Gracie, we're in the middle of a scene."

"Anthony Rinaldi is here," Gracie blurted out.

Logan grew rigid, his hands balling into fists. "Where is he?"

A different and more familiar kind of excitement pulsed through Rachel. How the hell did Rinaldi get out of prison? He'd been held without bond, and his trial wasn't for another two months. If she hurried, she could get the story on the air before any other reporter learned about it.

Gracie's eyes were wide with worry. "Outside the front entrance with Master Cole and Adrian. I think they could use your assistance, sir."

"Gracie, please help get Rachel out of the ropes. Since it was her first time, I didn't tie the knots tight." His eyes flashing a warning, he pointed his finger at Rachel. "Do not follow me outside." Before she could protest, he dashed away, leaving her behind and treating her as if she was a helpless little girl. Which, in these ropes, she kind of was.

Grinning widely, Gracie knelt and quickly worked to untie the knots. "So you and Logan, huh? I knew there was something going on. Every time you were together, I could practically see the sparks flying."

She raised her brow. "All we ever do is argue."

"Exactly," Gracie said as she untied Rachel's leg. "It's like foreplay for you two. He's a lawyer. He loves to argue. And you're…well, you're you. You need someone who will challenge you. Logan won't let you get away with the shit you pull on the guys you typically date." She bit her lip, her head tilting as if she was pondering something deep. "I never considered it before, but I think a Dom is just what you need."

"I don't need a Dom, Gracie. I'm not into kink," she said, disregarding the past few minutes as a fluke. "Tonight was about getting firsthand experience for my exposé on BDSM. Nothing more."

Talking a million miles a minute about her concern that Rinaldi was here to hurt Cole and Danielle, Gracie finished untying her. Rachel threw off the rope and gave Gracie a quick peck on the cheek before racing across the dungeon and hurrying up the staircase to the main floor. Thanks to Gracie's quick hands, she wasn't far behind Logan.

Somehow without checking, he knew it was her. "There's no story here, Rachel."

"Are you kidding me? Rinaldi's out of jail. That's an eleven o'clock top story, and I've got an exclusive. No way am I going to miss the opportunity."

At the top of the stairs, he stopped and turned, blocking her way. "Cole will never allow cameramen to get past his gate and onto his property."

Anger suffused her. "I don't need my crew. All I need to do is find out how he got out of prison and why he's here. This is my career, Logan. It's what I do."

"Do it and you'll likely lose your chance for an interview with Cole."

She held her ground, squaring her shoulders and looking Logan straight in the eye so he'd know how much this meant to her. "I'm willing to take that risk."

He clenched his jaw. "Well, I'm not. You'll only get in the way." He leaned toward her, getting in her face. "I see you out there and I'll make certain Cole throws you off the property. For good." He stormed off, heading toward the entrance of the club at the front of the mansion.

The hell she'd stay inside. She hadn't backed down from a story yet, not even when her life was on the line. She'd stared down the barrel of a shotgun of a disgruntled landowner, waded through sewage to find environmental dumping by a Fortune 500 company, and braved a pack of pit bulls during a raid on a dog-fighting arena. Placing her life on the line was the least she could do to keep the world apprised of the injustices.

With Rinaldi at the mansion, she had her chance to break the biggest story of the year. No way would she stay inside and cower like a prepubescent girl at her first dance.

Rachel climbed the last steps and went in the opposite direction of Logan. While she wasn't glad Rinaldi was here, she was grateful his arrival had interrupted her scene. If Gracie hadn't shown when she had, who knows what would've happened between her and Logan. His unfair view of her and his threat to have her permanently banned from Benediction confirmed he was wrong for her. No one, especially Logan, would prevent her from achieving her dreams. From this point forward, she'd stay as far away from him as she could.

Chapter Four

PASSING THE GROUP of members milling around the entryway of the club, Rachel tried to recall the layout of the house from the tour Danielle had taken her on earlier in the evening. Logan would be watching to make sure she didn't follow him out the front door. She needed to find an alternative exit. Going through the garage would draw too much attention, since she'd have to open it in order to get outside. But in the den, there was a sliding glass door that led to the backyard of the home.

She strolled into the room and smiled, trying to pretend she belonged there, even though she didn't fit in any better with this crowd than she had with those in the dungeon. Dressed in formal wear, the mingling guests drank champagne and chatted with each other as if they were at a black-tie affair rather than a sex club.

As she made her way through the space, averting her gaze so as to not invite any conversation, she recognized some of the guests as prominent members of the metro Detroit political and judicial system. Danielle and Kate hadn't been kidding when they'd told her she'd run into a few familiar faces. No wonder everyone at Benediction had to sign a confidentiality statement. She checked out the colored bands on their wrists to see what kink they were into, wondering what the green and blue ones meant.

Keeping her head down so that no one would recognize her and ask questions about why a nonmember reporter was roaming the rooms of Benediction without supervision, she edged her way to the door and stepped out into the night, breathing the spring air into her lungs.

Even from the back of the house, she could hear the angry voices coming from the front. She slunk around the perimeter of the home, staying close to the walls, until she reached the driveway by the garage.

A beautiful garden filled with ruby and white flowers, small blooming trees, and fat green bushes lined the front of the house. Avoiding the floodlights, she tiptoed behind one of the bushes and crouched down, slipping her hand into her pants pocket for her cell so that she could text her news crew and record Rinaldi. Coming up empty, she patted the other side, clenching her teeth when she remembered she'd left it in her purse at Benediction's coat check.

Staying low, she peered around the bush, spotting the arguing men. Flanked by Logan and his bodyguard, Adrian, Cole stood toe-to-toe with Anthony Rinaldi. She surveyed the area, sure she'd see a couple of Rinaldi's own men somewhere in the vicinity. Despite having spent the past several months in prison awaiting trial, he was still considered the head of the Rinaldi crime family.

Anthony Rinaldi looked surprisingly well for a man who'd spent his past months behind bars. His gray hair was cut short, and he'd lost some weight that his petite body really couldn't afford to lose, but if she didn't know better, she could've believed he'd come straight from a month-long stay at a luxury spa. How did he get out and why was he here?

"Your membership was revoked when you kidnapped my wife and the Feds uncovered the bodies on your property," Cole said, not yelling, but loud just the same. "I'm not sure how you managed to get past the gate, but I can assure you I will make sure it doesn't happen again."

Rinaldi didn't appear at all intimidated, his smile almost friendly. "All charges have been dropped, and I received a wonderful apology from the governor himself. I was set up for those crimes."

Cole's hands clenched into fists, and Rachel was sure it was taking everything he had not to beat up the man who'd planned on torturing and murdering Danielle. "I don't know how the hell you managed that, but regardless, you're not welcome here. If you want your money back—"

"Keep it." Rinaldi spread his arms out wide. "After I sue the government for false imprisonment, I'll start my own sex club. One with a real dungeon." He grabbed his crotch. "That way, when your pretty bride gets tired of you, I can show her how a real man fucks."

Growling, Cole lurched forward and grabbed Rinaldi by the collar, holding his fist back, prepared to punch. Adrian intercepted, pulling Cole off Rinaldi. "Cole, let him go. It's not worth it. You have a family to think about."

"Yeah, well, I don't," Logan said, stepping forward and punching Rinaldi in the mouth. "That was for Danielle. And this is for Kate." Before Rinaldi could recover, he punched him again, this time in the nose. Rinaldi fell to his knees, blood pouring down his chin and dripping onto the driveway. "If I ever see your face again, you're a dead man."

Rinaldi coughed and spit blood onto Logan's shoes. "Fine, I'll go. But you're the dead man, Logan Bradford. Enjoy your last few hours, because you just signed your death warrant." He stumbled as he got to his feet while Cole, Logan, and Adrian turned to go inside.

She remained hidden, watching Rinaldi begin the quarter-mile walk down the driveway toward the gate. Where were his car and bodyguards? The back of her neck itched, her intuition telling her there was more to the story here.

She had to follow him. She darted from her position behind the bush to the shallow woods that edged the length of the driveway. Staying on the grass, she remained twenty paces behind him, listening to him mumble and curse under his breath about his ride. He staggered as if he was under the influence of drugs or alcohol. Had he been like that before Logan had hit him or was it a result of the punches he'd taken?

When he got to the gate, he pushed a button to open it and ambled out, immediately turning to his left where he stopped by a Lexus parked on the side of the road. She deduced he must have gotten onto the Benediction property by following on foot behind a member's car as it entered through the gate. No wonder Cole's security hadn't known Rinaldi was on the property until he made it to the front door.

If Rinaldi was inebriated or physically impaired from Logan's beating, she didn't want him getting behind the wheel. She stepped onto the driveway, intending to stop him, but before she could speak, a dark sedan with tinted windows drove up and pulled to the side of the road behind Rinaldi.

Swaying, Rinaldi swore, sticking his hand under his coat jacket and patting down his pockets then pulling out his jingling keys. He suddenly seemed to be in a hurry, jamming his keys into his car door while looking over his shoulder at the sedan. Who was in the car?

Two men stepped out of the vehicle, dressed almost identically in dark suits. One of the men was massive, wide-shouldered and easily six and a half feet tall. If he wasn't in a suit, she'd peg him for a professional wrestler or football player. Knowing what kind of business Rinaldi was in, she'd wager that guy was an enforcer. The second guy was as tiny as the other was huge, but in this case, size didn't matter because in his hands was a gun, and it was pointed straight at Rinaldi.

She moved a little closer, trying to ascertain the men's identities. After covering the Rinaldi case, she was familiar with the major players in his organization, and she'd never come across these men in her research. With Rinaldi out of prison, it was possible that another crime family or someone within his own organization would take the opportunity to try to eliminate him. So why hadn't he brought his bodyguards with him?

The guy with the gun spoke, his voice betraying his anxiety with its shakiness. "We told you to lie low and enjoy our gift to you, Anthony. It doesn't appear you took our orders well."

Rinaldi showed none of the earlier signs of intoxication, as if the gun had instantly sobered him up. Like a true sociopath, the sight of the gun didn't seem to faze him, sneering at the men when others would have run. "That's because I don't take orders. I make them."

The man shook his head. "You're in no position to give us orders anymore."

"The fuck you say," Rinaldi said. "I don't care who the hell you two think you are, telling me—"

The big guy stood as still as stone as his partner did all the talking. Not that he had to speak. His mere presence was intimidating enough.

The man with the gun took a step closer to Rinaldi. "We're the ones who got your ass out of prison and helped you get away with murder."

Rinaldi clapped his hands once and spread them apart. "Quid pro quo, my friends. I helped you and you helped me. But we're done now."

"That's where you're wrong," the little guy said. "You don't get to be done. Not until..."

Rachel's body buzzed as an all-too-familiar scent engulfed her and a hand clutched her shoulder. She didn't even have to check to know Logan was standing right behind her, most likely foaming at the mouth because she hadn't followed his instructions like an obedient submissive.

"What are you doing?" Logan asked. "I thought I told you to stay inside."

She bit the inside of her cheek and silently counted back from ten to keep herself from going into a tirade. Then she glanced at him, hopefully conveying with her eyes what she'd like to vocalize. "Shh. Keep your voice down."

Logan tugged on her arm, trying to drag her away. "You do not need to overhear a mobster's conversation with his men," he whispered, although a little too loudly for her taste. They didn't need Rinaldi or the mysterious men to know they were hiding in the bushes behind the fence watching their little meeting. "That can only end in disaster."

She elbowed him in the gut, enjoying his wince. Crouching lower, she wrapped her hands around the cool metal bars of the fence. "They're not his men. Listen."

The little guy rushed Rinaldi, backing him up against his Lexus, and stuck the gun into his ribs.

"Fine," Rinaldi said, tripping over his feet before grabbing on to the side mirror for support. "Leopold arrives at Port Everglades at noon in two days."

Rinaldi continued talking, his speech coming out so slurred, she couldn't make out the words. If only she could record the conversation, she could decipher what he was saying later. She needed her damned phone.

She spun around and slapped her hands on Logan's chest. "I need a cell, and I left mine at the coat check, so give me yours."

He narrowed his eyes on her. "No, we're going back inside Benediction to get your things and then you're leaving."

"I'm not going anywhere. There's something weird going on with Rinaldi and those guys. Now give me your phone." She slid her hands to his hips, her fingers edging into his pockets, coming across a large bulge at the top of his left one.

Logan grabbed her hands and twisted her arms behind her back. "Watch it."

Not one to back down from a fight, she squirmed, struggling to get out of his hold without having to resort to kneeing him in the nuts and possibly alerting Rinaldi and those men to her presence.

His eyes flashing with warning, Logan backed her against the fence and pressed his hard body against hers, confirming the impressive bulge she'd felt in his jeans hadn't been her imagination. She cursed her reaction, liquid heat spreading through her pussy and her nipples tightening as if begging for Logan's touch. That's what happened when she went without sex for three months. Her body didn't care that she disliked the man holding her hostage or that she was in the middle of investigating a huge story. Her body wanted to finish off what they had started in the dungeon.

But her brain, not her body, was responsible for her success in the news industry. Nothing, *nothing*, kept her from her doing her job. Which was why it was strange that with Logan, her brain seemed to want to go on vacation and all reason fled out the window. That was the only explanation she had for rising on her toes, wrapping her leg around his ass, and tugging him closer so that she could grind her pulsing clit against said bulge.

Logan's lips parted, his breath coming fast and hot, and his eyes, still warning her of danger, grew hooded with lust. She was two seconds from begging him to fuck her where they stood. But at the same time, she couldn't allow herself to get distracted from her goal.

She needed that phone.

He released her hands and instead of taking the opportunity to push him away, she clutched the neck of his shirt, pulling him down to her. His long, tapered fingers delved into her hair, his palms cupping the base of her skull as his mouth dipping closer and closer. She coasted her hands down his arms, his muscles bunching and contracting under her touch, and rested them on his hips. As his lips lingered over hers, she slid her fingers into his pockets until she hit the jackpot, and then she wrapped them around the phone.

A sound like a firecracker going off in the street had them jumping apart as if someone had dumped a bucket of cold water on them. Phone forgotten, she whipped her head toward the noise just in time to see Rinaldi clutching his chest as another two explosions rang out and blood splattered from his head, landing on everything in its path. Rinaldi bounced off the hood of his car then slid onto the pebbles underneath his feet with a sickening thud.

"Oh, God," Rachel said, feeling as though her heart was in her throat.

Logan covered her mouth with his hand and tugged her behind the bush. As if they'd heard her, the two men crept toward the fence with deadly precision, armed and ready to shoot. She held her breath and flattened herself against Logan, trying to disappear. There was no way she was going to die before becoming an Emmy-winning New York news anchor. She'd worked too hard to die now, this way. She should at least get to report Rinaldi's murder on air before she literally bit the bullet.

An incessant buzzing of a phone broke the silence. The men stopped, the big one pulling his cell from his pocket then speaking into it. "It's done. Yes, right away." He slid the phone into his pocket and narrowed his gaze on the area behind the fence as if he could see them hiding behind the bush. He shook his head and turned to his partner. "It's time to go. We need to get Leopold from Port Everglades at noon the day after tomorrow and then get to the target in Las Vegas by Friday."

As soon as they drove away, leaving Rinaldi's body behind, Rachel broke out of Logan's arms and took a deep breath, blocking out the emotions threatening to bring her to her knees. Now that the imminent danger was over, it was time to get to work, fear be damned.

Calling to Logan over her shoulder, she began the short trek back to the club. "Let's go. I've got a story to report."

Chapter Five

In the two hours since she'd watched Rinaldi's brain matter splatter onto the ground, Rachel had run the gamut of emotions, and right now, she was pissed. She should be on television reporting the crime instead of drinking tepid tea from a foam cup as she and Logan sat in the interview room at the local police station waiting for Officer Hanover to finish his questioning. He'd left the room about twenty minutes ago to take a phone call and hadn't returned. Rachel hated to be left waiting. The police were reviewing Benediction's video feeds to determine if the murder had been caught on tape.

"Are you okay?" Logan asked from across the table, his voice laced with what she recognized as sympathy.

Why was he being nice? Despite what had happened between them at Benediction, Logan despised her and the feeling was mutual. Since the first time they'd met, they'd argued every time they were in a room together. It was as if she was dynamite and he was the fuse. What Gracie called "sparks flying" was more like a violent explosion. They simply tolerated each other for their friends' sake.

Which is why tonight had thrown her for a loop.

She lifted her cup and unnecessarily blew on the cooled liquid. "Sure. I've been around dead bodies before." In her profession, a trip to the county morgue was a regular occurrence. There wasn't a week that went by she didn't have to report a story on a child shot by a stray bullet or beaten to death by a parent. If she could handle seeing that firsthand, she could certainly handle seeing a murderer get his just deserts.

Logan reclined in his chair, crossing his arms over his chest, eyes narrowing on her. "But you've never seen someone killed before, have you?"

"No." She took a sip of her tea, taking the time to gather her thoughts about where these questions were leading. She didn't like the way he looked at her as if she was a witness on the stand. She'd seen him in the courtroom and this was definitely his defense attorney cross-examination mode. As her nana had taught her, the best defense was a strong offense. "You have though. In the military. You must be used to it."

"It's not something you ever get used to." He leaned forward in his chair, his hands steepled on the table and his shirt riding up, giving her a glimpse of the golden skin above his jeans. "It's okay if you need to cry."

She stared at him, wondering if he was serious. When his expression didn't change, she burst into laughter. "Are you kidding me? You think I'm going to break down?"

He gestured to her hands. "You're shaking."

She glanced at her fingers wrapped around the cup of tea. Huh, he was right. Still, that didn't mean she was a shrinking violet in need of a big, bad Dom to come to her rescue. This flower knew how to rescue herself. "Adrenaline." She set the cup on the table and dropped her hands into her lap. "When the police finish questioning us, I'm going out there to give my live firsthand-witness account on television. This exclusive will make my career."

His lips curled into disgust. "I don't believe you. A person is dead."

Antsy, wondering what was taking Officer Hanover so long to come back, she pushed back from the table and stood. "Anthony Rinaldi was a dangerous combination of psychotic, powerful, and wealthy. If he got the court to drop the thirteen murder charges of those women who were found buried on his property, then nothing short of death would stop him." She rounded the table, stopping next to Logan. "He's hurt people you and I care about. You can't say you're sorry he's dead."

Logan scowled. "No, I'm not sorry, but that doesn't mean his death should be used as fodder for your career."

Why shouldn't she benefit from it? She'd watched those men execute Rinaldi in cold blood. Surely there was a reason she was there to witness it. Why else would fate have placed her there?

She didn't bother arguing with Logan. He'd made it clear he held no regard for her career or for her advancement in it. Most people didn't understand what it was like for her. Maybe that's why she'd become such good friends with Kate and Lisa. They were both strong, capable, determined career women like herself and they let no one stand in their way. Even as Jaxon's collared submissive, Kate had created a successful law practice with Logan, and Lisa had started her own public relations firm that now represented half of Detroit's hockey team members. Of course, Lisa didn't date, so she didn't have any men trying to hold her back.

Rachel paced to the door, twirling her raven hair around her finger. "What do you think is taking Hanover so long to return?" As witnesses, they were free to leave whenever they wanted. It wasn't as if they'd been arrested. Hanover was probably outside the police station, giving her competition all the details of Rinaldi's death while she was stuck inside. No way was she going to miss this once-in-a-lifetime opportunity.

She creaked open the door and peered out into the hallway.

Empty.

"Rachel, do you ever do what you're told?" Logan asked, now standing right behind her.

She gave him a smile and wiggled her eyebrows. "Only if I would do it anyhow." With him or without him, she was getting out of there. Slinging her purse over her shoulder, she started down the hall toward the lobby, but before she reached the end of it, she spotted Hanover coming into the lobby from a different hallway. He walked up to a couple of men, but their identities were blocked from Rachel's view by the cops eating donuts.

She clenched her teeth. Those two could be reporters. Hanover was probably going to give them an exclusive on the Rinaldi murder. Well, she certainly wasn't going to stand for that. Prepared to give the officer a piece of her mind, she squared her shoulders and took a step toward the lobby. An arm snaked around her waist and dragged her backward until they were out of sight of everyone in the lobby.

"Slow down, Tiger," Logan whispered from behind. "Didn't you notice who Hanover's talking to?"

Keeping her body hidden behind the wall, she stretched her neck forward and peeked out into the lobby. Standing in the center of the room no more than twenty feet away from her, looking as if they had nothing to fear, were the two men who had gunned down Rinaldi in cold blood.

The hallway seemed to shrink and close in around her. She couldn't breathe, her lungs paralyzed from the shock of seeing the murderers here at the station. Why weren't they wearing handcuffs?

A lead weight lodged in her stomach, the nape of her neck prickling with intuition. No mobster would willingly walk into a police station and pal around with the cops. "Who do you think they are?"

The men turned toward Officer Hanover, flashing their badges and credentials.

The smaller man shook Hanover's hand, his nasally voice loud enough for her to hear. "Agent Seymour Fink from the county's FBI resident agency." He motioned to the larger man standing beside him. "And this is my partner, Agent Richard Evans."

Logan grew rigid. “Shit, they’re FBI. I don’t know what’s going on, but if they killed Rinaldi, they’re obviously dirty.” He grabbed her hand and pulled her down the hall toward the back of the station. “We need to get out of here.”

For once, she didn’t argue, allowing him to lead her down another hall while fleeing as quickly as she could in three-inch heels. “How? We’re literally surrounded by cops.”

He tightened his grip on her hand. “There’s got to be another way out of here.”

No sooner were the words out of his mouth than she spotted another exit. Warnings affixed to the door declared it as an emergency exit and restricted for police personnel, and an access control pad was located on the wall to the right of the door like the one they used down at the news station. “You need an ID card to exit,” she said, motioning to the pad. “If we set off the alarm, we won’t get out of the parking lot.”

“Not a problem.” He whipped out his cell phone and toyed with it, swiping through several pages of apps. She’d never seen anyone with so many apps on a phone. After opening one, he held his cell up to the access pad, and a quiet beep and the click of the door unlocking caused her jaw to drop. He threw open the door and waved her through it, following right behind her.

She’d known the man had mad computer skills, but messing with a police station’s security system exceeded her expectations. “How the hell did you do that?”

"It's an app that bypasses those kinds of sensors." Again, he took her hand, and together they crossed the parking lot, running to their cars while trying not to draw too much attention. "Pretty ridiculous the police use such a rudimentary system, but not surprising. The app interfaces with the system, working like a security badge."

She stopped between her car and his. "What are you, a jewel thief?"

"I gave that up years ago." He opened the driver's side door of his car and jutted his chin. "Get in."

She folded her arms. "Why do we have to take your car?"

"Rachel, we have about ten seconds before they figure out we're missing." He braced his hands on the roof, his jaw tense. "Get. In. The. Car."

Biting the inside of her cheek, she opened the passenger-side door and slid into his silver Mustang. That man was so bossy. She couldn't believe she'd forgotten how much his behavior infuriated her.

Within seconds, he tore out of the parking lot and zoomed toward the highway, each block taking her farther and farther away from the story that would have catapulted her to the top in her field. She held her breath, checking the mirrors for signs they were being followed. Part of her wanted to protest and go back to the police station, but rationally, she knew they had no other choice. They had to run.

A police car turned from a side street, merging into traffic and following right behind them. "We've got company," she said, wiping her damp palms on her pants. Neither one of them spoke, waiting for the cop to turn on his siren and demand they pull over. It was as if they were running out of oxygen and they were afraid to take a breath or move a muscle. Only when the police car switched lanes a couple of minutes later and drove past them did they relax. "You think they've figured out we're missing yet?"

"Even if they have, they'll waste time looking up my car's registration. By the time they do, we'll be in the city. We've got a few minutes before they can put out the APB." While zigzagging through lanes of traffic, he slid his cell from his pocket and dialed. "I've got a situation and need your expertise. I'm in the mood for a BLT. Heavy on the bacon. I'll meet you by our usual place. Ten minutes." She heard a man swearing on the other end. "I don't have an hour, Willie. Tell your date for the night you got somewhere to be. I'll make it up to you next time you need my expertise, you get what I'm saying?" He paused. "Yeah. Good deal."

Seriously, that was his plan? Hope the cholesterol in the sandwich would kill him before those FBI agents did?

She tapped her fingernails on the window. "A BLT? We've got the FBI and the police after us, and you're picking up a sandwich?"

Getting off the highway, he glanced over at her. "Willie's my client. I didn't order a sandwich from him. I let him know I've got the cops on me and that I needed some new wheels."

"He's going to give you his car?"

Logan's hands tightened on the wheel. "We're going to *trade* cars."

Understanding dawned. "Wait, he's one of your clients? You mean a criminal?"

The sides of his lips twitched. "He's never been convicted."

She didn't miss that he'd circumvented the question. The man was a car thief. She'd bet the only reason he hadn't been convicted of the crime was because he had Logan defending him in court. "He's giving us a stolen car? *Why* do we need a stolen car?"

"Rach, we're the only witnesses to the murder of a mobster by FBI agents. If it came down to it, who do you think the cops will believe? The FBI or two murder suspects? We need to go off the grid for a while until we can figure out what's going on."

For more reasons than she could count on both her hands and feet, going off the grid with Logan Bradford was the last thing she needed. Most important, she had to stay and report the story or risk losing her chance at winning a job in the New York market. The Rinaldi murder was the biggest story of her career. Plus, spending an extended period of time with Logan was bound to end in another murder because she'd likely kill him. There had to be another solution. "Don't you have a friend from the FBI who helped you when Rinaldi kidnapped Danielle? Why can't we call him?"

"I don't need to call him. As soon as he hears what's up, he'll start digging on his own." He frowned, driving into a Detroit neighborhood she reported from on a weekly basis due to its high incidence of murders. "The FBI works like the military. You follow the orders of your superior or risk court-martial. There's nothing he can do at this point. His hands are tied."

She unzipped her purse and pulled out her iPhone. "Let me call my boss from the news station. He can—"

"No." He grabbed it out of her hands and pitched it out the window. "No cell calls."

She didn't bother containing her anger. Who the hell did he think he was? Her father? "Why'd you do that?"

"FBI can trace it."

"You just called your friend."

He patted the pocket of his jeans where he'd placed his phone after his call to his car-thieving client. "I've got a signal jammer on mine to keep anyone from tracing our location or listening in on the conversation."

She huffed. On the run with Logan and without her cell was her version of hell. "Then why'd you speak in code with the BLT talk?"

"In case it didn't work." Shrugging, he pulled into a dark parking lot of a twenty-four-hour hot dog joint and cut the engine. "Nothing's foolproof. Always have a backup plan."

Craning her head to check the environment, she was relieved by the absence of cops in the area. Of course, this neighborhood, referred to in the media as "murder central," was known for the lack of police presence. While tonight that worked in their favor, she wondered why Logan didn't meet this guy at his law office like a *normal* attorney.

A metal banging coming from the back end of the car caused her to jump in her seat. Some guy walked around to the driver's side of the vehicle. She stuck her hand in her purse again, this time wrapping her fingers around her pepper spray.

Logan jutted his chin, his hand on the handle of the door. "Get out of the car."

She glared at him. "Stop ordering me around. I'm not one of your bondage bunnies from the club."

Sighing, he rubbed a hand over his stubbly jaw. "Sorry. Get out of the car. *Please.*"

Her friends had regaled her with stories of Logan's chivalry, but she had yet to see it. Apparently, Kate and Danielle got to experience Logan the knight in shining armor while she got Logan the Neanderthal.

Not taking her hand off her spray, she slid out of the car and got a good look at whom she assumed was Logan's client. With a baby face like his, he couldn't be more than twenty-one years old. "Hey, man," he said, shaking Logan's hand. "Gotta say, I never expected a call like that from you. Not setting me up, are you?"

"No." Logan slid his gaze toward her before returning to Willie. "I've got a little situation and just need to lie low for a bit. I really appreciate this."

"You've saved my ass. 'Bout time I got to return the favor." Willie lovingly caressed the hood of Logan's car. "I hate to chop your ride though. Why don't I just—"

"No, take it to your shop and do your magic," Logan said, tossing his keys to Willie. "I want it gone."

Willie pocketed the keys and did a double take as he noticed her standing to the right of the passenger door. Brows furrowed as he stared at her, he dropped a different set of keys into Logan's waiting hand. Willie's eyes widened in recognition and he snapped his fingers. "Hey, aren't you Rachel Dawson from Channel Five? You're even hotter in person."

"Back off, Willie," Logan warned.

Willie's gaze bounced between her and Logan, a slow smile breaking out. "Oh, that's how it is. I get it."

She waited for Logan to correct Willie's assumption but he never did. Instead he walked around to the back of his Mustang and popped the trunk, retrieving a duffle bag similar to the one he'd left behind at Benediction with all his kinky toys. Swinging it over his shoulders, he quietly shut the trunk and then moved to stand beside her. He slung his arm around her waist as if making his claim on her.

"Good luck, man." Willie hopped into the Mustang and, tires squealing, drove away practically before she could blink, as if he was afraid Logan would change his mind about the swap.

The silence unnerved her, her overactive imagination running rampant waiting for homicidal FBI agents, misinformed cops, or gangbangers to jump out of the darkness at any moment.

Logan led her to their new vehicle, a gray Monte Carlo. Despite having grown up near the "Motor City" of Detroit, she couldn't begin to understand the fascination of cars, but she could appreciate that Logan had traded in a beauty for something her parents would drive. Then again, Monte Carlos were so popular, they'd have no problem getting lost in a sea of commonality.

As she got into the passenger side, he threw his duffle into the backseat with a loud thump. "What the hell is in that bag, a dead body?" she asked, only half joking.

He sat beside her and started the engine. "It's my go-bag."

"Seriously? You keep a go-bag in your car?"

He shrugged. "Never know when you're gonna witness two FBI agents assassinate a mobster."

In no way was this fair. While he had a go-bag and a cell phone, she had nothing other than her purse, and even she wasn't dumb enough to use a credit card. She had exactly twenty-seven dollars cash and a package of mints to her name at this point. No change of clothes. No deodorant or toothbrush. No special hair care products to keep her thick hair from becoming a frizzy rat's nest. Nada. But Logan had a prepared duffle full of items that would no doubt keep him looking and smelling fresh as a damned rose.

Remembering she hadn't eaten dinner, she unwrapped the package of mints and popped one in her mouth. She'd have to make do because obviously, stopping at the McDonalds' drive-thru was out of the question. She held out the roll, offering it to Logan. He shook his head, declining, and fiddled with his phone.

"Where we headed?" she asked.

"I've got an old family friend who's a survivalist. Keeps to himself and lives out in the middle of nowhere in Florida, not too far from Port Everglades, where our friendly FBI agents are headed. We'll be safe there until we can figure out who we're looking for at the port."

He placed his iPhone into the cup holder and opened an app. Voices filled the car. She sat back and listened as the voices threw out a bunch of numbers and words she was familiar with from her job. Logan had accessed the local police scanner.

It was only moments before she heard them mention the APB out for her and Logan, telling police to look out for a silver Mustang and that they were armed and dangerous.

Hearing her name mentioned that way brought home the gravity of the situation. They really were being framed by the FBI for Rinaldi's murder. But the police weren't completely wrong. She was armed. Armed with the truth. And that made her dangerous.

She just wished she knew whom that made her dangerous to.

Chapter Six

"RACHEL, WAKE UP."

Blinking at the glare of the sun, she opened her eyes and stretched, turning her head to both sides to get the crick out of her neck. They were parked at a gas pump, the store's large sign at the entrance advertising Georgia peaches and salt licks. Beyond that was a two-lane highway with grass on both sides and not another structure in sight. "I wasn't sleeping."

She'd drifted off sometime after they'd passed Atlanta, but had woken up every few minutes, the sound of gunshots still lingering in her memory. The images of Rinaldi's blood splattering flashed like a slideshow through her mind.

Logan chuckled. "Sure you weren't. And you also weren't snoring."

"I don't snore." No one had ever accused her of snoring. Of course, other than her sisters, she'd never slept in the same room as anyone else, and it had been years since she'd done that. "Wait, do I snore?"

He only grinned.

She rolled her eyes, choosing to believe he was teasing over the alternative. "Where are we?" Checking the clock on the dashboard, she calculated the time they'd been in the car. They'd left Detroit around one in the morning, and it was now six at night. Logan had to be feeling the fatigue of driving for fifteen hours without a break, but he'd insisted he was too wound up to take a nap. More likely he was too much of a control freak to give up the wheel.

" 'Bout an hour north of Florida. This is the last stop before we get to our point of destination, so use the restroom and grab whatever you need. I'll meet you back at the car in fifteen. Keep your head down and don't do anything to draw any attention."

She got out of the car and slammed the door, her knees creaking from the hours of sitting. "You don't need to tell me that every time we stop, you know."

He dipped his head, a look of contrition on his tired face. "Sorry."

A sliver of regret managed to worm its way into her heart. On top of not sleeping all night, the stress of the situation had to prove just as difficult for him. She shouldn't have snapped like that. "No, I'm sorry. I'm always cranky when I first get up. Mainly because I don't get more than a couple hours of sleep at night and I survive on coffee, which I haven't drunk since this morning. I know you were only trying to help."

Something passed between them at that moment, as if they'd both finally accepted they were in this together. It was too exhausting to hate him. Even she could admit if he hadn't come along when he had last night, she may have lost it and given away her presence, getting herself killed as a result.

Together they walked into the dirty store of the gas station, avoiding making eye contact with the other customers. The place was falling apart with holes in the walls and cracked tiles in the floors. Her toes curled when she spotted a mouse darting under one of the store shelves.

Logan had mapped out a route to keep them off the highway, so they stuck to lots of back roads, making sure to stop at places that most likely wouldn't have surveillance cameras. No grainy black-and-white images of her and Logan showing up on the news. So far, the story hadn't hit the national airwaves. Hopefully, the FBI was assuming they were still in Michigan.

After using the washroom, she nabbed a coffee and a packaged cupcake and paid for it at the register, following Logan's instructions not to look the clerk in the eye. She took her meal outside, enjoying the fresh air. The weather was humid and much warmer than what they'd left back in Michigan. She took a deep breath and walked past the car toward the grassy area. It felt good to use her legs after being stuck in the car for endless hours. She wasn't used to sitting still for long. Which reminded her—she'd missed her private session with her Pilates teacher this morning. No wonder she was so stiff.

After sipping the worst coffee she'd ever drunk, she unwrapped her cupcake and took a huge bite, not surprised to find it stale. She dropped both her drink and the cupcake in the garbage. Guess now was as good a time as ever to start a diet.

"Stupid mutt," a male voice shouted, followed by a loud thud.

Across the field of grass, a man kicked a dog in its side for what she guessed was at least the second time. His head bowed in submission, the dog yelped and edged backward, trying to get away, but the man held its leash, still yelling at the animal as if it understood English.

Furious, she marched over. If there was one thing she couldn't stand, it was bullies. As the man raised his booted foot once more, she reached the scene and jumped in front of the dog, her arms spread wide. "Hey, you. Stop that. You're hurting him."

"Excuse me?" The guy sneered but, luckily for her, lowered his foot to the ground. She was in no mood to get kicked. "Why don't you mind your own business?"

She pointed her finger at him. "You made the dog my business as soon as I saw your boot connect with his rib cage."

"Dog ate my lunch when I went inside. He needs to be taught a lesson not to do it again."

The dog no longer bowed his head. Instead he was looking up at her with curiosity on his wrinkled face. She bent to rub his ears, loving it when the dog nudged her hand for more. He wasn't the most attractive dog she'd ever seen, but he was full of personality. With wet jowls and big brown eyes, he was wider than what seemed normal for a dog his size. She peeked underneath him, confirming his gender. "You can't discipline a dog for his nature. If you were stupid enough to leave food unattended around him, you should've expected it would get eaten. You're the one who needed the lesson not to do it again."

"Bitch, I don't know who you think you are acting all high and mighty, but this here dog's my property. I can train him however I want. Now, why don't you go run along before I train you like I train my dog?"

She stepped in front of the animal, her hands on her hips. "I'm not leaving until you promise you won't harm him."

"Fuck you." His face screwed up in a sneer and he spit some tobacco chew on the ground, just barely missing her foot. "I ain't making no promises to an uptight cunt who sticks her nose into other people's business."

He tromped forward, clipping her with his shoulder on his way to snatch back his dog. She twirled around, intending to scoop the animal into her arms, but before she had the chance, the asshole grabbed the dog's collar and twisted it, yanking him hard and eliciting a yelp.

"That's it." She pushed the dog's owner in an attempt to get him to release the strangling hold he had on the poor thing. "Give me the dog and I won't call the cops on you for animal cruelty."

The man turned, the unmitigated anger in his eyes now focused entirely on her. She took a step backward, but she wasn't quick enough. Forgoing the dog, he grabbed her by the shoulders and shook hard enough to snap her head back and to elicit tears. Then he raised one hand, readying to strike. She winced, preparing herself for the painful blow.

It never came.

"Take your hands off the lady," ordered Logan, his hand wrapped around the man's wrist midstrike. "Now."

She let go of the breath she hadn't known she'd been holding. Damn it, she wasn't the type of woman who needed a man to save her, but since last night, she'd been all too grateful to have Logan at her back.

The man released her with a shove and faced Logan. "This your bitch? You need to teach her a lesson about showing some respect."

While she crouched and reassuringly rubbed the dog's neck, Logan stood eerily still with his jaw locked with tension, somehow seeming much taller and formidable than he had a few minutes ago. "Seems like you're the one who needs to learn respect."

His gaze falling to the ground, the dog's owner took off his hat and rubbed the back of his neck. "You know what? This dog ain't worth it. Just took him to fuck with my ex in the divorce." He threw up his hands and took a step backward. "He's all yours now." He stomped away before getting into his truck and speeding away.

Typical bully. He could pick on something or someone smaller and weaker than himself but when confronted by a man equally his size, he ran with his tail between his legs.

"What happened to not drawing any attention?" Logan asked dryly.

She scratched the dog one final time behind his ears and stood with the leash in her hands. Yeah, she could admit she hadn't exactly stayed off the grid with her actions, but ever since she'd watched her friend suffer abuse in silence as a teenager, whenever she saw an injustice, she had a hard time keeping her mouth shut. That was one of the reasons she became an investigative reporter. It certainly wasn't for the low pay or the lousy hours. "I couldn't just let him hurt Walter, now, could I?" She tugged on the dog's leash and led him toward their car. He waddled alongside her, his tongue hanging out of his mouth making him look as though he was smiling.

Logan came up on the other side of her and seized her by her elbow, halting her in her tracks. "What are you doing? We can't take a dog with us on the run."

No, she supposed it wasn't ideal to add him to the chaos of the situation, but she couldn't just leave him here without anyone to take care of him. Besides, she'd always wanted a dog. With eight kids under eighteen in the house at once, her father hadn't let her have a pet, stating it was too much responsibility. Once she left home, she was too busy at school and then with her career to have a pet waiting for her at home. There were days she worked on a big story and never made it home at all. Not too difficult since she'd suffered from insomnia for years.

But this dog needed her and she wouldn't abandon him.

Figuring Logan required a little cajoling, she subtly batted her eyelashes at him. "It'll be fine. How much trouble could one little dog be?"

His eyes narrowed into slits. Figured he didn't buy her flirtatious act. Kate and Danielle had told her about Doms and how they could see through the bullshit. She hadn't quite believed them, but it appeared as though they hadn't been lying.

"Fine," he said, surprising her. "Just until we get to our first stop and then we'll figure out what to do with him."

She sighed dramatically. It wasn't worth arguing about right now. Once he spent some time with the dog and realized he wouldn't be a problem, he'd capitulate. "Uh-huh. Whatever you say."

"You're mocking me." He opened his car door, one hand on top of the car. "His name's Walter?"

She scooped up the dog in her arms and settled inside the passenger seat with the animal on her lap. "Yep."

"That's what it says on his tag?"

"No." Walter collapsed on her thighs with a sigh and began to lick her hand. "His tag says his name's Brutus, but he doesn't look like a Brutus to me, so I'm changing it."

Logan glanced at her as he started the car, lines creasing his forehead. "Why Walter?"

"I'm naming him after the man who inspired my career." She cupped the dog's face in her hands and turned him toward Logan. "Besides, this dog has the same eyebrows."

Driving down the road, Logan didn't smile at her attempt at a joke. Instead, he looked so deep in thought, she wasn't even sure if he heard her. And that bothered her. Not because he was ignoring her, but because she felt as though she'd done something wrong and she wasn't used to that feeling. Or at least she didn't normally care if she had. It came with the job.

Until she'd met Kate, she hadn't had a true friend since high school, too obsessed with school and her career to really put the energy into a friendship. Now she had three girlfriends—Kate, Danielle, and Lisa—who somehow didn't run the other way when they saw her coming. They called her out on her crap and accepted her into their little circle without reservation. She didn't have to worry about doing something wrong because they were used to it. They even expected it.

The silence in the car was deafening. Uncomfortable by it, she wiggled in her seat. After a few minutes, she blew out a breath. "You're not really upset that I caused a scene, are you?"

Drumming his fingers on the steering wheel, he didn't respond for a couple of beats. Then he glanced at the dog before returning his attention to the road ahead of him. "No," he said quietly. "You surprised me, that's all."

"Why?"

"You stuck your neck out for a dog." His eyes briefly met hers. Just long enough for the heated intensity of them to make her shiver. He ground his teeth, jerking his gaze away all too soon. "That man could've hurt you."

She shrugged, her lips tugged up in a half smile. For a moment, she could almost believe he cared about her. But she wasn't deluding herself. It was obvious to her that Logan was in love with his law partner—her best friend Kate—despite Kate being in a collared relationship with

Jaxon Deveroux. It was Rachel's job as a reporter to dig deeper than the surface and examine subtleties. Maybe other people couldn't see it, but whenever Kate was in the room, Logan's eyes, filled with longing, tracked her every move.

Petting the dog, she peered out the passenger-side window at the miles of browning grassy fields. Logan didn't feel anything more than a little lust and a whole lot of disgust for her. No one really understood her, and she couldn't blame anyone because she rarely gave a person the chance. She realized she put people off with her brash manner and her singular drive to be the best of the best professionally, but it had never bothered her.

Until now.

And she didn't like it one bit. He meant nothing to her, and she meant even less to him. So why had a ball of disappointment settled in her belly?

"If I believe in something, I don't let anything stand in my way." Needing a distraction, she switched on the radio. "Mind if I put on some music?" She settled on a popular song and sat back in her seat.

He huffed out a laugh. "Uh, I'm pretty sure Britney Spears doesn't qualify as music."

She whipped her head toward him. "I like Britney Spears, so sue me."

"Believe me," he said, his lips turned up, "if I could sue you for liking Britney Spears, I would."

Annoyed, she folded her arms, the sudden movement startling Walter awake. He perked up his head, looked around, then put it back down again and resumed his nap. "If you're so particular about what we listen to, why don't you choose the music then?"

Smiling, he leaned forward and turned the dial, stopping on classic rock. Obviously satisfied with his choice, he sat back and tapped his fingers on the steering wheel to the beat.

"Who is this?" she asked.

"The Who."

"Yeah, who is this?"

He laughed. "The Who. That's the name of the band."

Weird name for a band, but she liked their sound. "Oh. Never heard of them."

His brows furrowed as he slid her a look of incredulity. "How could you not know of The Who? Where do you live? Under a rock?"

She chuckled to herself. He wasn't far off. Since going out into the world on her own, she'd tried to learn as much about pop culture as she could, but even now, more than ten years later, she always felt one step behind everyone else. "I didn't really get to listen to popular music until I moved out of my parents' home to go to college."

Living on campus had been an eye-opening experience for her. From fashion to speech, she'd mimicked the girls around her. No one had ever guessed she'd spent her years growing up in an extremely religious household, covered from head to toe—even in the sweltering heat of summer. In her small community, women popped out baby after baby and were expected to cook and clean while the men worked and attended religious services. Her family and the members of their church were cut off from modern technology like music, computers, and televisions and restricted from reading anything not approved by the church leaders. And since her father was one of those leaders, he expected a model family that adhered to all of his rules.

Within a few months of leaving home, she'd added a couple of notches to her bedpost and drooled over Ryan Gosling, just like her roommates. She'd read classics such as *To Kill a Mockingbird* and *Pride and Prejudice.* She had gotten drunk and smoked pot. Skipped class. Took naps before going out to the bar at ten o'clock on a school night. But she also spent plenty of her time pretending she knew about things like everyone else. Pretending to be someone she wasn't. It had been exhausting. Even now, she kept her past hidden away as if it was a dirty secret.

Confusion remained on Logan's face as if he couldn't understand how anyone could have gone through life without hearing The Who. "Didn't you have a radio in your house?"

She shrugged. "My parents kept an emergency radio in their closet, but it never occurred to me to use it." Contrary to the way she lived her life now, she'd always followed her parents' rules. She hadn't known any different until that fateful day when she'd learned that ignorance wasn't bliss and knowledge was power. "Other than that, they had a CD player, but they only played classical and religious music. We didn't even have a television."

But although she'd seen some family programming at other people's houses, the awe of it hadn't permeated until she'd snuck into her cousin's den and caught her uncle watching a report about the fallen Twin Towers. She'd heard about the terrorist attack, of course, but seeing the reality of it and hearing the victims' accounts of what they had gone through had changed her irrevocably.

He turned down the radio's volume. "And now you're a television reporter. What do your parents think of that?"

She recalled her father's angry words and her mother's cries when she told them she was leaving for college to become a journalist. According to her sisters, they still had hopes that she'd leave her career and "return to God."

Swallowing the lump that had formed in her throat, she put on the brave face she'd worn for ten years and shoved down the feeling of rejection. "My parents don't approve. I speak to a couple of my sisters, but we're not close." At Logan's frown, she jumped to defend her family and clarify the situation. As sad as it made her to no longer have a place in her family, she couldn't blame them for their beliefs or the way they chose to live their lives. "Don't get me wrong. They're not forbidden to associate with me, and my parents would never refuse to welcome me into their home, but I just can't bring myself to do it."

It was bad enough that she wore clothes that didn't cover her shoulders, but to choose a career over family was something her parents could never understand. That's why she'd made it easy on them and stayed away. Legally changed her last name and created a public bio that made no mention of the parents who believed by leaving home to have a career she was living her life in sin and would spend an afterlife in hell.

Logan turned and looked at her, his eyes flashing with pity. She hated that look. That's why she'd kept her past hidden. She hadn't suffered tragedies like her friends Kate and Danielle. She'd been loved. Who was she to complain?

"How many sisters do you have?" he asked, surprising her with the question. She would've thought he'd ask why, if she was so brave when looking for a story, she was such a wimp when it came to her family. And she really didn't have the answer.

Relieved he hadn't asked anything more personal, she smiled as if it didn't hurt to think about what she might be missing by choosing to live her life on her own terms. "Five sisters and two brothers. I was the fourth child." She shifted in her seat, angling her legs toward Logan. His gaze dropped to the exposed skin of her calves before he returned his attention to the road. "What about you? Are you close with your family?"

He coughed, his voice coming out a bit raspy. "Yeah. I've got a big family too. Four older brothers."

"You're the baby?" She shook her head. "I'm surprised. I figured you for the oldest 'cause you're so bossy."

He grinned. "You think I'm bossy, you should meet my brothers. They're navy SEALs."

Five Bradford brothers? Judging by Logan, her hormones would go on overload if she ever found herself in the same room as all of them. Strange that he would go into a different arm of the military from the rest of his brothers. "You were in the army, right? What did you do for them?"

His hands tightened on the wheel. "Intelligence."

The reporter in her smelled a story, but the woman in her knew better than to piss off the man she was stuck with until they resolved this mess. Still, she couldn't resist asking, "Why did you leave?"

"Army and I weren't a good fit," he answered, his line sounding dull and rehearsed. He conveniently ended the conversation by switching the radio to AM and turning up the volume. Yeah, there was definitely more to the story. But they weren't friends. He owed her no more than she owed him.

He stopped on a news station and they listened to the day's top stories. A foiled terror attack on some obscure African country. Another shooting of a minority by a police officer. A debate in the Senate between Senator Hutton, who was calling for additional funding to protect the nation in case of viral warfare, and Senator Byron, who wanted to cut federal spending on homeland security. Rachel should be at her office right now, in the thick of it, reading the Associated Press wire and watching her network's national station.

Walter whimpered in her lap, making little doggie noises in his sleep. Did dogs have nightmares? Patting his head, she jerked at the sound of her name on the radio. "The FBI is unable to comment on that. However, the public should consider them armed and dangerous. I'd like to reiterate that if you see Logan Bradford and/or Rachel Dawson, please do not approach them, but instead, call 911 to report the sighting to the police or call the FBI's Major Case Contact Center. That's all we have for now. We won't be answering any questions at this time."

Her mind whirled with the knowledge that she no longer reported the story.

She *was* the story.

"It doesn't make sense," Rachel said as the station switched from the FBI media coordinator to another story. "How did the FBI get jurisdiction over Rinaldi's murder?"

Worry was etched on Logan's face. "I'd assume from the organized crime angle, but there's much more going on here than a couple of agents taking out a multimurdering mobster no one would mourn." He rubbed his hand over his head. "You know what this means, don't you?"

"Yeah. It means we've just become national fugitives." She heaved a sigh, soothing the whining Walter. "It means we're fucked."

Chapter Seven

STARING IN THE full-length mirror, the Senator straightened his tie and practiced his speech, the words he'd spoken dozens of times before but nevertheless continued to rehearse. There was nothing worse than a man who stumbled over his words. Appearances were everything, which was why men like him could tell a thousand lies and yet no one bothered to question him. He was American royalty, the son and brother of former United States presidents. His family had dirt on every CEO of every major news outlet as well as the most influential politicians on both the federal and state level, from their addictions to underage hookers to their penchant for cross-dressing to rape of senatorial interns. None of them dared speak out against his family for fear of exposure of their dirty little secrets.

Arms circled around him, a naked body pressing against his back and a hard length digging into the crack of his ass. His eyes closed and he suppressed a groan, knowing it would only excite his lover and invite another round. He was still sore from last night.

Everyone had a secret.

Even him.

Especially him.

Hands drifted down his chest over his thickening cock to his balls and squeezed. Hard. Harder. The pain mounted until he couldn't stop the moan from escaping his lips.

The hands released him only to unbuckle his belt and yank his pants to his ankles. Then they returned, rolling his testicles.

"You're nervous about your speech," said his lover, the admonishment in the tone shaming him. "I've told you, there is no place for fear in politics."

Since the age of six, he'd been trained to fear nothing. By the time he'd turned ten, the methodical whippings and food deprivation were as commonplace as a wet dream for a thirteen-year-old boy. He didn't fear the rituals or the way his father and brother watched without blinking, their stares as harsh as the tail of the whip cutting into his flesh. He thrived on it. Exulted in it. Embracing the history of his family that would one day take him all the way to the White House. He grew to love the pain that reminded him he was still alive.

When he wasn't in trouble for stuttering in a school speech or trembling from receiving only a B on a history test, he was ignored, his parents too busy campaigning or running the fucking country to care about their son in his room with a 104-degree fever from the flu. His youthful indiscretions brought plenty of wrath from his father's political management team, but nothing got the man's attention like fear.

Their attempt to condition him had somehow warped into a fetish. He craved sexual domination, his only chance to relinquish power for a time and beat the fear that remained with him like a second skin. It wasn't unusual for men in politics to submit to a professional dominatrix, but his sexual desires and his daily life intertwined until he could barely function without a beating. When he was younger, he purposely started fights in order to get the release he needed. Of course, that got his parents' attention once the press caught wind of it. They had paid for professionals to visit him daily, but when one had threatened to go to the media about it and was eliminated by one of his father's cronies, his parents found a permanent solution to his "problem."

Nails jabbed his balls, forcing him out of his head. "Focus on the pain," said his lover, the husky timbre of the voice making his dick throb. "What does it mean?"

"I'm weak." The Senator hissed as the nails pierced his skin. "Fear is for pussies."

His lover quivered behind him, aroused by his pain. "Are you a pussy?"

He shook his head vehemently. "No."

"I don't believe you." The grip on his balls tightened and the nails sunk deeper. Warmth welled and dripped down his testicles, blood he couldn't afford to lose after the amount he'd lost last night. "If you can't convince me, how will you convince the American public?"

"I. Am. Not." He punched the mirror hard enough to create a fissure in the clear glass. "A. Pussy." His knuckles stung but he didn't bother to check. Any sign of weakness on his part would prolong his torture. And although he got off on the pain and humiliation, he couldn't be late for his speech. Any form of unprofessionalism was grounds for a beating that would leave him pissing blood for days.

"Much better. I almost believed you this time," crooned his lover. "Maybe after I fuck you without any lube, you'll sound more convincing. Bend over."

He trembled as he complied, excitement replacing the fear and erasing all the doubts from his mind. A gag fastened over his mouth, his lips around the red ball in the center. Drool gathered in his mouth almost instantly and his cock hardened, the tip bouncing up to his belly button.

Without warning, his lover thrust inside him.

This is what he needed. To be dominated and forced to surrender. To endure pain so that he could inflict it on others without fear or remorse.

Plenty of heads would roll for fucking up the Rinaldi assassination.

Beginning with Logan Bradford and Rachel Dawson.

Chapter Eight

SHE DIDN'T WANT to admit to it, but Logan had been right. Walter whined every couple of hours to go to the bathroom, slowing their journey to their final destination. Wherever the hell that was. "Are you sure you know where we're going? There's no way anyone lives out here. We're in the middle of nowhere."

With her behind the wheel and a yet-again sleeping Walter on her lap, they were driving down a two-lane road somewhere in the Florida Everglades. She hadn't seen a single car pass by in an hour, and the last time they'd stopped, she spotted a sign to beware of alligators.

Alligators.

She'd given Walter just enough time to pee before dragging him back to the car. It would be her luck to rescue the poor pooch from an asshole of an owner only to have him eaten by a giant lizard twelve hours later.

Tall reeds surrounded both sides of the roads, and as the sun set, sounds of different animals in the swampland increased until she could almost believe she was in the African jungle. There were no lights anywhere to be seen down this stretch of road. The last sign of civilization she'd seen was over an hour ago as they passed a road that led to an Indian reservation and a board advertising fan boat tours and alligator-wrangling shows.

"Trust me," Logan said reassuringly. "Uncle Joe made us memorize his coordinates before us kids knew how to read."

"Uncle?" She couldn't believe anyone from the civilized world would choose to live out here. Even at night, the humidity was thicker than beef stew. Not to mention the crazy bugs she'd encountered in the past few hours. What the heck were they feeding the mosquitoes down here to grow them so large?

"Honorary title. Joe and my father grew up together in Detroit and became SEALs during Vietnam. Dad says Joe was always paranoid. You know, worried about Big Brother watching. After the war, he bought some property with cash and built a secure compound for himself. Turned survivalist. He'd visit each Christmas and give me and my brothers something new to add to our go-bag. About five years ago, he stopped coming. He doesn't leave his land anymore." He motioned to the road with a jut of his chin. "And we're here."

Looking ahead, she slowed at the sight of the smooth road turning into a dirt one. At the bumps, the dog woke up, his body shaking. He hopped into the backseat and curled up on the floor behind her. About one hundred yards down, an enormous barbed-wire fence blocked them from going any farther.

She stopped at the fence and put the car in park. “What should we do? Drive through the fence?”

He snorted. “Not unless you have a desire to try electrocution.”

A visual of it playing in her mind, she swallowed down her fear. “Seeing that it’s secure, how are we going to get in? It’s not as if we can go to his front door and ring the doorbell.”

Logan grinned, folding his arms. “Oh, he already knows we’re here.”

Lights bright enough to blind an entire baseball stadium full of people shined on them from somewhere above the car. She squinted, covering her eyes with the top of her hands. “What the hell is that?”

“That’s my uncle’s welcome.” She peeked through her fingers and saw Logan swing open the car door and climb outside. After a minute, the lights turned off and a piece of the fence in front of them had disappeared. Logan dropped back into his seat and slammed the door shut. “You’ve got thirty seconds to get through before the fence returns.”

He didn’t have to tell her twice. She hit the gas and plowed through the opening. “How the hell did the fence disappear into thin air?”

“Optical illusion. That part of the fence is actually a gate. You couldn’t see it open because the lights were too bright.” He pointed to a shadowed house up ahead.

"You can park in front. Uncle Joe's already there with his shotgun."

Where the heck was Logan bringing her? She slowed and parked the car. "I thought he knew it was us."

"He does." Logan reached in the backseat and snatched his go-bag. "But until he knows we're alone, he's gonna have that shotgun glued to his hand."

As Logan jumped out of the car, she cooed at Walter to lure him from the floor behind her. He hopped up and over the console, landing on her lap. She scratched him behind the ears and let him out of the car without his leash.

Taking a deep breath, she got out of the car, ready to face the man Logan called Uncle Joe. He didn't look anything like she expected a man who lived off the grid to look. Wearing jeans and a knock-off polo, he was clean-shaven, with silver hair kept short and combed to the side. Of course, none of that was really relevant since the man was still pointing his shotgun at them.

"Didn't I warn you?" Joe chastised. "Our government is more corrupt than those third-world countries they look down upon."

"Yes, you warned me," Logan said in a placating tone. "It's good to see you, Uncle Joe. Now put down the gun. You're scaring the lady with it."

As if he hadn't noticed her before, Joe turned his head and narrowed his gaze on her. A slow grin formed on his face before he leaned the shotgun along the wall next to the front door. Then he threw his arms open wide, stomped down the steps of the porch, and headed in her direction. "Rachel Dawson, you're even more beautiful in person."

Glued to her spot out of fear of setting the man off, she slid a glance to Logan, who didn't appear at all worried, a slight smirk tugging up his lips. He hadn't called his uncle first, so how did the man know her name? "Thank you, but how do you know who I am? Do you watch me on Detroit Channel Five?"

With a frown, Joe stopped in front of them and gave Logan a hug, thumping him on the back. "You two are all over the news. You're like the modern-day version of Bonnie and Clyde."

"What are they saying?" she asked.

"That Logan shot mobster Anthony Rinaldi at your urging," Joe said, pulling back from Logan. "That you two are sexual deviants on a cross-country crime spree doing everything from robbing sex toy stores to beating up some guy and stealing someone's valuable dog. Ridiculous, right?"

Walter chose that moment to sidle up and plop down on her feet.

Eyeing the dog, Joe scratched his head. "Or maybe not so ridiculous."

She straightened her spine and placed a hand on her hip. That's what was wrong with the media these days. They didn't dig any deeper than the surface before running with a story. Her, a sex deviant? Anyone who had ever slept with her knew she was as vanilla as they came.

Thank goodness her parents didn't have a television. She didn't want to think what would go through their minds when they learned she was on the run for murder. "We didn't steal Walter. His owner was abusing him. And we never laid a hand on that man."

"Shit, that means the FBI will have an idea of where we're headed," Logan said. "They'll know to look for us at the port."

"Port?" Joe asked, looking at Logan through narrowed lids.

She lifted Walter off the ground and into her arms. "We overheard a conversation between two FBI agents and Rinaldi right before one of them shot Rinaldi in the head."

Joe rubbed his chin. "Explains who's behind the phony story being fed to the media." He motioned to the house with a tip of his head. "Let's go inside. I'd hate for this conversation to get picked up by some CIA satellite."

The three of them walked toward the house, the dog still in her arms. Hopefully, Joe wouldn't mind her bringing an animal into his home.

On closer inspection, the two-story farmhouse looked as if it should be condemned. Maybe it had been nice in its day, but Joe obviously hadn't maintained it. There were wooden boards nailed over some of the windows, missing pieces of siding, and cracks in the wraparound porch. She could almost imagine how peaceful it would've been for a couple to sit on one of those gliders at the end of a hardworking day, drinking an ice-cold beer and watching the children playing in the yard. She wondered if Joe had ever been married or if his brand of crazy had kept him isolated and alone all these years.

Joe grabbed his shotgun then opened the front door, ushering them inside with a wave of his hand.

"Does the word *Leopold* mean anything to you?" Logan asked as soon as the door closed.

Rachel blinked in disbelief as she took in the interior of the home. It was as if she'd stepped into an alternate universe. Joe may have not updated anything on the outside, but inside, everything was immaculate from the crystal chandelier hanging over their heads to hardwood floors beneath their feet. The walls were painted a soothing pale yellow, and as they progressed farther, she noted the gray leather furniture and massive flat-screen television in one of the rooms. He may not get out much, but somehow he'd appropriated the modern items. Not what she would've expected from someone living off the grid, but what the hell did she know? Maybe there was an underground network for people like Joe. She filed that away as a question to ask. Just because she was running from the law didn't mean she couldn't pick up a story or two for later.

"Leopold," Joe repeated. "Someone's name?"

"Possibly. I'll need to use your computer to see what boats are coming into Port Everglades this Friday and then hack into the cruise lines to check their passenger lists."

"If you live off the grid, how do you have electricity and Wi-Fi?"

"I generate my own power through a combination of solar, wind, and micro hydroelectricity. It's fairly simple and a lot cheaper than the energy the government mandates you use. Here in Florida, lots of municipalities make it mandatory to hook your home up to an electrical grid, but I know my constitutional rights. They can't make me. Besides, they don't know I'm here anyway, and I plan to keep it that way. Wi-Fi was a bit tougher, but I managed to hook into a satellite and now I have both Wi-Fi and ten thousand television channels from all over the world."

She'd heard about a couple of different companies trying to start up something they termed the "Outernet," which would provide international access to Wi-Fi for free, but she hadn't known the capabilities were already available. "Aren't you worried you'll get discovered and thrown in jail?"

Joe laughed, his teeth stained yellow and a couple of them missing toward the back. "Been living like this since the seventies. Feds haven't discovered me yet. Doubt they will now. According to their records, I died in Vietnam in a helicopter crash, my body never recovered. Not quite sure how they missed that I'd never been in the helicopter in the first place. Could have knocked me over with a feather when Logan's dad, whom I'd listed as my next of kin, had showed me the letter he'd gotten from the government notifying him of my death." He shrugged a shoulder. "I figured I might as well remain dead." He moved closer and whispered to her, his eyes wild. "You're talking to a ghost." Leaving her spooked, he backed away with a smile and headed toward a staircase. "Come on. I'll show you to your room. You both look like you could use a good night's sleep."

It was only nine at night, but they'd been on the go for twenty-four hours and Logan hadn't slept at all in that time. She'd slept a couple of hours that afternoon as was typical for her. In fact, she wasn't tired at all.

They followed Joe up the stairs, and it was then she noticed that he walked with a bit of a limp. It didn't seem to slow him down at all though. He led them past a couple of closed doors before bringing them to the spare bedroom.

"You both can stay here. I'll take the dog with me. Give you two some privacy," Joe said, giving them a wink as he took Walter from her arms.

Privacy? That's the last thing she and Logan needed. "That's kind of you, but we don't need—"

"Thanks, Uncle Joe. See you in the morning." Logan hugged his uncle, who left, shutting the door behind him.

There wasn't much to the room, but then again, why did he have an extra bedroom at all when he lived out in the middle of nowhere by himself? The room had a tropical feel to it, decorated in teal and tangerine colors with artwork of ocean scenes and a ceiling fan with blades resembling palm tree leaves. The queen-size bed in the center of the room was covered by a seashell-themed comforter and matching throw pillows.

Heat bloomed in her core and her muscles tensed.

One bed.

She may have fucked plenty of men, but she'd never slept with one. Bad enough she had insomnia, but to have someone sleeping next to her while her mind raced all night long…

"We can't share a bed," she said.

"Why not?" Logan smirked as he prepared for bed, pulling down the blankets and tossing the decorative pillows on the floor. "Afraid you won't be able to keep your hands off me?" He clutched the bottom of his shirt and, in a single move, drew it over his head.

"I just don't…" She lost her thought, distracted by the sight of Logan's bare chest. Her heart began to flutter and her throat went dry. Dear God in heaven, the man was cut for being so lean. Her fingers itched to play with the light patch of hair sprinkled over his sternum and to explore the chiseled planes and contours of his abs.

Logan's brows furrowed as he unbuttoned his jeans and slid them down his thighs, leaving him clothed in only a pair of tight navy boxer briefs that did nothing to conceal what hid underneath. "Don't do what? Share a bed?" He dropped onto the mattress, putting his hands under his head.

Before she did something she'd regret, she sat on the edge of bed, linking her fingers together on her lap and keeping her gaze focused on them. "Couldn't you ask Joe if there's somewhere else you can sleep? I mean, he probably just assumed we were together since the media made it seem that way. Just tell him the truth."

"The truth?"

"Yes." She refused to look at him. "That we can hardly stand one another."

The ensuing silence made her uncomfortable, something she wasn't used to feeling. What was it about Logan that set her on edge? She was balls-to-the-wall Rachel

Dawson, Detroit's number one investigative reporter. Nothing fazed her. She didn't get camera shy or stage fright. She'd interviewed foreign dignitaries and cold-blooded murderers. So why couldn't she handle sleeping next to Logan?

And why did it bother her that he hadn't immediately repudiated her claim that they couldn't stand one another?

"Rachel, I'm tired," he said on a sigh. "It's been a long forty-eight hours, and before I start figuring out why a couple of FBI agents are trying to frame us for murder, I'd like to get some rest. I promise I won't touch you. Now get in bed."

She jumped up, nearly stumbling over her own feet, and hurried toward the door. "I'm not really tired. Maybe I'll go see if I can find Joe's computer and start on our research."

"Get. In. Bed."

A full-body shiver stopped her cold at the deep tone of his voice. She twirled around. "Is this how you usually get women to sleep with you? You just order them?"

Humor lit up his eyes. "Only the ones who want me to."

Exasperated, she turned off the lights. She wasn't going to win this battle. She was trapped for the next eight hours without her phone, computer, or even a book. Forget waterboarding. This would be pure torture for her.

She stomped across the floor and tugged her pants off before climbing into bed and pulling the comforter up to her neck. She lay on her back, staring up at the ceiling.

Her eyes adjusted to the darkness, and she watched the fan whirling around and around.

He rolled to his side, facing her. Her body shivered from the awareness of him, practically naked, lying next to her. Although she didn't look for confirmation, she could feel the heat of Logan's stare. "Good night, Rachel."

"Night, Logan."

It wasn't thirty seconds before his breathing evened out. Typical man.

She flipped to her side and forced herself to relax. Following advice she'd gotten from a sleep specialist a few years ago, she tensed all her muscles for ten seconds then relaxed them one by one, beginning with her neck. By the time she got to her toes, she'd identified every noise in the room. The ceiling fan, while pretty, made a whooshing sound; the house creaked; and she was pretty sure she could make out the ticking of a clock from another room.

Huffing out a sigh, she closed her eyes and replayed the past twenty-four hours in her head, beginning with the conversation she'd overheard between Rinaldi and Cole DeMarco. Something hadn't sat right with her, and it bothered her even more now. Why had Rinaldi come to Benediction when he knew he'd never get past the front door? And how had those agents known he would be there? It was possible they'd followed him or perhaps they'd placed a tracker on his vehicle, but her intuition told her there was a reason he'd shown up at Benediction as soon as he was released from prison.

If only she was back home, she would have access to her computer and she could investigate the story. She'd start with the FBI and find out which office and which division those agents worked for. She rolled onto her back again and interlaced the fingers of her hands together, over her chest. Eyes open again, she drew her knees up, pressing her feet into the bed. Were those agents even assigned to Rinaldi's case? They must have been if they needed a legitimate reason to be at the scene of his murder.

"What's wrong?" Logan asked, his voice startling her from her thoughts.

"I can't get comfortable."

He rested his head on his hand. "What can I do to help?"

"Nothing. It's always like this."

"When you sleep in a new bed? Or when you sleep with someone else?"

Not wanting to respond to that last loaded question, she kept it simple. "I don't sleep."

He sat up, leaning against the headboard. "What do you mean you don't sleep? You slept in the car."

She mirrored his action. "Right. That's it. I got my two hours."

"That's all you get? Two hours?" he asked incredulously. "No one can survive like that."

"It's been that way for me since I left home." Her old therapist said it was caused by guilt and the inability to feel safe outside the strict structure she'd grown up in. But Rachel called bullshit, figuring it was because she'd suddenly woken up for the first time in her life and didn't want to miss out on all the possibilities. She quit going to therapy after that session.

"You're telling me you've been running on two hours of sleep a night for more than ten years?"

Why did he care? Despite not sleeping much, she was physically and mentally healthy. Her doctor figured she'd sleep if she needed it, but two hours was enough for her. "Yes. It's not a big deal."

"Have you tried sleeping pills?"

"I've tried everything." And she had. Not because it worried her to go without sleep, but because she wanted to be normal. "Nothing works."

He shifted his legs and angled toward her. "What about sex? Does that help?"

She laughed, ignoring the tingles racing through her at Logan's mere mention of sex. "I don't know about you, but I like to be awake when I have sex."

He nudged her with his foot. "I mean after, when you and your partner have exhausted each other from hours of hot and sweaty, mind-blowing, animalistic sex. After you've come."

She let out a shuddered breath as she tried to visualize what animalistic sex would look like. Had she ever had that kind of sex? Not that she could recall, and let's face it, that wasn't something she was likely to forget. Whatever sex she did have never resulted in an orgasm. But she couldn't blame the men. She was obviously one of those women who couldn't come during sex.

"Rachel?" Logan edged closer. "I'm assuming you're not a virgin."

She laughed nervously. "Of course I'm not a virgin. I'm twenty-nine years old."

"Then why the silence? If you've had sex…" Stopping, he must have noticed her head hanging in mortification. "You've had an orgasm, right?"

She really didn't want to discuss this with him. Or anyone. "I've had orgasms. They're fine."

"Fine? What the hell kind of orgasm are you having?" he said, sounding outraged.

She snapped up her head. "I'm guessing the same kind that everyone else has. I just don't see the appeal. I mean, sure, it feels good for a minute or two, but it's not worth getting sweaty over. Not that I make myself sweaty."

"Yourself?" His voice cracked. "Don't your partners give you orgasms?"

"You say that like it's a crime that I can only come through masturbation. I'm not alone. One-third of women can't come during sex. Eighty percent require clitoral in addition to vaginal stimulation while other—"

"No wonder you can't sleep. Does that brain of yours ever stop?" He suddenly rolled out of bed and crossed the room. "I've got an idea, but you're going to have to trust me."

She exhaled a loud breath. "Logan, we're in the middle of nowhere with a couple of rogue agents who want us dead and your uncle, who probably has a shed filled with enough weapons to arm a small country, is down the hall. I have no choice but to trust you."

"Great," he said, flicking on the lights, giving her another view of Logan in nothing but his boxer briefs.

This time, she didn't bother averting her eyes, raking her gaze over the toned muscles of his abdomen and following the trail of hair down. "In that case, I'm going to blindfold, gag, and tie you up. And then I'm going to show you what a real orgasm feels like."

Chapter Nine

HER HEART WAS beating so quickly she was sure it would fly out of her chest. Did Logan just offer to give her an orgasm? It was one thing to let him tie her up at Benediction, where things couldn't go too far, but she couldn't do it here. "Logan, I don't think that's a good idea."

"Too bad." Folding his arms across his chest, he leaned his back against the door, the muscles of his forearms rippling. "Because I think it's a great one. Otherwise, you'll just keep me up all night, and we both need to rest if we're going to get ourselves out of this mess."

She bunched the comforter in her hands. "So you're taking one for the team and having sex with me to get some sleep?"

"Hell no." He pushed off the door and stalked closer, heat banked in his eyes. "First of all, if I fucked you, I'd be doing it because I wanted to and not because I wanted to get some shut-eye. And second, the last thing we'd get was any sleep because if I fucked you, I'd do it hard and all night long. We don't have that kind of time."

All night long? The room suddenly seemed a lot smaller. "Then I'm confused. I thought you said you were going to give me an orgasm."

Now beside her, he braced a hand on the wall over her head and leaned toward her, his scent doing wicked things to her insides. "There are other ways for me to do that for you."

She couldn't count the number of times a guy had thought he had a magic tongue, and she was tired of faking her orgasms to conserve a man's ego. "It won't work. I'll get frustrated and you'll get mad—"

He scowled, tilting up her chin with two of his fingers. "Has some guy made you think it was your fault he couldn't make you come?"

Although only one of them had actually called her a frigid bitch to her face, they'd made it clear they'd done the same moves on other women with a 100 percent success rate. Most of them didn't care so long as they got off. And she always got what she wanted too—information. "It is my fault. These guys, they knew what they were doing. A couple of them had a reputation for it, you know? So it had to be my fault. I don't know why I'm telling you this."

Somber, he shook his head. "There's nothing wrong with you. You're a strong woman. You require someone stronger than you who can shut off that brain of yours for a bit."

Comprehension of what he was suggesting slammed into her. "Oh, God. You want me to submit to you."

"I bet you always stay in control during sex. Am I right?"

What was wrong with that? She was the one who knew what felt good and how to move to get the right things stroked in the right way. "So you're saying it *is* my fault they can't make me come."

He picked up a piece of her hair and slid it between his fingers. "I'm saying it's time you let someone else be in charge for once. You and me, we're in this together. I don't know how long it's going to take or what's going to happen in the future. All I know is we've been skirting around this attraction between us for more than a year."

Attraction? Sure, he might get her motor running, like now, with him standing so close, gently fondling the strands of her hair, which for some reason she felt all the way to her clit. But all they did was argue. "We hate each other."

His gaze dropped to her lips. "I don't hate you, Rachel. I never have," he said softly. "When Kate first introduced us a few months after you two became friends, I didn't want to like you. She'd told me previously about how you'd met during the Alyssa Deveroux murder investigation. That you were just one more reporter who'd vilified Jaxon because he practiced BDSM and that you'd do anything it took to get your story. I didn't care that Kate had forgiven you. I still held a grudge." He paused. "But even though I didn't want to like you, I did. And it pissed me off because I liked you a lot."

He liked her? Those pesky oversized butterflies flew around in her belly. "You sure didn't act like you liked me. You argued with me over everything."

"It was easier to argue with you than to do what I really wanted."

"What was that?" she asked, noticing the way her voice trembled.

"Kiss you senseless." He cradled her face in his large hands. "You wanted to learn more for your exposé. Let me show you. Until this is over, submit to me."

Her throat contracted, and for a moment she couldn't breathe. "What does that mean? I'm supposed to do whatever you say?"

He laughed. "No, I'm not delusional. That would never happen. Just when it comes to your sexual pleasure."

She swallowed thickly. "In bed, you mean."

"In bed." His eyebrows rose. "Or wherever else I decide."

"Just until we clear our names?" Her heart beat in triple time as she considered his offer.

Could she really do it? She'd lived on her own terms for so long, she didn't know how to answer to anyone. What would it be like to give up control during sex? Would it really help her achieve an orgasm? She doubted it, but what could it hurt to find out? Even if Logan failed to deliver, she could justify it as professional research. But the minute he thought he could control her outside the bedroom, she'd end it.

Pushing against his chest to move him away, she got to her feet. She'd do it, but on her terms. No pretending this meant anything more than just an experiment for research's sake. How many reporters could use firsthand experience as a part of their story on BDSM? It was just the angle she needed to get the feature noticed by the national network execs. As long as she stayed professional, she could do this. She gripped the bottom edge of her shirt and began sliding it up her torso. "Fine."

Logan stilled her hands. "What are you doing?"

Frowning, she thought it would be obvious. "I'm taking off my clothes."

He smiled and motioned to the bed with a jut of his chin. "Not yet. Lie on your stomach. I want to relax you first."

She rolled her eyes as she established herself onto the bed. A massage? Really?

Lying flat with her arms stretched out in front of her, she closed her eyes, feeling the dip of the mattress from Logan's weight. She felt the heat radiating off him as he straddled her and sat back on his haunches. An image of him pulling her onto all fours and taking her from behind crashed into her. She could almost imagine him using her hair to propel her body backward onto his cock as he controlled her every movement.

His rough hands glided down the length of her spine, causing goose bumps to pop up in their wake and a shiver of desire to pass through her core, tightening and clenching muscles deep in her pussy. They were like ghosts of a whisper, relaxing. Soft. Barely touching her, but she felt them deep below the surface. His hands were learning her body, exploring every curve and plane of her back just as she'd desired to do with his chest only minutes before. His hard cock brushed against the bottom of her spine, letting her know he was just as turned on by her as she was for him.

She melted into the mattress, her nipples rubbing almost painfully against the fabric of her shirt with every pass of his hand. Fingers kneaded the tight muscles of her shoulders, loosening the tension that had been there for far too long. She'd had professional massages before. Had even had a man or two rub her muscles in an attempt to get her to relax, but nothing, nothing, had ever felt like this. Logan didn't just touch her. He commanded her body. Took control of her mind, leaving behind a quivering mess of a woman with no thoughts or feelings other than how blissfully relaxed she felt.

In silence, he worked his way down, his hands pressing and kneading and rubbing while she unabashedly ground her pussy against the mattress in anticipation. When he worked his magic fingers into the muscles of her ass, she heaved a loud sigh and fell even deeper under his magnetic spell. Arousal coursed through her body, her nipples hardening and her pussy growing wetter and wetter, so wet she'd bet anything she was leaving behind a spot on the sheets. But she didn't care about that. She didn't care about anything at the moment but how good this man could make her feel. And he hadn't even touched her sexually.

Yet.

She trembled as his hands glided down the back of her thighs, his fingers so close to her pussy she could almost feel them parting the lips through her underpants. It took her a moment to realize she wasn't imagining it. His thumbs were over her panties, spreading her open, giving her clitoris a chance to poke out and rub against the sheets. But all too quickly, his hands moved on to her inner thighs, leaving her desperately aroused and aching to be filled. She squirmed, trying to get his hands back on her pussy, but all she got was a chuckle from him. Knowing she had no control over his actions, she allowed herself to drift away on a sea of calm, concentrating only on her breathing and the sensation of warmth permeating through her body as if she'd downed a shot of whisky. This wasn't sleep, but she'd take it.

After he finished molding her feet, he removed himself from the mattress, his missing weight noticeable despite her dream-like state. His scent tickled her nose, and warm breath blew on her ear. "Turn over," he whispered.

She didn't hesitate before slowly flipping onto her back. He inched her shirt up, exposing her breasts to his view. Maybe she should care, but at this point, the only thing she was concerned about was getting those hands on her again. She heard him groan, the sound of it reverberating through her and perking up her already hard nipples. And then those hands were massaging her collarbone, drawing her out of her body as if she was floating above the mattress, only the sexual awareness remaining. All the fear, the guilt, the drive to always work to be better, the best, so that the sacrifice she'd made in giving up her family would all be worth it, melted away like chocolate on her tongue.

His hands were on her heavy breasts now, kneading in a way that wasn't sexual, but rather clinical, and yet each scrape of his hands along her sensitive skin sent a dart of lightning to her clit. Her dry lips parted and her tongue bathed it with the moisture pooling in her mouth. He squeezed her breast harder, and she briefly wondered if it was in response to her tongue, but the thought quickly disappeared, her mind too foggy to retain it.

He'd promised to relax her, but this...this was beyond relaxation. It was pure and total abandonment, and she didn't know how he'd managed to make good on his promise. She didn't care how he had done it. Only that he had. He'd kept his promise to her, which meant he'd keep his other promise to her. He'd give her an orgasm.

As soon as the word flashed in her mind, her body tensed. Even with good intentions, Logan would fail on that promise of an orgasm. It was one thing to relax her with a massage, to get her motor cranking for sex, but it was an altogether different story when it came to a climax. Oh sure, she would get to the edge, but she never fell over. She'd just teeter there on the apex of the climax mountain and slide back down the wrong way after the guy got discouraged.

"You know, I can hear you thinking, Rachel," Logan said softly, his hands no longer moving. "You were relaxed for a while. Want to tell me what happened?"

No, she didn't. She just wanted to get back to that place where fear and recrimination didn't exist. Kate and Danielle had spoken to her at length about the high they got from surrendering to their lovers, but she never quite got it. She still didn't. Not completely. But she was beginning to understand it. She'd taken care of herself for so long, she didn't know how to let anyone else do it for her.

"I don't know," she said, opening her eyes. He didn't press her for more. Just nodded, clearly not buying the lie, but having the decency not to confront her on it. Her body hummed with arousal as she realized Logan was straddling her again, the only thing separating his cock and her pussy, tiny bits of fabric covering them both. If she raised her hips and he pulled aside the cotton, he could drive himself into her, filling her and stretching her with what appeared to be an above average-sized dick. Maybe she wouldn't come, but she'd still enjoy it. And even better, she could take back the control she desperately craved. Make him come hard so at least he'd go to sleep and leave her alone with her racing thoughts.

His hands braced her hips as he stared at her, his eyes crinkled in curiosity. When he removed himself from his position over her body, she couldn't help the knot of disappointment stuck in her throat. He was giving up. She should be used to it, but she had a moment of weakness, believing he might be different.

He strode over to the window and bent, retrieving his duffle bag. Well, she wouldn't be getting an orgasm, but at least she'd gotten one hell of a massage out of it. Maybe now he'd help her find a computer and she could get to work while he slept. That way, by the morning, she'd have a lead on who this Leopold was and why those agents were so interested in him. Once they got back on the road, she'd get her two hours of sleep and she'd be golden by the time they showed up at the port tomorrow afternoon.

Jarring her, he dropped the bag on the mattress. With a purposeful stride, he returned to stand by the side of the bed and rifled through his bag, coming up with rope and three bandanas.

Her stomach performed somersaults over the items in his hands and the wicked gleam in his eyes.

He hadn't given up.

He'd just gone for reinforcements.

Heaven help her, she was about to be inducted into the kinky hall of fame.

Her eyes settled on the growing bulge behind his boxer briefs. Hell, the tip of it was peeking out at the top. He wasn't just packing. He was huge. No wonder he was so cocky. He had the goods to back it up.

At the lick of her lips, he scoffed, catching her eying him appreciatively. "I told you, I'm not going to fuck you tonight, so stop looking at me as though you're starving for me, because no matter how much you want it, you're not getting it tonight."

"But, if I'm willing and you're aching, what's the problem with me relieving that ache for you?"

"The problem is you're not ready to be fucked by me yet." He bounced the rope between his hands, his voice taking on a deeper, stronger tone. "Baby steps, Tiger. You need to learn how to give up control before I reward you with my cock. I won't die if I don't come tonight, so don't worry about taking care of my needs. In this room, I am in control and the only thing I want is you naked right now, so while I stand here and watch, I want you to take that shirt off and slide those panties that are teasing me out of my ever-fucking mind because I want to see what belongs to me now. I need to play with those gorgeous tits of yours, see how sensitive they are, get my lips around those nipples that are poking out at me through your shirt, begging me to suck on them. I want to check if that pussy is as spicy as that mouth of yours during our verbal sparring sessions or as sweet as it is when you're crooning to that ugly-assed dog of yours. And darlin', the only thing I want you to do is nothing."

He placed one knee on the bed and leaned toward her. "You're not responsible for your orgasms, you got me? They're mine. Mine to give. Mine to take. And trust me, when I want something, I get it."

She made her living with her voice, but she was struck speechless. No one had ever spoken to her like that in her life. Her friends had laughed about a dominant man and how they could use their voices to train their pussies into coming on demand. Rachel had always assumed they were full of shit, exaggerating. No one could come on demand without physical stimulation. Now, hearing those words come out of Logan's mouth in that panty-melting, pussy-creaming way of his, she could believe it. Her clit was pulsing, swelling from his voice. If he could manage that from just his voice, what the hell would it be like when that mouth actually touched her?

She exhaled a loud breath, thinking about his tongue flicking at her clit and his breath bathing her in its fiery heat. "You keep your kink junk in your go-bag?"

As if he could see straight through her defenses, he smirked. "None of this is 'kink junk' as you put it. They're essential items for any go-bag. You can turn any ordinary household item into something kinky. Since I'm going to blindfold, bind, and gag you," he said, picking up the bandanas and then dangling them in his hand, "you'll need a way to communicate if you want me to stop." He handed over one of the strips of fabric. "If you drop the bandana, I'll remove the gag so you can talk. Now let me see what's mine."

She swallowed hard, nodding. Trust didn't come easy to her. Even her friends didn't know who she was underneath the woman they knew as Rachel Dawson. How could they when she could barely remember? But for some reason, she did trust Logan Bradford, and that had to mean something. Maybe, just maybe, he was seeing the woman she'd kept hidden away from the rest of the world. She trembled, the thought equally exhilarating and terrifying. What if she bared herself to him and he found her lacking?

Logan claiming ownership of her shouldn't set her blood on fire, but it did. *It's temporary*, she reminded herself. There was nothing wrong with giving up control and gifting it to another. She'd done the countless hours of research for her exposé on BDSM and had spoken at length with both Danielle and Kate. There was strength in submission. She couldn't deny it. And she was strong.

She just wasn't sure if she was strong *enough*.

Guess there was only one way to find out.

Chapter Ten

"STAND UP," LOGAN said, hauling her to her feet. "Now take off your clothes, starting with your shirt."

Man, he was bossy. Yet somehow, the bossier he was, the slicker she became between her thighs. She wondered what he'd do if she refused. Would he spank her? Did she want him to? She smashed her lips together to keep from giggling. Maybe another time she'd try it and find out.

She slid her shirt up her body and over her head, dropping it on the floor. Logan's heated gaze went straight to her chest as she reached around to unclasp her bra. As it fluttered away from her breasts, he inhaled sharply and bit down on his lower lip as if this was the first time he'd seen them. His hands were clenched into fists and she watched his Adam's apple bob up and down as he swallowed.

He might be in charge, but she still had the control, the power to make him crazy with lust for her. She snagged her panties with her thumbs and slowly slid them down her thighs, stepping out of them and leaving herself bare for his hungry perusal.

He blinked rapidly, his gaze falling to her bared pussy, and he hummed in the back of his throat. She was proud of her body. Several men had complimented her on it, but never once did those compliments make her feel the way she did right now with Logan. He didn't need to use any words because everything he was thinking could be found on his face. His nostrils were flared, his eyes hooded.

He wanted her.

Which made it that much more confusing that he refused to fuck her.

"Come closer," he ordered, his voice thick with arousal.

Her heart banged a staccato beat as she took a step toward him.

He placed the bandanas on the bed and dangled the rope from his hand. "I'm not going to gag you or blindfold you until I'm finished binding you because I want you to see what I'm doing and to let me know if the ropes are too tight." He motioned for her to turn around with his finger.

She faced away from him and hissed out a breath as his arms circled her under her breasts. "I'm going to start like I did at Benediction. And for your research, this is called Shibari."

"Japanese rope bondage, right?" she asked, trying to distract herself from the fact Logan's fingers were brushing the sides of her breasts and that her nipples had perked up, as if begging to get in on the action.

"Did your homework, huh?" She heard the amusement in his voice. "Anyone can tie a knot, but there's something esthetically beautiful in Shibari. It turns rope into art." While he placed the rope under her breasts, his thumbs stroked lazily over her distended nipples, back and forth, as if they had all the time in the world.

Her breath whooshed out of her, half hiss and half moan. She trembled, already feeling as though she was losing control of her body, and he'd only barely touched her. "I know for a fact you weren't into kink when you met Kate, so when did you start practicing Shibari?"

Logan and Kate had interned at the same law firm their final year of law school when Kate had gone undercover at Benediction to help prove her then-client, Jaxon Deveroux, innocent in the murder of his wife. Because Logan had helped them solve the murder and because he was now Kate's law partner, Jaxon returned the favor by buying him a membership to Benediction.

His breath blew on her ear. "I guess it depends on how you want to define kink. I didn't participate in the BDSM community or join a club until recently, but that doesn't mean I wasn't tying up women and having my way with them before. I'll admit, Shibari is new to me. When Cole discovered my interest in bondage, he introduced me to a friend of his who mentored me in Shibari and Kinbaku, which is another kind of Japanese rope bondage. But yeah"—he bit down on her earlobe and then sucked it into his mouth, easing the sting—"I've always been kinky."

All too soon his mouth disappeared and he went back to work. She looked down, admiring the way he'd secured her heavy breasts with the silky rope. They swelled, aching for his caress. She wanted his mouth on them now, using his teeth and tongue just as he had on her earlobe, and with any other man, she would've demanded it. But there was something about trusting Logan would get there on his own time frame that amped up her arousal.

Her breathing slowed even as her pulse raced, a warm, syrupy sensation sweeping her body, and her eyelids grew heavier with each slide of rope on her feverish skin. The room shrunk so that all she knew was Logan. The crinkle of his brows, the beads of perspiration dotting his forehead, the slide of his tongue across his bottom lip as he concentrated on his task of tying her. He smelled like sex on a hot summer day, his scent dizzying and stimulating all at once. She couldn't remember a time when she had been so aware of another person or when she'd enjoyed a man's touch this much.

And he'd barely even started.

She closed her eyes and sunk into the moment, allowing herself to let go of all her thoughts and fears and just once—for research's sake, of course—truly give her power over to another. Swaying on her feet, she trembled as Logan's hands splayed her inner thighs, her clit throbbing and moisture slickening the folds of her pussy.

"Easy there," he said roughly, his hands moving to her hips rather than going where she needed him the most. "You're tipping over. Before you lie down, I want you to look at yourself in the mirror." With a hand on her lower back, he directed her across the room. "Open your eyes, Rachel."

Her eyes fluttered open to a vision of her reflection in the mirror hanging over the dresser. The rope criss-crossed over her breasts, creating a makeshift harness that both lifted and showcased them, her erect nipples darkened from a pink to reddish-brown. From there, the rope descended down the center of her abdomen and over the glistening dark curls of her labia, spreading them wide and exposing her wet crimson folds. It could've appeared crude—should have appeared crude—and yet instead, the view was highly erotic.

"You look gorgeous in my ropes," he whispered into her ear. "And I can't wait to get my mouth on you."

Yeah, he wasn't the only one.

Their gazes collided in the mirror, almost tangible electricity arcing between them. Her skin felt tight, her body on fire with need. In this moment, with her breasts and pussy on display, she'd never felt more vulnerable. More desirable. More alive.

Logan stroked his hands down her arms and turned her around to face him. He tucked a piece of hair behind her ear and then cradled her cheek, his lips inching their way closer and closer to hers. Her eyes closed in anticipation.

His lips brushed against her forehead before he released a sigh. "I want you on the bed." Gripping the rope underneath her breasts, he pulled her flush against him so she could feel the steel of his covered erection pressing into her belly. "Now."

A thin thread of uncertainty trickled into her consciousness. Why hadn't he kissed her? If it wasn't for the proof of his arousal, she would've thought he wasn't attracted to her, but what she had felt stirring beneath his briefs left little doubt as to how she affected him physically. He wanted her as much as she wanted him, so why wouldn't he kiss her?

The answer hovered right below the surface, but she didn't want to think right now. Maybe Logan had done her a favor. At least now, she wouldn't confuse their sexual intimacy as anything more than a limited beneficial agreement for them both. She'd hopefully get an orgasm, and he'd get some sleep.

He led her back to the bed, each slide of the rope against her damp skin making her shiver. Then he picked up one of the bandanas, situating it over her eyes and plunging her into darkness. "Before I gag and finish binding you, how are the ropes? Are they too tight?"

She swallowed and gave him a smile. "They're fine. Good, I mean."

He placed a piece of fabric in her palm and closed her fingers around it. "Remember to drop the bandana from your hand if you need to stop." On her nod, he slipped it between her lips and tied the back of it.

Her pulse pounded in her ears, the heady rush of excitement speeding through her. She allowed him to lay her back onto the bed and manipulate her limbs into position. Ropes bound her wrists together and drew them above her head. Within a minute, her arms were immobile, most likely tied to the headboard. He spread her legs and pushed her knees up, so that her feet rested on the mattress. Then ropes circled her ankles, keeping her pussy open wide for him.

Heat unfurled in her belly, spanning outward, the anticipation of what he'd do nearly driving her insane. She clutched the bandana in her palm as if the world would end if she dropped it. Without the use of her voice to command, without the use of her eyes to direct, without the use of her hands to caress, without the use of her feet to walk away, she was free to just be. To savor the moment.

Something stroked the length of her neck. It lacked the calloused roughness that she'd felt before, so she knew it wasn't his fingers. It took her a moment to register that it was his tongue, bathing her with its moist heat, only to have the air cooling his trail as his mouth slid lower. The contrast of hot and cold caused her body to shiver.

And then his wicked tongue laved a circular path on her breast, each pass of it coming closer and closer to her nipple until it was finally there, jolting her into a sexual frenzy of need. Her muffled moan filled the room as she unsuccessfully tried to arch her nipple farther into his mouth. The ropes held tight, preventing even the smallest of movements. She was completely at his mercy, dependent on him for her pleasure, and apparently, he wasn't going to rush it.

Even though she couldn't see, she closed her eyes beneath the bandana, sinking even further into the experience. Her abdominal muscles clenched as he sucked her nipple farther into the cavern of his mouth, his teeth, tongue, and lips pulling and releasing, teasing and nibbling, sending waves of bliss permeating from her breasts to her pussy, until she was almost certain she would orgasm from that alone.

It had never been like this for her before. Sure, it always felt good when a guy used his mouth on her, but it was like comparing a typical downpour of rain to a hurricane. The wet proof of her arousal dripped out of her, her legs shaking from need. He was winding her up and up and up, just from the suction of his mouth on her nipple. As if he was enjoying every second of it, he made a humming sound in the back of his throat.

She almost couldn't stand it. Muffled pleas for more fell from her lips, her head shaking back and forth. The ache in her pussy morphed into a pulsating blaze.

He released her nipple and worked his way over to the other one, beginning the tantalizing process all over again. His tongue was like a key to the engine of her pussy, revving her up.

She tried to buck, to squirm, to ease the building tension with a clench of her thighs, but all to no avail. Her brain went fuzzy, the normal pictures and thoughts running through her mind suddenly disappearing, leaving behind only a black slate with bursts of multicolored stars.

All too soon and not soon enough, Logan began gliding down her torso, nipping her sensitive skin along the way. "Fucking responsive as hell," he murmured. "Just as I knew you'd be. Now let's see if you taste as good as I've imagined."

Her mind repeated one word over and over.

Yes, yes, yes.

Until now, she'd never really craved a man's mouth on her pussy.

"Ever taste yourself, Tiger?" He caressed the skin above her slit. "I bet you haven't." His tongue dipped into her channel, sampling her. "I'm not gonna give you bullshit about you tasting like honey or peaches or some crap like that. You don't taste sweet. You're like a hot exotic spice on my tongue. So I'm going to enjoy the hell out of this pussy right now and you're just gonna lie there and take everything I give to you."

She jerked, crying out when his fingers rubbed on each side of the hood of her clitoris. And when his lips sucked it into his mouth, her entire body bowed. Deprived of most of her senses, she indulged in the sensation of touch, hypersensitive to every ridge and bump of his rough-yet-gentle tongue as he languidly caressed her exposed bud with it. Nothing... *nothing* had ever felt so exquisite. That was until his fingers breached her entrance and slowly began pumping in and out of her. She bit down on her gag, her arms quaking from the intensity of pleasure coursing through her.

Her toes curled into the comforter as Logan continued to stroke her clit with his tongue, the stubble that had grown in on his face in the past day rubbing against her exposed folds. A fire blazed deep in her pussy, building stronger and stronger with each pass of his tongue and quickening thrust of his fingers. Dizzy and breathless, she felt as if it was whirling like a spinning top. She dangled on the precipice of climax, her muscles growing rigid before she plunged over the edge, waves of ecstasy flowing outward from her pussy to every part of her body.

Logan had not only delivered on his promise, he'd surpassed her expectations. She'd never come like that. Didn't even know it was possible. What did it mean? Would she require a massage and bondage every time in order to achieve orgasm? Was she truly submissive?

The thoughts flitted through her mind before scattering away like a feather on the wind. Murmuring words of praise, Logan released the bindings on her hands and rubbed her wrists then removed the gag from her mouth. She wanted to say something to tell him she appreciated the care he'd shown her tonight. Tell him thank you.

But before she could find the right words, her mind quieted. The last thought she had was that Logan would prove more dangerous than the FBI chasing after them.

Chapter Eleven

She'd actually slept.

The bright sun streamed through the window blinds, hitting Rachel's face. She stared at the digital clock, shocked it was after eight in the morning. The last thing she remembered was Logan removing the bindings from her after she'd experienced an orgasm that had made all the other ones she'd had before pale in comparison.

What did that say about her?

In her head, she knew that didn't make her weak. She would never, ever associate that word with Kate, who was collared by Jaxon. During the day, Kate ran a successful law practice and battled for the rights of those discriminated against, but at night, she surrendered to her lover, enjoying the bite of the whip. Kate was the strongest woman she knew.

A twinge of remorse unfurled in Rachel's chest. She wasn't the only one who thought that about Kate. Last night, she'd ignored the fact that the man who licked greedily at her pussy was in love with her best friend, but now, in the stark light of morning, the knowledge rushed back into her like a tidal wave.

She couldn't help feeling like second best.

It didn't matter because it wasn't going to happen again.

She'd promised him her submission until they cleared their names, but if all went well, they'd figure out how to do that today when they found Leopold at the port. By tonight, she might finally have the story to catapult her career to the next step—New York. It was everything she'd been working toward for the past ten years. Every long night studying in the library, every time she'd run errands for the news producer at the station, every man she'd screwed or screwed over to get the information she needed. All of it would prove worth it when she became an anchor at a big-market news station.

She'd miss her Thursday bar nights with her friends, but she had no other reason to stay in Michigan. Hell, she lived only three miles from her parents, and she never saw them or her siblings. She had few ties and no personal entanglements to complicate her life, and that's exactly how she wanted it. No one would ever tell her how to live her life again, even a Dom as sexy as Logan.

She rolled out of bed then picked up her pants off the floor. After putting them on, she snagged a T-shirt from Logan's go-bag and slipped it over her head, tying off the bottom edge to make it fit better. Although others might consider her high-maintenance, she didn't require much.

But clean clothes, deodorant, and a toothbrush were absolute must-haves she needed to survive this ordeal.

Swinging open the door to search out Logan, she found Walter instead waiting for her in the hall and crouched down to pet him. "Hey, boy. Want to take me to Logan?"

The dog turned and waddled away as if he understood her question. Laughing, she trailed him down the stairs, hearing voices and the clacking sound of keystrokes on a computer's keyboard as she neared the landing.

Following the voices, she was about to step into the room, but stopped when she heard Joe mention her name.

"You and Rachel been together long?" he asked.

She held her breath, waiting for the answer, not quite knowing what she wanted to hear. She'd already made up her mind about no repeats, but she was curious how Logan would respond.

"We're not together," Logan said after a long pause.

"Didn't look that way to me."

"Before everything happened, she and I fought every time we were in the same room. Now we're just making the best of a bad situation. Don't read too much into it."

Making the best of a bad situation. Last night meant nothing to Logan but a way to get her under his control and make her sleep. If she'd been a different kind of a person, someone who allowed a man to wrap his hand around her heart and crush it, she might be upset right now. But that wasn't her. She was a realist. What Kate and Jaxon and Danielle and Cole shared was an anomaly, not the norm.

Reality was her parents. A marriage practically arranged by her grandparents. They each played their traditional roles in the marriage, but there was no passion. No spark. Her mother spent her life raising her brood of children and caring for the home. Her father owned and managed a successful jewelry store, and when he wasn't working, he was praying. When the two were together, they were cordial and friendly, but she could tell they didn't love each other in a romantic sense. When she was twelve, she overheard her mother crying with her aunt about a man whom she had lived next to as a child, someone outside their church who had died in a car accident that day. That was the first time she could remember her mother crying, and she realized, even at that age, that her mother had loved that man at one time. Rachel had never spoken to her mom about it, but she knew now her parents had both fulfilled their duties to their families. They made the best out of a bad situation.

Just like Logan.

Walter sat in the doorframe and barked, looking back at her as if inviting her inside and, no doubt, alerting Joe and Logan to her presence.

She flipped her hair and squared her shoulders then, with a smile, entered the room. "Good morning."

"Morning," Logan said, not looking away from the computer screen in front of him. If his words hadn't been clear enough for her, his reaction upon seeing her this morning certainly were.

Joe, on the other hand, greeted her with a big, knowing smile. "Help yourself to breakfast. There should be some bacon and eggs left unless your friend here gave it all to the dog," he said, nodding at Logan.

She silently cursed the warmth spreading in her chest. "You fed Walter?"

"Yeah." Logan didn't stop typing as he slid her a glance. "Let him out and gave him breakfast. Didn't want to wake you. No big deal."

She flipped her attention to the jumble of numbers, symbols, and letters on the computer screen. "What is all that?"

"The back door to the cruise line's passenger list," Logan said. "First thing this morning, I pulled up the schedule of cruise ships arriving at the port today. There are four. I already broke into three other lines, but none of them had a passenger by the first or last name of Leopold."

"Won't the companies be able to know they were hacked? What if they trace it?"

Joe huffed out a snort. "You don't know my boy here too well, do you? There's nothing he can't hack."

"Now, that's not true. But if I can't hack it, I've got a couple friends who can." Logan twisted around to look at her. "Don't worry. I'm good enough to not leave a trail."

She curled her fingers along the back of his chair. "How did you learn how to hack?"

"I've always been into computers. By the time I was sixteen, I could hack into just about any database. While other kids were playing football and basketball, I started my own business testing companies' mainframes and making recommendations on how to tighten them, so they didn't leave any holes that would allow security breaches. After I graduated, I got dual degrees in computer science and communications and put some of what I learned in the army doing military intelligence. Now I design role-playing computer games for those in the military to practice combat tactics in my spare time."

He didn't fit the image of what she assumed a hacker would look like. Shouldn't he look more like Clark Kent than Superman?

She raised a brow. "You're a computer geek?"

He shrugged. "It depends on your definition of a geek. As a kid, I made enough money to buy a car and take girls out on dates. Oh, and I was homecoming king senior year of high school." Flashing her a bright smile, he turned back to the computer screen. "Damn it, there are no Leopolds listed as passengers or employees on any of the ships."

Her mind went to work, cataloguing the other possibilities. She itched to do her own computer research. "What if we're wrong? What if Leopold isn't a person? Maybe it's a ship."

Before he could respond, a loud siren wailed throughout the house. She froze while Joe burst into motion, grabbing keys from the desk drawer before opening a closet.

"Shit. Is that who I think it is?" Logan asked, pointing to the security screen in the corner of the room.

The monitor revealed a stream of black cars kicking up dust as they headed down the road leading to the fence. It had to be the FBI. They'd found them. But how?

"Son of a bitch," said Joe, grabbing two bags from the closet and throwing miscellaneous items into them. "You must have led them straight here. Got a tracker on you somewhere. We've got two minutes tops before they create a bypass for the electric fence."

That didn't make sense. They'd "borrowed" Willie's car, and there was no way that had a tracker on it. She'd done everything Logan had told her to do. She hadn't used a phone or a computer. There was no way to trace her, and Logan sure as hell hadn't done anything to jeopardize them either.

"How can they do that?" she asked.

"Insulated wire," Joe said, throwing a couple of guns and boxes of bullets into the bags. "You attach it at two different points in the gate and you can cut the middle. The electric fence keeps most people out, but with the FBI, it only buys us some time to escape."

Logan tugged her away from the monitor and down the hall, following the cursing Joe. As they came to the staircase, Joe pressed on the side of it, opening a secret panel. He stepped inside, ushering them in with a wave of his hand.

A bark came from behind her, and she whipped her head toward its owner. Walter hurtled himself at the front door, barking and snarling as if defending them from intruders. As Joe moved farther into the hidden passageway, Logan pulled on her arm, urging her forward.

She stopped in her tracks, looking back at the dog. She couldn't leave him here. Who knew what they'd do to him. He belonged to her now, and that meant he was hers to protect.

"I have to get Walter," she said, pulling out of Logan's grasp and running back toward the front door.

Logan growled but didn't stop her. "Hurry. We're running out of time."

Walter continued his assault at the door until she scooped him up in her arms. From behind the curtains at the side of the door, she could see at least two dark sedans driving up the road from the gate. If it had taken the FBI only minutes to penetrate the fortress Joe had spent years building, how the hell would she and Logan ever be able to escape from here?

"Come on," Logan shouted, hurrying her back under the stairs.

Once she and Walter entered, Logan reached around her and shut the door. The dog was still barking, his heavy little body shaking with fury. She quietly shushed him, petting him gently as she followed Logan and Joe down a narrow tunnel lit only by the flashlight in Joe's hand. "Where does this lead?"

"Goes under the stream in the backyard," Joe responded breathlessly. "About a quarter mile down, there's a shed hidden by the Everglades with a car in it. Let's just hope the battery isn't dead. I haven't had the need to start it lately."

"I'm really sorry about this, Uncle Joe," Logan said. "I promise to make it up to you."

"Nonsense, boy," Joe said. "I wouldn't have given you the coordinates if I didn't want you to use them. But you might want to figure out how they followed you here, so you don't make the same mistake again."

Logan looked back at her, accusation in his eyes. "Did you use my phone or anything else since we've gotten here? Call into work to coordinate our nightmare as your big story?"

Seems trust went only one way with him.

And here she'd thought things had changed between them after yesterday's conversation and last night's nonconversation.

Clenching her jaw to keep from giving him a piece of her mind and holding Walter tighter to keep her fists from flailing, she took a deep breath and exhaled before responding. "No. I've done nothing since I've gotten here but submit to you, sleep, and come downstairs to find you. If one of those things was the cause of alerting the FBI to our whereabouts, then I apologize." Nope, she couldn't do it. She added, "And I'll make sure never to do it again."

His eyes softened. "I didn't mean—"

"Mind having your lovers' quarrel a little later? I don't think this is any of my business," Joe said gruffly.

She didn't embarrass easily, but her cheeks heated at her oversharing. Still, she didn't regret defending herself. It was one thing to submit in bed, but hell if she'd ever submit outside it. She fought for herself as hard as she fought to right wrongs through her investigative reporting, and she wouldn't change for anyone, including Soldier Boy.

They continued down the tunnel until it ended at a ladder. Joe climbed up and threw open a hatch.

Logan started his ascent, and held out his arms out as he neared the top. "Give me Walter." She handed him the dog so that she could use both hands to climb, and he passed Walter to Joe.

She followed Logan up the rungs of the ladder, blinking away the spots in her vision caused by the brightness of the sun. In front of them was a brown wooden pole barn, which, from the looks of it, had been slowly decaying for the past thirty years. But she had to hand it to Joe. If she'd stumbled upon it without the knowledge of what lay inside, she would walk past it, never thinking twice about inspecting the contents. Although it seemed odd to find a structure like this in the middle of a swamp.

A splash from the stream behind startled her. She whipped her head around, seeing nothing but a circular ripple spreading out from the center, and turned back to Joe, questioning him with a raise of her brow.

Joe wiped the sweat from his forehead then worked the combination on the lock of the barn. "You might want to keep the dog in your arms for now, Logan. We grow the gators big down here."

She didn't know what was worse at this point, gators or FBI agents. "What's the plan here? We're just gonna drive away and hope they don't follow us?"

Joe removed the lock and swung open the doors of the barn to reveal a Jeep inside. She and Logan were about to follow when Joe held up his hand to halt them. "You're not coming with me."

Chapter Twelve

"What?" she asked. "You're going to leave us here for the FBI?" With a wave of her arm, she motioned to the estuary. "And the gators?"

"No." He pointed to a cluster of bushes. "Right behind the red mangroves over there, you'll find a fan boat. Head west and keep going until you see a bunch of small buildings. That'll be the town. Dock the boat over there and find the purple house in town. Ask for Morrie. Tell him I sent you and you need the truck. While you're doing all that, I'll be taking the FBI on a wild-goose chase. By the time they catch up with me, you'll be long gone."

Logan shook his head vehemently at Joe's attempt to hand him one of the bags he'd taken from the house. "No. I can't ask you to do that for us. There's got to be another way."

Joe grabbed Logan by the shoulders. "You just figure out who's behind this setup and don't worry about me.

I'm sure I can keep them up to their eyeballs in paperwork while they try to figure out how a dead man has aided and abetted two criminals."

As soon as the words *dead man* left his mouth, she realized how the FBI had found them. She bit her lip, hating she was about to burst the man's bubble. "I hate to be the bearer of bad news, but I think they already know you're alive."

Joe released Logan and narrowed his gaze on her. "Why would you think that?"

Her ability to string together facts to come to the right conclusion was one of her strongest attributes. "It's the only thing that makes sense. Once they got the tip from Walter's previous owner about our location, the FBI probably checked to see if Logan had any contacts in Florida." She gave him an apologetic smile. "Sorry, Joe. Apparently, the FBI already knew where to find you before we got here."

The men froze. She transferred her weight from foot to foot, watching Joe's puzzled expression as he processed her theory.

Laughing, he pounded Logan's back. "You've got yourself a smart one, Logan. Don't fuck it up." He jutted his chin toward Walter. "Morrie just lost his dog. Might want to consider giving him Walter. The man could use a companion." On a salute, he climbed into his truck and slammed the door shut. The engine roared to life and he drove off, waving his hand out the window as he headed back toward the direction of the house.

She and Logan started for the boat that was allegedly hidden behind the bushes. What if they couldn't get it working? They'd be stuck here in the middle of a swamp.

"Know how to drive a fan boat?" she asked, trying to get her mind off the danger hiding all around them.

"No, but I have a feeling I'm about to learn unless you've got some experience with them."

She puffed out a breath. "Closest experience I've got is a canoe in summer camp. You're military. They must have trained you for things like this."

"Sorry. There weren't many opportunities to go boating where I was stationed. But unlike you, I've driven a boat with a motor before. Fan boats can't be too different from a pontoon, right?" he said teasingly.

Rounding the other side of the bush, she got her first sight of what Joe had left them to use as their getaway vehicle and stopped in her tracks. The boat looked like a tin can sliced in half with a huge fan stuck on the back. There were only two rows, each wide enough to accommodate one person.

The boat tipped as Logan stepped onto it with Walter tucked under his arm like a football. In her mind, she saw herself falling into the open mouth of a waiting alligator.

No way was she riding that thing.

Logan set Walter down and held out his hand to her. "Hop on."

"No, I think I'm going to find another way to get out of here."

"Rachel, there's no other way." His voice softened. "Trust me."

She must be out of her mind to trust him after he'd practically accused her of inviting the FBI to find them, but when he used that voice on her, she couldn't resist. She did trust him to keep her physically safe.

Emotionally was a whole other matter and one she didn't have time to explore at the moment.

"Fine," she said, taking a deep breath as he helped her onto the boat. She sat in the front, taking Walter from Logan and putting the dog on her lap.

Logan unknotted the rope anchoring the boat and dropped it in the back before getting behind the wheel. "This should be easy. It's just like a car." He handed her a pair of headphones. "I think we're supposed to wear these." After they placed them over their ears, he turned the key and put the boat into drive.

They started out slowly, gliding on the water with little noise. The boat rocked slightly from side to side, making it clear to Rachel it was a good thing she hadn't eaten breakfast this morning. The sun was high in the sky, the heat and mugginess increasing as they ventured farther into the swamp. She couldn't identify any of the foliage, but the beauty and splendor of it all was breathtaking. Some trees grew out of the water, the branches winding together to create platforms with wild grass growing out of them, while other trees shaded them with their hanging limbs.

Similar to the ones she heard last night on the drive to Joe's, all sorts of noises, from chirps and whistles to splashes and knocking, came from deep inside the swamp. But these were amplified by the fact they were now *in* the swamp rather than driving beside it in the safety of their car. Her heart had barely slowed from their dramatic exit down the tunnel and now it was racing again from all the unknowns hiding within the wetlands.

As they cleared the constricted passageway, they came to a body of water resembling a small lake. Before she could relax, Logan hit the gas and the boat began to speed away, the wind smacking her cheeks and blowing her hair in all directions.

Walter sat up, bliss on his scrunched face and his jowls flapping. For a moment, she allowed herself to forget the past thirty-six hours and the fact they were currently speeding away from the FBI. She tipped her head back and laughed, enjoying the sensation of flying above the water and the slight bumps as they landed. The fan was loud, blocking out the earlier swamp noises. Pelicans flew overhead, their wings spanned out as they dived through the blue sky and into the sparkling water before flying off again with fish in their beaks.

If they'd been down here on vacation, she might be able to fully immerse herself in the experience, ask him to explore the various wildlife and plant life in the Everglades. But who was she kidding? She didn't take vacations, and if she did, she certainly wouldn't be on vacation with Logan.

After confiding in him about her parents, she'd stupidly thought they had made some kind of connection, and because of it, she'd trusted him with her submission. For the first time in her life, she'd allowed herself to be vulnerable with a man, and at the first opportunity he'd proved to her that nothing that happened between them in the past twenty-four hours meant anything at all.

As she'd overheard him say to Joe, they were just making the best out of a bad situation.

Even though she was angry with him, she still trusted him to protect her. Logan was one of the good guys. That much was clear. He'd defend her with his life. And she would count on him to help her get out of this mess. But he couldn't hold her to the agreement to submit to him, and after the way he'd so casually disregarded her feelings, she wouldn't be so quick to do it again. She wasn't a doormat, and she wouldn't allow him to treat her as one.

A realization struck as they zipped across the lake toward the buildings Joe had referred to. Earlier she'd been looking at Rinaldi's murder from the wrong angle. The dead mobster wasn't the story. She and Logan were. The press was already creating a buzz, but she had something they didn't. Inside information of what it was like to be framed for murder and chased by the FBI. It was the kind of story every two-bit reporter would give his or her firstborn child to have an exclusive to. When this was all over, she wouldn't sit down with the highest bidder. She'd be the one reporting the story. Not only would she and Logan find a way to prove their innocence in the murder, but she'd also report on what it was like to run for their lives without having the protection of those who had sworn an oath to protect.

This was who she was. An independent career-driven woman who'd do anything for a story. At least that's what Logan and everyone believed. New York was waiting for her, and what better opportunity would she find than the one that had metaphorically fallen in her lap? This story had the possibility of Emmy Awards and Pulitzers.

Nearing the row of buildings, Logan slowed the boat, the whirring of the fan quieting. Now that it was no longer windy, Walter flopped back down onto her lap and rested his head on her knees. They slowly floated to a dock where Logan jumped out and secured the boat to a piling. She dropped Walter onto the wooden planks of the dock and took Logan's hand for help out of the boat.

Running her fingers through her windblown hair, she avoided Logan's eyes and scanned the area, looking for any sign of the FBI or police. Fishing poles in hand, a couple of men sat on the other end of the dock, a six-pack of beer beside them. Beyond that, a line of people stood waiting to get onto a fan boat. A quick glance at the sign on the building told her it was a fan-boat ride business. On the other side was a tackle and bait shop. None of the structures were anything close to purple.

"Are you sure we're in the right place?" she asked Logan as he lifted Walter into his arms.

Logan unzipped his bag and dug through it, retrieving Walter's leash. "No, but I didn't see any other towns, so we'll just have to hope this is it." He clipped the leash onto the dog's collar and handed it off to her, striding away from the water and hopefully toward the town.

Clearing the buildings, she was surprised to find a vibrant small town with a myriad of stores, houses, and churches. Sweat dripped down between her breasts and her shirt stuck to her back. It had to be at least ninety degrees out. Her mouth watered at the thought of stopping for a bottle of cold water and a breakfast burrito. Was it too early for ice cream? She started walking in the direction of the convenience store, only to be yanked back by Logan.

He pointed in the complete opposite direction. "There's the purple house. Let's go."

She put her hunger and thirst on the back burner as they crossed the street toward the house. It stuck out from the others, not only because of its color, but also because of the signs warning of the forthcoming apocalypse should anyone trespass onto the property. Hopefully that meant the guy had a sense of humor and wasn't a loon. If he was one of Joe's friends, it could go either way.

They climbed the porch and opened the screen door to knock. She heard some banging inside and then the sound of turning locks. The door creaked open a bit with two chain locks still attached, and a man with curly gray hair and thick glasses peeked out.

"Who are you? Didn't you see the sign?" he asked gruffly.

"Are you Morrie?" she asked softly, trying not to scare the man into shutting the door. He definitely seemed a bit off his rocker.

The man's eyes narrowed. "Who wants to know?"

"Joe sent us," said Logan. "There's been a situation, and we need a car."

The man slammed the door. A few seconds later, he removed the chains and opened it fully. "Did they follow you here?"

"No, sir," Logan answered. "Joe's leading them away from us in his car."

"Good. Good." Nodding vehemently, he kept his gaze on his bare feet. "Meet me 'round back," he whispered before slamming the door in their faces again.

Grinning, Logan turned to her. "Well, he seemed nice."

She snorted and started down the steps of the porch. "Let's hope he's not leading us to his secret laboratory where he'll take us captive and do experiments on us."

Logan laughed. "I think we're safe, at least from him." Meeting her down at the foot of the porch, he pressed his hand on her lower back and leaned to whisper in her ear. "Did I forget to mention you look incredibly sexy wearing my shirt?"

Even though she was boiling from the morning's extreme temperature, the warmth of his hand permeated through the shirt to her overheated skin. Damn him for his sexy talk. She'd already forgotten why she was angry with him.

They walked around the back and found Morrie waiting for them, a rusted old pickup truck beside him. She couldn't imagine that thing would start much less serve as their getaway car.

He slapped the hood a couple of times then held out a set of keys. "Been waiting to get this atrocity out of my backyard ever since Joe left it here ten years ago. 'Course, he comes by to start it up every few days and brings me my groceries. I sure do appreciate his company. He's not dead, is he?"

She stepped closer to him, taking the keys from his hand. "No. He's fine. I'm sure he'll be by your house to see you real soon."

His gaze fell to Walter. "That's a nice dog you got there."

She took the leash from Logan and offered it to Morrie. "He's looking for a new home. I don't suppose he could live with you, could he?"

Morrie's eyes glistened and his hands shook as he accepted the leash. "Ever since my dog, Rocky, passed, I've been wanting a new friend. Got bags of dog food and brand-new chew toys that Rocky never got to enjoy." His voice wavered. "Thank you."

"No, thank *you*," she said, looking at Walter wistfully. As much as she had already become attached to Walter, he'd be better off with someone who didn't work long hours…or have the FBI in pursuit. "It's too dangerous to take him with us."

Morrie grabbed her wrist. "They're after you, aren't they?"

She gasped, wondering if he recognized her and Logan from the news. "Who do you mean?"

His eyes widened and his lips trembled. "The aliens. Do they want you to go back to Vietnam too?"

Her heart broke for him. "No. No one's after us. We just need to borrow Joe's car for a couple of days." She threw her arms around the old man. "I promise you, the aliens will never take you back to Vietnam."

He sighed and pulled away, his head hanging as he shuffled toward his house. "I can't escape. They take me there every night."

Logan brushed his knuckles down the apple of her cheek. "Hey, he'll be okay. He's got Walter now, and Joe wouldn't have suggested it if he didn't think he'd give Walter a good home. But right now, we need to go before the FBI figure out we aren't in the car with Joe."

She nodded, trying to smile, but she just couldn't make herself do it. She gave him the keys and hopped up into the passenger side of the truck.

She held her breath until they made it onto the highway without incident. In less than two hours, they'd make it to the port. She didn't know what they'd find there, but she did know one thing.

If they didn't find Leopold, they'd lose the one lead they had to prove their innocence.

Chapter Thirteen

Rachel would've thought there'd be a breeze coming off the water of the port, but the air was stagnant and humid, and the afternoon sun beat down on them with its relentless heat. She could barely smell the salt of the ocean underneath the heavy scent of motor oil and car fumes. Sweat collected on the nape of her neck, and if there was one thing she hated, it was sweat.

At least outside the bedroom.

Her stomach cramped from anxiety, and she silently cursed the gas station hot dog and slushie she'd eaten for lunch. Without knowing what or whom to look for, they were running blind. It wasn't as if they could start asking around, or they'd draw attention to themselves. At this point, their only hope was to find Evans and Fink and spy on them in order to discover what they were up to without getting caught. Of course, since she and Logan couldn't exactly show their IDs at the staffed access-control gate, they'd parked off-site and hiked it. Unfortunately, there were several fenced-in restricted areas that not only required an ID, but a port-issued badge. Not to mention, the entire port was monitored by security cameras.

It would've been better if she and Logan were armed with more information than the word *Leopold*. Were they about to stop a murder? She shook her head, pursing her lips. The area was too busy and exposed for that. The agents couldn't risk any witnesses.

She hadn't felt this helpless and ill-informed since she'd lived with her parents. Once she'd gotten access to the Internet in college, it was as if the whole world opened up to her. While other students had complained about the amount of homework, she'd spent countless hours online sifting through websites, from international news sites to Bloomingdale's. She'd read about other religions and crammed in as much as she could in a short period of time in order to catch up to her peers.

There was no question she was book smart, but she'd lacked street smarts. She hadn't known how to react when her roommate had woken her up at three in the morning having sex with her boyfriend on the bunk above her. Or when she attended her first party and she didn't know not to accept drinks from strangers and ended up in the hospital after imbibing a drink laced with Rohypnol. There were times she wanted to give up and return home to her parents, and others when she wanted to curl up in her bed and forgo any social interaction. But she hadn't. Instead, hungry for knowledge, she'd immersed herself in every possible experience.

As an investigative reporter, she had access to databases and dozens of contacts for finding the information. Now it was as if she was going through withdrawals, her hands shaky from the lack of technology at her fingertips. Joe's old truck picked up only AM radio stations, and there was very little news about the manhunt for them, the reports simply replaying the same bogus sightings and the FBI's official statement.

They walked to a sanctioned public viewing area where they could get a good look at the port. In addition to the gigantic cruise ships, several cargo ships were docked. Using forklifts and cranes, the workers at the port busily loaded and unloaded crates, oblivious to the unknown danger that lurked within the gates. "So what's the plan?" she asked Logan, hoping he'd come up with something better than hanging around the perimeter and hoping they spotted something or someone marked "Leopold."

Logan scratched his scruffy cheek, looking sheepish. "Before you came downstairs this morning, I put in a call to some friends of mine to check the inventory of the cargo ships. Once they had the results, they were going to send it to a secured e-mail that I can access from my phone."

She crossed her arms. "Why didn't you tell me this before now? Didn't you trust me?"

He squinted and shielded his eyes from the sun. "It had nothing to do with trust. I just figured I'd tell you if they found anything."

She bit her lip, knowing now was not the time to have this kind of conversation. But after accusing her this morning of tipping off the Feds and withholding this information from her, she couldn't help feeling slighted. "So your friends are hackers? Like you?"

He shook his head. "Better than me. I served with them in the army's intelligence unit. I'm good, but there's nothing they can't hack." He opened an app on his phone. "Once they figured out which cargo ships were arriving at one today, my friends accessed those ships' records. All the ships are required to have documentation of what's on board, especially if it's international cargo. Then it has to go through customs."

She moved closer to him, trying to make out what he was reading on the screen. "Do you see anything?"

He looked up at her. "There are only two ships that arrived at one. Both of them were scheduled to dock at the cargo terminal yard a few blocks away from us. They guys didn't find anything called Leopold."

Of course not. That would be too easy. "What did the ships have on them?"

He took her hand and steered her in the direction of the cargo terminal yard. "The *Triple Green* carried fruit from South America, and the *Media Congo* originated from the Democratic Republic of Congo with copper and inorganic chemicals."

Fruit and copper? What was so special about that? "So what are Fink and Evans doing here? Maybe the South American ship was carrying drugs? Or the African ship was smuggling diamonds?"

"Only one way to know." He pointed at the fenced-in yard. "We've got to get in there and find them."

He was crazy. The port had security monitoring almost every portion of the property. "And how are we going to do that?"

He held up his phone and waved it in front of her. "We're going to jam the camera feeds by disrupting the signal. My app will jam every camera within thirty meters and play the previous few minutes of video on a loop. But we'll need to move quickly and stay out of sight as much as possible." They stopped in front of the fence, and he squeezed her hand. "Ready?"

She tilted her head back. "That's a really high fence."

He frowned. "Rach, can you climb a fence?"

She shrugged. There weren't many opportunities for climbing fences in her childhood, but she couldn't imagine it was too difficult. "I've never tried. Guess there's only one way to find out."

Logan played with his phone. When he was done, he began to climb. "Come on. We've only got a couple minutes to get over the fence."

She grabbed on to the fence and lifted herself up, sticking her feet into the holes. Then she hoisted herself higher and higher until she came to the top. She got into a squat and turned herself around, creeping down the other side of the fence. With Logan waiting for her on the ground, she released her grip on the fence and jumped down.

"Not bad for your first time," Logan said with a grin. He took her hand and pulled her between the high towers of shipping containers. "This way toward the ships."

They ran down the aisle, the noises of the port getting louder and louder the closer she and Logan got to the water. Her heart thudded against her chest, adrenaline shooting through her. At the end of the aisle, they stopped and peered out onto the dock. Workers unloaded crates and containers from the large white ship marked *Media Congo.*

Logan nudged her and pointed to the left of the ship. "There they are."

Inconspicuously dressed in dark business suits, Evans was shaking the hand of a customs agent as Fink bent to pick up a slim green tubular object. Then they strode away, heading in the direction of her and Logan.

She couldn't make out the green object. "What is Fink carrying?"

His brows wrinkled. "It looks like a gas canister." As the agents moved closer, Logan grabbed her hand and pulled her back, flattening them against the shipping container.

"You think they saw us?" she asked.

"FBI! Freeze!" one of the agents shouted.

"I'd say that's a yes," Logan said. "Run!"

Trapped between the rows of shipping containers, they raced up the aisle. It wasn't as if the agents would shoot them in the back in front of witnesses. Then again, she and Logan were two of the most wanted people in the country right now and allegedly armed and dangerous. It's possible no one would bat an eye if an FBI agent shot and killed them during capture.

The booming noises of guns firing startled her, causing her to stumble.

"They want us dead," she said breathlessly, wishing she'd taken a spinning class rather than Pilates. The reality of the situation crashed into her. They weren't going to arrest her. There'd be no opportunity to prove her innocence. No trial. The agents needed to pin Rinaldi's murder on her and Logan. Evans and Fink couldn't afford the risk of them telling the authorities what they had witnessed.

"Really? I couldn't tell by the bullets flying at us," Logan quipped.

Looking over her shoulder at the agents, she tripped and fell forward, smacking her hands and knees on the ground. "Logan!"

From ten yards ahead, Logan stopped and turned around, his eyes wide with fear. He raced toward her.

Her heart jumped into her throat, beating faster than she would've thought possible, and her breath caught in her chest. She'd always wondered if what they said about life passing before your eyes was true.

It wasn't.

The only thing going through her mind at the moment was how angry she'd be if the sons of bitches got away with her murder.

A sadistic smile spread across Evans's face as he raised his arm and aimed for her head. She winced, anticipating the kill shot and hoping it wouldn't hurt.

Logan bent and grabbed her from under her arms, heaving her to her feet and yanking her away just as a bullet pinged by and embedded itself in a nearby container.

He flung himself in front of her, a gun suddenly in his hands. "Go," he shouted. "I'll meet up with you."

It was a suicide mission. If he stayed, she'd never again see him alive.

She wouldn't leave without him.

Fink shouted at Evans. "We're not supposed to be here. If you shoot them, we'll have to answer questions, and we'll never make it on time for Friday. We've got to let them go."

Evans kept his arm raised, a scowl on his face. The second he holstered his gun, she and Logan took off, not waiting around for him to change his mind. With trembling hands, she climbed back over the fence.

She and Logan returned to the truck and sped away, neither of them speaking about how close they'd come to dying.

Logan drove south, taking them onto the crowded highway where they could disappear into the chaos of Miami traffic.

The adrenaline from the past couple of hours wore off, leaving her hungry and restless. She rested her head against the glass and peered at Logan. "Where are we going?" she asked.

"I'm going to find us a hotel to stay at for the night."

"What if someone recognizes us?"

His lips quirked up. "The kind of place we'll be staying at won't ask any questions."

She lifted her head and tapped her nails on the window. "Ew, we're going to stay at one of those rent-by-the-hour places, aren't we? Have you seen those exposés on what shows up on ultraviolet light in hotel rooms? Not to mention the bedbugs. If they grow mosquitoes that large down here, how big you think the bedbugs will be?"

Cocking a brow, he glanced at her. "Well, if you'd rather skip the hotel, we can camp outside somewhere. They don't have as many gators or black panthers down in these parts."

As many? One gator or panther was one too many for her.

"Evans had mentioned the target is in Las Vegas on Friday," she reminded Logan, recalling the conversation they'd overheard after Rinaldi was killed. And Fink had mentioned Friday again today. "That only gives us a couple of days to get there and stop whatever the hell they're planning." She paused. "What do you think is in that gas tank?"

"I wish I knew. But whatever it is, it can't be good, especially coupled with the word *target.*"

"Maybe a weapon?" she said, theorizing. "But what kind of weapon could you get from the Congo that you couldn't get anywhere else? And why hide it in a gas canister?"

"Because all ships have canisters of oxygen on them in case of emergency." Logan glanced at her. "Either someone slipped something inside it, or they exchanged one canister for another."

After an hour without incident, they pulled into the parking lot of a decrepit motel, the sign in front advertising rooms for ten dollars an hour and ninety-nine-cent shrimp cocktails.

While Logan went to check in, she sat in the truck, her gaze darting to every slam of a door and to every car that drove by. She kept waiting for the agents to arrive and finish what they started.

For some morbid reason, she wondered if anyone would really mourn her if she died.

Would her parents? Or had they already mourned the daughter they had lost?

She sighed, pinching the bridge of her nose to ward off the tears. She would not die. They'd figure it out, and when they did, she'd return to her real life, where she wouldn't feel so helpless.

A sudden knocking on the window ripped her from her thoughts and sent her pulse skittering. She snapped her head to the right and sighed in relief at the sight of Logan holding a key in his hand. After she caught her breath, she got out of the car.

"We're in room seven," Logan said, dropping the key into her waiting palm. "I'm going to go get some supplies."

As he headed off to the store across the street, she found their room and got her first look at where they'd be spending the night. It was small, but then again, how much space did they need? It had everything she required—a shower and a television. She tried to ignore the single bed in the middle of the room and the fact that once again, she and Logan would have to share it. This time, though, he'd just have to accept she wasn't going to sleep more than a couple of hours because there was no way she'd allow a repeat of last night.

Besides, he'd left his rope and the bandanas at Joe's, so there'd be no tying her to the bedposts tonight. Not that this bed even had posts or a headboard to tie them to.

Settling on the bed, she switched on the television and flipped the channels to her favorite cable news station.

It didn't take more than a minute before her and Logan's photographs flashed across the screen. At least they'd used her publicity shot. Logan's photo was of him in his army uniform, his youthful face free of hair and the lines of hard experience that roughened his appearance now. His eyes were different then too. Less guarded. Less…haunted. Since she'd known him for only a year, she had no foundation for what he was like before he'd joined the army, but she'd interviewed several men and women who had served, and they had all acknowledged a loss of innocence that had nothing to do with age.

The news anchor reported an exclusive from someone "close" to Rachel, who alleged Rachel was having an affair with both Rinaldi and Logan. The anchor and two other guests debated the validity of the story, one of the guests proposing Logan may have killed Rinaldi in a jealous rage.

Rachel chuckled, wondering who claimed to have inside knowledge into Rachel's love life. The jealous-lover theory made for a great news clip, but as soon as the FBI dug into her history, it would deflate like a soufflé taken out of the oven too early. She wouldn't have slept with Rinaldi even if he'd promised her an exclusive that would've won her a Pulitzer. The man had tortured and murdered numerous women then buried them in the woods behind his cabin.

Even she had some standards.

A firm knock shook the door. She slid off the bed and checked the peephole before opening it. Carrying two brown bags, Logan strode into the room and dropped them on the floor beside the air-conditioning unit.

Logan kicked off his shoes and picked up one of the bags, bringing it with him to sit next to her on the bed. He motioned to the television. "Anything good on?"

She laughed. "Us. Did you know we've managed to rob three different gas stations from New York to Texas? And that I was having an affair with both you and Rinaldi, so you killed him in a jealous rage? I can't believe they're reporting this crap."

"Don't you normally report crap as well?" he asked, holding out a turkey sandwich for her.

She tried not to be offended by his question. "No, unlike anchors, I'm responsible for my own stories and not a mouthpiece for the network. As an investigative reporter, I sift through the mountains of crap to uncover the truth."

She unwrapped her sandwich, cringing. Ugh, mayo. She despised the condiment, but right now if she had been a vegetarian, she'd kill her own cow if she needed to in order to eat. She wolfed down a couple of bites before noticing Logan staring at her intensely. "What?"

Exhaling loudly, he ran his hand over his scalp. "I'm sorry. You know, about this morning when I unjustly accused you of making a phone call and compromising us. I know you would never use our predicament to advance your career."

She shrugged. The fact was she *would* do almost anything to advance her career, but she prided herself on following a strict moral code. She'd never endanger someone else for a story. "It's okay. You don't know me well enough to trust me. I understand."

"You're wrong. I do know you. You're a woman who will risk her own safety to protect a dog." He turned down the television. Then he put his hands on her hips and lifted her onto his lap, so that she straddled him. Sliding the ends of her hair through his fingers, he stared at her intently. "Back at the port, you had a chance to escape when Evans had his gun on me, but instead, you stayed. Why?"

She lowered her gaze. "We're in this together. You would have done the same for me."

"Look at me." He tipped up her chin, so that she had no choice but to look into his warm eyes. "I've never been more scared in my life as when I thought Evans was going to shoot you."

"Me? He had a gun on you a minute later. You put yourself in front of me, protecting me from Evans."

He caressed her cheek with the tips of his fingers. "I wasn't worried about myself. I wanted you safe. That's all that mattered to me. Do you understand what I'm saying?" He wrapped his hand around her nape and drew her face closer. "*You* matter to me." He blew out a breath. "Since leaving the army, it has all been about control for me. I'm not impulsive and I don't act based on emotion.

At least I didn't." He swallowed hard. "When I'm with you, all rationality flies out the window. I may have control over you in the bedroom, but you have to know you have more power over me than anyone else in my life. Do you get me, Tiger?"

Hummingbirds fluttered their wings in her belly. It sounded as if he was saying he was falling for her.

"What about Kate?" she blurted out.

Frowning, he cocked his head. "What does Kate have to do with you and me?"

"You know..." She waited for him to figure it out, but he stayed quiet, his brow raised in question. "You're in love with her."

He reared back. "I'm not in love with Kate. I'll admit I had a crush on her before she shot me down, but since that time I've only considered her a friend and law partner. If anything, I look at her as more like a sister, which is why we make sure not to play at Benediction on the same night." Cupping her cheek, he stared into her eyes. "I misjudged you, and for that I'm truly sorry. Because now that I've gotten to know you, I realize how much time and energy I've wasted fighting my attraction to you this past year. The woman I've come to care about is selfless, compassionate, and sexy as hell. I apologize for having accused you of having less than noble reasons for doing your job. You've trusted me these past couple of days, and I want you to know I trust you too. I know we agreed to an expiration date, but I'd really like to see how far we can take this."

Hope bloomed in her chest. He wasn't in love with Kate. But how would Logan feel about her when she told him she was going to do a story about what it was like when they were on the run? Would he understand or would he try to stop her?

She leaned in and kissed him softly on the cheek. "Me too." She quirked up her lips. "This may surprise you, but you're not the only one with control issues."

He grinned. "You don't say?"

She took a breath, preparing herself to tell him something no one knew about her. It had taken her several years after leaving home before she was no longer embarrassed by her upbringing, but by then, Rachel Kaczynski had faded into a distant memory and it had seemed easier to keep her that way. Unlike Rachel Kaczynski, Rachel Dawson didn't take shit from anyone. No one could ever confuse her with the girl who'd grown up believing women were subservient to men.

"Remember I mentioned I had been raised in a religious household?" she asked, linking her fingers together on her lap. "What I didn't tell you was that my father was our church's leader. Our preacher." She huffed out a laugh at the shock on Logan's face. Sometimes, she couldn't believe it herself. "Calling it a church gives it much more credibility than it deserves. In a lot of ways, it was more like a cult. Even though I grew up in suburbia, surrounded by people of all faiths and cultures, I may as well have lived in the middle of nowhere like your uncle Joe. We were kept isolated from the rest of society, deprived of televisions, Internet, radios. We were only allowed to associate with other members of our church. Our school was at the church and taught by church congregants.

Boys were encouraged to go to college and have careers while girls were expected to marry young and have lots of babies. I was taught that my opinions didn't matter. That I was less than boys simply because I had a vagina. That as a female, it was my job to serve my father and then my husband."

She paused to clear her throat, years of resentment toward her parents bubbling up from deep inside her and spilling from her mouth. But as difficult as it was to finally reveal the truth about her past, it was equally as freeing. Because if she continued to keep it a secret from Logan, he would never really know her. And she wanted that. She wanted that more than anything.

Logan brushed his fingers up and down her arm. The gentle strokes on her skin soothed her, encouraging her to continue.

"When I was sixteen," she said quietly, "I discovered my friend Leah was being physically abused by her father. She had bruises all over her body. At first she denied it, making those excuses you hear about falling down the stairs, but I didn't believe her. I mean, I could see the fingerprints on her arms. As the daughter of our church's religious leader, I felt it was my duty to tell him. She was so scared. I can still picture her shaking and sobbing in my arms in the girls' bathroom at our school. I went home that night and sat with my father in his office, telling him all the horrible things I'd learned about what went on in Leah's house. I was sure he'd call the police. Instead, he scheduled some counseling sessions with her father."

He resumed holding her hand and squeezed it. "It wasn't enough to stop him, was it?"

She sighed. "No. It was the first time I saw my father as fallible. Not only did the abuse not stop, it got worse. Leah wasn't allowed to speak with me anymore, and she no longer changed her clothes in front of me, but I saw the stiff way she moved and the way she'd wince when anyone touched her. I begged my father to call the police, but he refused. It was a 'community problem.' So for the first time in my life, I broke one of my father's rules. I called the police myself and reported the abuse."

It had torn her up inside to go against her father's wishes, but she was sure he'd forgive her.

"Did it help?" Logan asked.

She shook her head, remembering. "Leah lied to them and said she'd fallen down the stairs. Her father stormed over to my house, sure my father had called the cops on him. Instead of being proud of me for standing up for the weak and defenseless, my father apologized to the abuser and grounded *me* for breaking the rules. I realized at that time I couldn't stay in a community that was more worried about showing skin than the bruises hidden underneath the clothing. In my senior year of high school, I secretly applied to state colleges and got loans to afford it. I left for college the day after I graduated high school."

The two years between the incident and leaving for college were the longest of her life. In some ways she wanted to savor each moment spent with her family, knowing her time with them was limited. In others, the inability to speak her mind or act on her beliefs caused her to resent her parents.

She loved them. She missed them. But she'd never become them.

Logan kissed the center of her palm. "What happened to Leah?"

"I'd been expected to marry the son of my parents' best friends." The boy whom she'd given her virginity to a month before she left for college. "It wasn't an arranged marriage per se, but if I'd stayed in the community, I have no doubt I would've married him to please my father. Jacob was a good man. Before I moved away, I encouraged him to take care of Leah. They were married a few months later, and they now have five kids."

She needed him to understand what drove her. "When I left my parents' house, I swore I'd never be powerless again."

He drew her in for a kiss, his warm lips lingering as they breathed into one another.

She'd do just about anything to hold on to what she and Logan were building together. He was nothing like her father, and yet doubt lingered. Logan was a Dom. Didn't that mean he expected his partner to be submissive? Just because Rachel allowed him to take charge during sex didn't mean she'd take that role outside the bedroom.

She hadn't lied when she swore she'd never be powerless again.

Even if it meant losing Logan.

"The store carried clothes, so I got you a pair of University of Miami shorts and T-shirt. I bought us some toiletries. I don't know about you, but I could use a shower."

A shower sounded heavenly, especially if Logan would be joining her. But right now, she needed food more than anything.

Logan turned up the television volume, and they listened to the news as they ate their sandwiches and washed them down with ice-cold bottled water.

The reporter segued into the chaos that had erupted on Capitol Hill within the past two days. Senator Hutton, the chairman of the United States Senate Committee on Health, Education, Labor, and Pensions, had successfully filibustered Senator Byron's bill to cut the budget of Homeland Security, taking the Senate floor for a record eighteen hours. As a result, he delayed the vote until the Senate reconvened from a two-week nonlegislative period, giving him time to launch a campaign to sway public opinion and swing the Senate votes in his favor. A panel of political analysts debated whether Senator Hutton was paranoid or justified in believing that a bioterrorism attack was imminent.

The report cut to a part of Senator Hutton's speech.

"No one thought Ebola would ever make it to our homeland, and yet recent events have proven otherwise. Our country was caught unprepared, and now, more than a year later, we've done nothing to address the issue. Imagine what would happen if a virus worse than Ebola crossed into our borders. Now is not the time to decrease the Homeland Security budget, not when terrorists all over the world are plotting attacks on the United States. Do we really believe we can keep our people safe from the greatest threat to our national safety? Bioterrorism isn't a possibility. It's a reality. With the amount of power and money these terrorist groups are accumulating, how long before they get their hands on a biological weapon and release it in our country? Viruses including Ebola, but also Marburg, dengue fever, smallpox, and malaria. Or possibly even the obscure Leopold virus, an airborne pathogen originating in what was formerly known as Leopoldville, Congo. This virus is similar to Ebola, but far deadlier…and airborne. According to the research performed by the Centers for Disease Control, this virus has the potential to wipe out the entire United States population within days of initial infection."

Rachel froze. *Did he just say Leopold?* She elbowed Logan in the gut. "Did you hear him say Leopold, or am I going crazy?"

Pale, he shook his head. "You're not going crazy."

At the end of the short news clip, the anchor added that Senator Hutton would be speaking to some of the wealthiest businessmen in the country during an upcoming appearance at the Tuscany Hotel in Las Vegas, in an attempt to sway influential public opinion and to prevent Senator Byron's bill from passing in the Senate.

She didn't know much about viruses, but she didn't have to in order to know that the Leopold virus would spread easily in a crowded place like a resort casino. "Could Fink and Evans be transporting the virus in the gas canister?" she asked Logan, a chill running down her spine.

Swearing loudly, Logan whipped out his phone and dialed. He put it up to his ear, his jaw tight and his eyes worried. "Looks like we're going to Vegas."

Chapter Fourteen

"So ARE YOU going to tell me who the hell this friend is who is flying us up to Vegas?" she asked as they parked the truck across the street from a house with its own runway. Seriously, even the president didn't have his own runway at the White House. And she'd thought Cole DeMarco, the owner of Benediction, was filthy rich.

They'd left the motel at the crack of dawn and had driven three hours down to a private strip of land in the Florida Keys, where Logan's friend had arranged them to take a corporate jet.

"Yeah," Logan said sheepishly, scratching his freshly shaven cheek. "You may have heard of him. Sawyer Hayes."

Her jaw dropped just a little bit. "The billionaire?"

Everyone in America had heard of the man who'd become the youngest billionaire in the country at age eighteen when his parents died, leaving him as the sole heir to the entire Hayes estate. She'd been the same age and a freshman in college at the time, and although their reasons for not having family were vastly different, she'd identified with him and had thought the way the media had hounded him after he'd gone through such a tragedy was in poor taste. Then months later, he'd suddenly disappeared from the news, and she'd rarely heard his name mentioned again except in passing.

"Not anymore." Logan tossed the keys in the glove compartment. "Some woman stole a big chunk of his money, but he still has more than anyone could spend in a hundred lifetimes."

They got out of the car and headed up the patch of grass to the back of the palatial home where Sawyer's plane was supposed to be waiting. Even with all her professional contacts, she didn't have anyone who could not only give them a plane but owned a mansion with a private runway that lacked the typical security found at airports.

Must be nice to have friends in high places.

A knot settled in her stomach. "Are you sure the FBI won't be able to trace us to this plane or to Sawyer?"

"There's no official flight plan, and Sawyer sent one of his employees here on legitimate business. Plus any record of it will disappear a minute after we get into the air. It's one of the perks of having friends who also happen to be the best hackers in the country."

From what she could recall, Sawyer originally hailed from Arizona. "You mentioned you met your hacker friends in the army. Did that include Sawyer?" she asked.

"Yeah, I met him during basic training."

That explained where he'd disappeared to all those years ago. It would be hard for the media to follow him while he served in the military, especially while overseas. Still, that seemed awfully extreme to escape the scrutiny of the media. With all that money, couldn't he have just bought a private island to disappear?

Sticky from the morning's heat, she lifted her shirt away from her chest a few times, fanning herself. "Why would anyone do that if they didn't have to?"

Logan's blue eyes darkened, his gaze colliding with hers. "I didn't become a soldier because I had to."

She stopped. "Really? So if your brothers hadn't been marines, you would've still joined the armed forces?"

"Sawyer had something to prove, and that's all I can say about him." He thumped his chest with his fist. "I did it because I wanted to serve our country like my father had and my brothers do. I made that choice all on my own. My family would have supported any decision I made, but for me, the only decision was what branch. Only, after a few months, I realized the armed forces weren't for me. So after serving my four years, I didn't reenlist and got out."

"And went to law school."

He shrugged one shoulder. "There are a lot of people out there who need defending. Too many innocents go to prison. They need someone to believe in them."

Innocents like them.

The people Logan defended were blessed to have a man like him on their side. Not because he rarely lost, but because he truly gave 100 percent to everything he did. He believed in them.

Did he believe in her?

Exhaustion settled like a weight around her neck. "Do you think we'll get out of this mess?"

Nodding, he wrapped his hand around her neck. "I do. I promise we'll find out who's responsible for all of this and we'll take them down."

She took a breath. "I'd like to believe you."

His gaze dipped to her lips, and a flare of lust bloomed low in her belly. How could he arouse her from just a look? With a hand splayed on the bottom of her spine, Logan steered her around the corner of the house. As the plane with the Hayes Industries logo came into view, her heart flopped into her stomach, and perspiration that had nothing to do with the heat popped up on her nape.

Growing rigid, she froze. "We can't fly on that."

The sleek white-and-blue plane had two propellers, which meant it had two engines, so if one of them stopped working, they wouldn't fall out of the sky. But what if they hit a bird and it took out both engines at once?

Logan frowned. "Why not?"

She balled her hands into fists, her nails digging into the flesh of her palms. "It's not safe. He's a multimillionaire with a private plane. Shouldn't it be, you know, bigger, like the ones they'd show in the movies with a bedroom and a fully stocked bar? This thing would fit in my apartment."

He slung his arm around her waist and propelled her closer to the plane. "It is perfectly safe, and it's plenty big for the two of us. Haven't you ever flown on a small plane before?"

"Sure." She gulped around the lump of fear in her throat. "One of those commercial planes with fifteen rows rather than the usual forty. I prefer my plane to come equipped with flight attendants and alcohol. Lots of it. In addition to the two Xanax I take an hour before the flight just to set foot on it."

Before the events of the past couple of days, she'd always considered herself courageous. But braving the Everglades, rogue FBI agents, and now this deathtrap on wings was way outside her comfort zone.

"Don't worry." Logan smiled as they boarded the plane. "I'll keep you safe."

"How?" she asked, stepping inside the narrow aisle of the plane. "If the pilot passes out, would you know how to fly this thing?"

A man dressed in a Hawaiian shirt, board shorts, sneakers, and a pilot cap appeared from the cockpit. "Don't worry, miss. I don't plan on dying today, so you'll be fine." He laughed at what she guessed was his idea of a joke and stretched out his hand. "Captain Ivan Rothschild at your service. I take it you're Mr. and Mrs. Smith?"

Mr. and Mrs. Smith? Did he really believe those were their names? And that they were married?

Logan shook the pilot's hand and they spoke about altitude and flight time for a couple of minutes while she checked out the interior. There were four rows of leather seats. The seats were wider and the rows roomier than on commercial flights, but the plane itself was narrower and seemed to be shrinking by the second.

"Relax, Rachel," Logan said, rubbing the back of her neck reassuringly. "You're in good hands."

Hyperventilating, she blinked a few times and realized the pilot had gone back into the cockpit already. Since she couldn't get her feet to move, Logan helped her advance farther into the plane and into her seat. A few moments later, he waved a mini-bottle of vodka under her nose. "Take a drink."

She knocked it back in two large gulps, the burn of it sliding down her throat and warming her belly.

Working in the high-pressure field of journalism, Rachel couldn't show weakness or the people waiting in the wings for their chance would snatch up the opportunity to upstage her. Since she'd started at the station fresh out of college as a lowly assistant to the producer, she'd taken every precaution to shield herself from looking as if she had any vulnerabilities. It was sink or swim in her profession, and in seven years, she'd managed to keep her head above water.

But now she wasn't only sinking, she was drowning. And Logan got a front-row seat to her humiliation.

Beside her in the aisle, he crouched, placing his hands on her knees. "Rachel, you need to breathe. Concentrate on my voice," he said, his tone firm but soothing, as it had been the other night as he'd bound her. "I'm going to count back from thirty, and I want you to repeat each number after me."

She nodded mindlessly. By the time they'd counted to one, her breathing had normalized and the pressure from her chest had lifted.

"You know why you have a fear of flying?" he asked as he settled in the seat beside her. He reached over her lap and grabbed the buckle, belting her in before clicking himself into his own seat.

The whir of the engine started up, but she was too agitated by his question to care. "I don't have a fear of flying. I have a fear of crashing."

A slow smirk spread across his face. "No, you have a fear of losing control. When you fly, you're completely dependent on someone else for your safety. There's a great amount of trust that comes from handing over your power to another, and you have a hard time doing it."

"That's not true. I did it the other night with you." The words popped out of her mouth before she could stop, and she immediately regretted them.

"Yes, but I had to tie you up, blindfold, and gag you in order to get you to relax."

As the plane sped down the runway, she crossed her arms over her chest. "Too bad that's never going to happen again."

He leaned into her, his eyes daring her to lie to him. "Oh no? And why not?"

"I've decided."

"You've decided." He cupped her chin, tilting her face toward him. "What happened to our agreement?"

She licked her lips. "You can't hold me to it. It's not as though it was binding."

His mouth inched closer, hovering over hers. "Are you saying you're a woman who goes back on her word?"

"Yes." Confused, she shook her head. "No." They were in the air, the ocean below them, and she wasn't freaking out because all she could concentrate on was the faded scar on his bottom lip. What had he asked? "I can't think."

"Exactly," he murmured as his lips brushed over hers.

In that moment, she decided that thinking was overrated.

She should've known by the way he'd used his mouth on her pussy, but wow, the man could kiss. His lips slanted softly over hers, teasing and coaxing her to part her lips so their tongues could dance in a passionate tango. She sighed into his mouth, the tension in her muscles ebbing away like a mirage in the desert. With a rumble from deep in his throat, the kiss changed, Logan apparently no longer satisfied with soft exploration. Instead he devoured her, his palm wrapped around the nape of her neck, holding her captive to his domination of her mouth. Heat suffused her body, a heady rush that left her dizzy and aching.

She didn't know a kiss could be like this, as if he was making love to her with his mouth. It absolutely terrified her. Because love had nothing to do with what was going on between them. It was simply lust. Only nothing about this situation was simple.

But the intensity of his kiss made her want to dive headfirst into the tempestuous sea and forget that falling in love with a Dom who craved control would only end in her drowning alone. Because no matter how much she liked him, she wasn't a submissive. She couldn't give him control over anything outside the bedroom, and although he swore he didn't require it, she couldn't take that risk. Maintaining control was equally as important to her.

As long as she didn't fall in love with him, was there any reason to deny herself a few orgasms? She wasn't sure if her climaxes were a result of the man himself, his talents, his domination, or, like a perfect storm, a combination of all three, but she wasn't naïve enough to believe another man could produce the same outcome. Not after more than ten years of lovers who had tried their damn hardest to give her an orgasm and failed. Logan had shown her climaxes were half-physical and half-mental, and only those who could break through the barrier and quiet her thoughts would be the ones who could give her the ultimate pleasure.

Now she would return the favor.

She moaned as he thumbed one of her nipples over her shirt. The captain's voice came on over a speaker announcing they were at a cruising altitude, but it was dulled by the thudding of her heart. Ripping her mouth away, she unbuckled her seat belt and fell to her knees, situating herself in front of him. She spread his legs, moving between them, and released his seat belt before going to work on the button of his pants.

His hand covered hers. "Rachel, you don't have to do that."

She'd heard that line from guys before, but this was the first time she believed it. Logan truly didn't expect anything in return for the orgasm he'd given her the other night. With him, it wasn't quid pro quo when it came to pleasuring his lover.

Which made her want to do it for him even more. "I want to. If we're going to do this again, I don't want to be the only one getting off. I want to please you."

And she did. Those words had never been uttered by her to a lover. Pleasing them was nothing more than a means to an end. It wasn't something she'd wanted to do. With the exception of the boy who'd taken her virginity, sex had never been about affection. It had been a mutual agreement between two parties for business purposes. Her agreement to temporarily become lovers with Logan had started much the same way. But a couple of minutes after he'd started her massage two nights ago, she had realized there was something different about what was happening between them. Without having experienced anything like it in the past, she just didn't know what it was. Even as her heart pounded and her palms sweated, she was calmer around Logan. Her thoughts slowed and her breathing deepened. It was as if her body was attuned to his. But what she felt for Logan went beyond physical attraction. Until him, no man had ever made her feel safe. There were people out there who wanted them dead, and yet he had a way of making her forget it. With him, she discovered a sense of peace that she hadn't realized was missing from her life. From his seat, he gazed down at her with indecision in his eyes, his pupils dilating and cock growing under her fingertips. He swallowed hard and nodded. "Pick a safe word."

"Family," she said automatically, her eyebrows raised in question. Why would she need a safe word to give a blow job? Besides, it wasn't as if she could talk with his dick between her lips.

Not for the first time in the past couple of days, he read her expression. "If your mouth is busy and you need to stop, snap your fingers." At her shuddered breath, he hooked his hands under her armpits and pulled her to her feet before hurtling himself out of his seat. He tugged her to the aisle of the plane, then, with his hands on both her shoulders, pushed her gently to the floor again. "I'm gonna teach you how to please me."

Rather than offend her, the demand sent shivers down her arms and across her chest, hardening her nipples. Still, as she unbuttoned his pants, she rolled her eyes, not wanting him to see the power he had over her. Right now, she was supposed to be in charge. "I know how to give a blow job."

He held her chin firmly between his thumb and index finger, tilting her face up. "Don't want a blow job. Giving me a blow job requires you to think. Puts you in control."

Her eyes widened. This was about his pleasure, not hers. He was the one who was supposed to lose control. Her lips parted in protest, but he hushed her by plunging his thumb between them.

He smiled darkly at her. "I'm taking that control from you. Now, unzip me and pull out my cock. I'm dying to get inside that hot sassy mouth of yours and fuck your face."

Tremors raced down her spine to her pussy. She worked over a swallow, the crude vision of Logan using her mouth for his own pleasure playing in her head like a pornographic movie. It was filthy. Repugnant. Wrong.

Wrong had never felt so right.

Chapter Fifteen

Slowly unzipping his pants, she was filled with as much anticipation as opening up a birthday present. By the time she got to his boxer briefs, she'd had enough of slow. She yanked down his pants to the floor and stared at the covered erection in front of her. She could see the outline of his cock through his underwear, and although she'd yet to see it, she could tell it was much larger than average. Wanting to know how much larger and too impatient to wait, she rubbed her knuckles over it, feeling it jump from her touch.

Logan ripped her hand away. "I didn't tell you to use your hands on me." He grabbed her other hand and set both of them on the sides of his hips. "Get me naked now, Rach. I'm done playing."

One touch of his cock over his underwear, and he thought she was playing? She thought briefly about showing him what playing meant, but this wasn't about her.

It was about pleasing him, and if that meant following every one of his domineering commands, she'd do it. She was just as eager to take him in her mouth as he was to get there.

She drew his underwear down his solid thighs until they joined his pants on the floor. He stepped out of them and kicked them away. Spreading his legs a bit, he placed a hand on top of her head.

His thick cock bobbed in front of her, the tip of it springing toward his belly button. It was darker than the rest of his skin, as if blushing from the blood that was coursing through it. A drop of precome dripped from the slit, running down the underside of his tip. How would it taste? She inhaled, taking in the spicy musk of his arousal.

"Open that mouth of yours, gorgeous." The hand on her head remained, his fingers tangling into her hair, while the other hand wrapped around the base of his dick.

Knowing he'd fill her mouth completely, she opened it wide as he fed his cock to her inch by inch.

"That's it," he crooned. "Wrap those lush lips of yours around my cock and take as much as I give you."

The breadth of his cock stretched her lips as far as they could comfortably go. The taste of his precome hit her tongue, its slight saltiness reminding her of the ocean they'd left behind in Florida.

Before he got to the back of her throat, he stopped his intrusion, his hands moving to her cheeks. "Ah, yeah. You're such a good girl. Now keep your head just like that while I slide my cock along that tongue."

Her pussy's walls quivered at his words, her arousal drenching her panties. She'd never been so turned on from pleasuring someone else. Until now, she would've never imagined it was possible. But hearing the breathlessness in his voice, seeing the flare of excitement in his eyes, tasting his tangy precome on her tongue, made her feel powerful even as he controlled her. She didn't have to think or worry about whether he was enjoying it. He showed her with every thrust, every word he uttered, every low groan. And because of that, she was free to lose herself in the moment. She may not want a man to control her outside of sex, but judging by her body's response to his domination of her, submitting to him aroused her.

He pumped slowly in and out of her mouth, careful not to gag her. "Slide your hand under your bra and squeeze your tits for me."

Following his directive, she hummed around his cock, the pressure she exerted on her breast relieving a bit of the building ache in them.

"You like to play so much, why don't you play with that hard nipple that's been teasing me."

She pinched her nipple and rolled it between her fingers, her eyes practically rolling back in her head from the darts of pleasure zipping from her nipple to her pulsing clit.

As if he was losing a bit of his control, Logan increased his pace, his fingers pressing harder into her cheeks. "Later, I'm gonna tie you to the bed, bind your breasts, and then I'm gonna slide my cock between them and fuck you that way. Come all over that pretty face of yours." He tapped her cheek. "You like that idea? Does it make you wet to think about me using your body to get myself off? 'Cause I'm gonna do it."

She closed her eyes and surrendered to the moment, consuming every filthy word he spoke and picturing the fingers on her nipple were his.

"There's not a single part of you I'm not going to mark with my come," he murmured. "It'll be dripping out of you, I'm gonna fill you so good." He exhaled as if imagining it. "Are you aching for me? Does your greedy pussy want my cock?"

She couldn't speak or nod her head, so by pleading with her eyes and humming in accord, she attempted to convey to him how much she wanted his cock inside her right then.

He groaned, picking up her message loud and clear. "I want to see how much you want it. Show me. Rub your fingers on the outside of your pussy and get them nice and shiny. Don't touch your clit or put your fingers inside you. You're gonna have to wait for me to do that."

Oh, God, she was never going to survive if he made her wait much longer. She eagerly slid the hand she wasn't using on her breast into her pants and underneath her panties, not surprised to find herself slick and slippery with her pussy's moisture.

"I can hear how wet you are," he said after a minute of her running her fingers up and down her slit. "Now I want to see it."

She pulled her hand out of her panties and held it up over her head.

Logan licked his lips. "Oh yeah, you're desperate for me to make you come, aren't you? Soon, Tiger. I'm almost there." He ceased thrusting and withdrew from her mouth, grasping her hand and wrapping it around his cock. "Paint my dick with your juices."

She glided her hand up and down the length of him, coating him in her arousal.

He tapped her cheek again and stayed her hand. "Open." He pushed his cock between her lips and pumped it into her mouth at a quicker and jerkier pace than before. "Taste yourself. Taste good?" he asked breathlessly.

To answer his question, she hollowed her cheeks to increase the suction around him. Drips of his salty pree-jaculate splashed on her tongue, mixing in with the spice of her juices.

Logan's legs trembled. "Fuck, I'm gonna come." He tangled his fingers into her hair and left the other on her cheek as his cock twitched and shots of hot come jettisoned into her mouth. "Drink it down. Drink it all down."

She swallowed over and over, the endless streams of come sliding down her throat. As if he'd finished a marathon, Logan breathed heavily, the tension of his muscles visibly more relaxed and his eyes sleepy. When his dick slipped from her mouth, she looked up at him and smiled.

Damn it, he'd been right. There was a big difference between a blow job and face-fucking. Face-fucking had made her horny as hell. Amazing what the loss of control and some dirty talk could do to her. It was almost as good as coming herself, but her body was still hanging on the precipice, waiting for the touch to take her over the edge.

He turned and went over to the seats, giving her a great view of his perfectly muscled ass. He bent slightly, reclining the back of one of the seats before striding to her and lifting her to her feet. He led her to the seat and playfully pushed her into it. "Lie back."

Like a man on a mission, he went straight to work on getting her out of her pants and divesting her of her soaked panties. He dropped to his knees and hooked her legs on each of his shoulders, opening her to his heated gaze. He'd seen her like this before, but since the last time she'd been blindfolded, it was the first time she got to witness the hunger in his eyes as his mouth descended onto her pussy and his tongue made contact with her swollen, exposed clit.

"Oh, God. Fuck me, you taste sweet," he said between licks.

Her eyelids began to close, but she forced them to remain open, not wanting to miss a moment of watching this dominant man eat her pussy as if she were a delicacy. Hot liquid pleasure flowed outward from her core as he stroked her bundle of nerves with his tongue.

She reached for climax, but despite the winding tension building between her thighs, her mind continued to throw up roadblocks, preventing her from truly surrendering. Maybe she should fake it as she had with some of the others. Clearly by his demonstration the other night, it wasn't Logan's fault if she couldn't climax.

He lifted his mouth from her pussy and glared at her. "I can tell I lost you, Tiger. Guess I need to remind you who holds the control right now." He slid two thick fingers into her slick channel and curled them upward. "You ever had a man play with your G-spot, baby?"

She shook her head. G-spots were a myth like Santa Claus and happy marriages. At least when it came to her. A few guys had tried to find it, but apparently she didn't have one.

Logan shifted his fingers a touch and smiled, his cock lengthening against his thigh. "Ah, there it is."

His fingers tapped a spot inside her. A bolt of lightning electrified her cunt, and her body thundered in response, shaking uncontrollably. "No, no." The foreign sensation was too intense.

He tsked at her, increasing the rate of the tapping. "You don't say no to me. I want you to come this way, and unless you say the safe word, you're gonna do it. Don't analyze it. Just feel it. I'm getting hard again just from the feel of your pussy walls tightening around my fingers. You're so slick. So hot. Gonna feel like heaven on my cock."

Her hands gripped the seat. She couldn't catch her breath. "Logan?"

"I'm here," he said reassuringly. "You're safe. I'll catch you when you fall."

She didn't hold back. She closed her eyes, sinking into the sensation and surrendering to it and to Logan. Her legs trembled violently and a scream ripped from her throat as the orgasm slammed into her, over her, and through her like a tidal wave taking along everything in its path. The most intensely pleasurable contractions she'd ever experienced rolled through her body until they slowly died down, leaving her boneless and replete.

After a few minutes, she got the energy to open her eyes. Logan was already dressed and had thrown a warm blanket over her. Sitting beside her, he held out a bottle of water. "Drink."

Common sense returned as she took in her surroundings. They were on an airplane with the captain behind closed doors only feet away. There was no way he missed her scream or the reason for it.

She took the water, refusing to look at Logan. For some reason, the blanket and the water annoyed her. She wasn't sure why. Maybe it was because it was proof that she'd given up control for a few minutes. Or maybe it was from that sub drop she'd read about, the temporary depression that sometimes followed a scene when the endorphins decreased. Either way, she just wanted to get dressed and forget it happened. "I'm fine. You don't have to give me aftercare."

He toyed with strands of her hair, sliding them through his fingers. "Aftercare isn't just for the bottom. Maybe I need it too."

She turned her face toward him. "I'm not comfortable with it. Please, Logan."

"That's because you're thinking again. Eventually, you're gonna trust me enough to do the thinking for you in other times except sex."

She jumped out of her seat and picked up her pants off the floor. "Just because you gave me a couple orgasms doesn't mean I'm going to let you control me outside of sex. It's never gonna happen."

Stepping into her pants, she choked on her disappointment. She'd thought maybe Logan might be different from other men.

Logan didn't argue, just cocked a brow and let her stew in her anger. The rage she'd been feeling quickly dissipated, leaving behind only exhaustion. She plopped down in the seat next to him, and when he patted his shoulder, she accepted his offer to rest her head on it.

She tried to fall asleep, but she couldn't keep her thoughts from racing. What would happen when they got to Las Vegas? How would they stop Evans and Fink from releasing the virus? He caressed his hand down her head, playing with her hair. "How'd you sleep last night?"

"Fine," she said, lying.

While Logan had made plans for their flight to Vegas, she'd taken a shower. After running around for two days, it was heavenly to wash the grime, dirt, and sweat from her body. She had never appreciated deodorant, toothpaste, and razors until she went without. She must have spent an hour in the bathroom cleaning and shaving. She'd hoped Logan would've joined her, but he'd taken his shower after she finished, taking nearly as much time in the bathroom as she had, shaving the light beard that had grown in over the course of the two days.

Both of them exhausted, they'd climbed into bed before nine o'clock. With his leg thrown over hers and his hand possessively placed on her stomach, he'd held her all night. But while he'd easily fallen into a deep slumber, she'd found sleep elusive, too worried about what would happen in Vegas.

Logan chuckled. "You didn't sleep at all, did you? We've got a few hours until we get to Vegas. Go to sleep. I promise I'll keep you safe."

Eyes closed, she felt his lips press against her forehead.

She knew he meant his promise to keep her safe.

Too bad he couldn't honor that promise. Because the more she trusted him, the more she depended on him, the harder she fell for him. But as he'd told her, he craved control. And ultimately, she couldn't give that to him. She wasn't a submissive. Retaining control was just as important to her.

What she couldn't say, what he didn't realize, was no one was more dangerous to her well-being than him.

Because he was the only one with the real power to break her.

Chapter Sixteen

SHE'D SLEPT.

Again.

She had to hand it to Logan. He'd not only learned how to play her body as if it were his own personal instrument, he'd become her favorite kind of sleeping pill.

They'd landed in the backyard of Sawyer Hayes's mansion, which was located outside the Las Vegas city limits, only a half-hour drive from the Vegas Strip. According to Logan, the man had homes all over the country, each equipped with its own landing strip since he traveled frequently on business. But unlike the lush tropical backdrop of Florida, this yard had red mountains as its scenery. Instead of grass, his desert yard comprised dirt and rocks. And yet it was equally as beautiful, the swimming pool a desert oasis lined by palm trees and cacti.

If she'd thought it was hot in Florida, it was only because she'd never been to Vegas. As soon as they'd deplaned, her throat had gone bone-dry. It was like walking into a sauna fully clothed.

She'd never been to Sin City. She'd seen photos, of course, but nothing could've prepared her for the awe of the city's impressive skyline nestled between majestic red mountains.

Rather than having gone inside Sawyer's home, they were whisked away by a stretch limo. Along the ride she stared out the window, taking in the sight of all the city's hotels, shops, and restaurants.

After salivating from the thought of tacos, burgers, and steaks, she was thankful to find Sawyer had thoughtfully provided a full meal for them to eat in the car. As she feasted on chicken Caesar salad and French bread, the limo drove down the highway, leaving the Las Vegas city limits and the Strip's skyline behind them.

When she'd asked Logan where they were headed, he'd only told her they'd be staying somewhere safe. She supposed it didn't matter anyway since she didn't know one place from another in Nevada. As long as they had access to computers and could figure out a way to stop Evans and Fink from carrying out their plan, she didn't care where they stayed. Her fingers twitched with the urge to feel the keyboard under them. Two days without the Internet was long enough. It was time for her to do what she did best.

Expose the truth.

An hour after they landed, they drove up to the Paradise Lost Hotel. The sign seemed a bit understated for what she'd expect of a Nevada hotel, lacking the neon lights and pizzazz of those found on the strip. The two-level hotel was a dingy white brick building with a working fountain in front. It didn't look like much from the outside, but she was sure if the wealthy Sawyer had set them up here, it couldn't be as bad as the place they'd stayed at in Florida.

The driver opened the door and she slid out of the limo. She held a hand over her eyes to shield them from the sudden light.

With the duffle Joe had given them, Logan wordlessly sidled up beside her as the door opened and Sawyer Hayes appeared.

He was just as handsome as she remembered. His blond hair fell in soft waves to just above his shoulders, and his eyes were a piercing shade of jade. The youthful innocence of his face had disappeared in the decade since she'd last seen him on television, and deep laugh lines were etched around his eyes and the corners of his lips. The few days' worth of stubble on his chin failed to hide his dimple. In his torn jeans and a simple navy T-shirt, it would be impossible to guess his net worth by his clothes.

The nondescript lobby of the hotel was decorated in beige and crème with a Berber carpet and aerial photos of the Vegas strip. She found it odd that the front desk had two computers but no people working behind it. The place was strangely quiet, as if they were the only people here. Maybe business wasn't doing that well and that's why Sawyer had chosen this location as their hideout.

Smiling wildly, Sawyer shook Logan's hand and gave him one of those typical guy half hugs while pounding his back. "Good to see you, man. Even if it's because you're on the run from the Feds. You never do things easy, do you? I remember that one time you got caught with those twins—"

"Sawyer, this is Rachel," Logan said, efficiently and thankfully cutting him off before he could expound on his trip down memory lane.

Sawyer took her hand and kissed the top of it. "Sorry to meet you under these circumstances, Rachel, but it is a pleasure nonetheless."

Even though she didn't buy his suave act for a second, she was still affected by his flirtation and felt her cheeks heat with a blush. "Thank you."

He released her hand. "If you'd like to join me downstairs tonight, I'd be happy to find some appropriate clothes for you to wear." He lowered his voice, raising his eyebrows. "Unless you prefer to wear nothing at all."

Was Sawyer still flirting, or was she missing something? "I'm sorry. I don't think I understand."

"You didn't tell her?" Sawyer asked Logan, shaking his head.

Logan shot Sawyer a deadly look before turning to her. "The Paradise Lost Hotel isn't actually a hotel. It's a sex club."

"We're staying at a sex club?" she asked shrilly. "Like Benediction?"

Was everyone into the lifestyle these days?

"Tell me you're a submissive," Sawyer begged, taking a step closer to her. "My cock will wilt in disappointment if you're a Domme."

"Hands off," Logan said, practically growling as he yanked her under his arm. "Keep them and your damned cock away from Rachel."

Sawyer threw up his hands. "Sorry. Didn't know she belonged to you."

"I don't," she said, neither of them listening.

Logan's eyes flashed a warning. "Well, now you do."

Shocked, she peered up at him, wondering what the hell had gotten into him. Sure, he'd agreed to figuratively and literally show her the ropes of BDSM for as long as they were on the run, but since when did she belong to him?

"It's not like you to be so territorial," Sawyer said, his lips tipped up in a grin. "You used to share your toys."

"I'm no one's toy," she declared with her hands on her hips, although neither of the men seemed to hear her. They were acting like cavemen. She half expected Logan to beat his chest and drag her by her hair to his cave.

Coming from anyone else, she would've been offended and given him a piece of her mind, but with Logan, she was oddly aroused by his display of ownership. It reminded her of how Cole treated Danielle and how Jaxon behaved with Kate. Logan was acting as if he was her Dom, and rather than anger her, it made her feel secure. She wanted to belong to him. Did that mean she wasn't only submissive in bed, but in other aspects of her life? How could she be submissive and, at the same time, want to be in control?

She frowned. And what did Sawyer mean about sharing toys?

Heat unfurled in her belly. She had a feeling they weren't talking about Legos.

She followed Sawyer and Logan down a hallway of what would normally be hotel guest rooms. Her mouth watered and her stomach rumbled as they passed a vending machine filled with chocolate bars and bags of chips. Even though she'd eaten in the limo, she had a couple of days of calories to make up for, and she didn't plan on doing it with steamed vegetables and broiled fish.

When they reached room number 109, Sawyer swiped a key card through the reader on the door and then handed a card to both of them before opening the door and ushering them inside. "The guys are on their way. We've all been waiting for your call."

Whatever expense Sawyer had saved on the exterior of the hotel and the lobby obviously went into the bedrooms. Everything about the room screamed "luxury." Here the crème-colored carpet was thick and lush, and the walls were painted a light gold. The mahogany king-sized, four-poster bed had one of those gauzy canopies hanging over the top of it, and it was covered with a gold-and-crimson brocade comforter and throw pillow. A crimson cushioned bench sat at the foot of the bed.

After spending one night in a car and two in less refined bedrooms, she could definitely get used to it here.

"Knew I could count on you," Logan said, dropping the duffle on the bed.

"The guys?" she asked, confused.

"Our friends Oz, Hunter, and Rowan," Logan clarified.

Sawyer leaned casually against the doorframe, his arms folded across his chest. "Yeah, well, not so easy with the Feds on your asses, but Oz created credible stories and the appropriate backup trail to throw them off their scent. He made it look as though we were meeting you at Mount Rushmore in South Dakota."

She sat down at the bottom of the mattress and practically moaned at its softness. "That'll help thwart the FBI, but Evans and Fink will be looking for us in Vegas."

Sawyer smiled. "Not here, though. There's nothing tying me to this place." He pushed off the frame of the doorway and straightened. "There's food in the mini-fridge and everything in the vending machine is free, so help yourselves. I bought you each a few days' worth of clothes and already put them away in the dresser." He pointed to a closed door across the room. "You can find toiletries in the bathroom, so feel welcome to take a shower."

Clean clothes and a shower that didn't have mold growing in it sounded like heaven right now.

Sawyer checked his watch. "I'll call you when the guys get here, and we can figure out your next move."

Logan strode to Sawyer and shook his hand. "Thanks again for sticking your neck out for us."

Sawyer nodded, smacking Logan's shoulder. "My club, Paradise Found, opens at nine downstairs. There's a separate entrance at the back that leads directly to it, so if you choose to remain up here, you'll have all the privacy you need so long as you stay in your room. The others will be…occupied during club hours." He turned, his gaze lasering in on her. "And Ms. Dawson, I do hope I'll get the pleasure of your company in the club tonight. If you're worried about being recognized, you're welcome to wear a mask. We don't have the same exclusive requirements that you find at Benediction. For thirty-five dollars and a waiver, you get entry into the club for the night. For that reason, several of our guests choose to wear masks to maintain anonymity." He tipped his chin and shut the door behind him as he left.

With him gone, she felt as if she could breathe again. Despite his flirty demeanor, there was an underlying intensity that seemed to suck the oxygen out of the room.

She and Logan had plenty to discuss, but right now she had only one thing on her mind. "What did Sawyer mean about sharing your toys?"

From across the room, Logan winced, his body growing rigid before he blew out a breath. "The guys and I used to share women."

Her stomach flip-flopped and her skin grew tight. The guys. As in plural. "Share? You mean you'd all have sex with one woman? At the same time?"

Maybe to buy him some time before answering, he pulled some men's clothes out of a drawer before turning around to answer. "Usually only two of us, but yeah." He brought his clothes over the bed and sat next to her. "Does that bother you?"

Bother her? She guessed that depended on his definition of *bother*. Because she was bothered, all right. Hot and bothered. Her body flushed with arousal, her heart racing and her pussy growing wet. She didn't want to think about Logan and other women like that, but her body was totally on board with her in the middle of Logan and another man.

Still, she played it cool, uncomfortable by her body's reaction to the idea. "No, not at all. Maybe it should, but my friendships with some of the kinkier women of Detroit have enlightened me about sexual relationships."

"Yeah?"

"Yeah. Safe, sane, consensual. As long as all parties agree and no one is harmed, it's none of my business what people do to get off. And that includes you."

Her comments were rational and mature, and her voice hadn't cracked once. There was no way he'd guess the storm of arousal raging inside her at the moment. She took a breath and smiled. "So, I understand guys like the idea of having sex with two women, but what do you get out of sharing? Are you bisexual?" Because the mental picture of a naked Logan and another man kissing and touching each other was almost as good as the one with her in the middle of it.

He sputtered. "No, I'm not bisexual." His gaze snared hers and held tight. "Sharing is one of my kinks. The idea of giving the woman so much pleasure she can't control herself," he said softly, a fevered light in his eyes. "The tight way her inner muscles clamp down on me as she's filled with a cock in both her pussy and her ass and watching her completely come undone." He swallowed thickly. "It's a rush."

His words aroused her to the point of pain. But since Logan had warned Sawyer away from her, he clearly didn't want her with two men. She wouldn't ruin what limited time they had together by asking him to do something he obviously didn't want to do. After all, she should be flattered he didn't want to share her.

Nervously fumbling with the neck of her shirt, she leapt to her feet and crossed to the dresser to find some fresh clothes. She was shocked and flattered that Logan had paid enough attention to know her sizes. She picked out some jean shorts and a black blouse as well as a set of black lace panties and matching bra that she was certain Sawyer had chosen for her to wear in the club tonight.

"I'm going to take a shower," she announced, not looking at Logan before taking her clothes with her into the bathroom.

And what a bathroom it was.

It had to be close to the same size as the bedroom.

Everything was done in gold-and-crème marble from the heated floors to the double sink. There was a Jacuzzi tub that could fit more than two people comfortably and a huge glass-enclosed shower with multiple showerheads. Mirrors hung on the walls and, oddly, in the shower. There were fluffy throw rugs that looked soft enough to sleep on and pristine gold towels with the word *Paradise* on them.

She chuckled, the meaning behind the name of the hotel, Paradise Lost, and the club, Paradise Found, suddenly dawning on her. One would acquire paradise only within the club and its bedrooms.

Indecision warred within her as she debated whether to shower or take a bath. A Jacuzzi would soothe her muscles and relax her, but she was dying to try the shower. She opened the door and turned the knob, cranking it to the hotter side. Water sprayed from five different spots, three from the ceiling and two from the sides, seemingly coming from out of the mirrors. Bizarrely, there were several suction cups with large metal rings resembling bracelets on them stuck to the mirrors too.

She undressed, ready to burn those filthy clothes. By the time she'd thrown them in the trash, the room had filled with steam. She stepped into the shower, groaning when hot water rained down on her. This was so much better than last night's excuse of a shower.

Finding shampoo, she flicked open the spout and poured some into her waiting hand. She sighed at the soothing scent of lavender permeating throughout the shower.

After she massaged the shampoo into her hair, she closed her eyes and braced her hands on the wall in front of her as she tilted her head back under one of the showerheads and soapy water cascaded down her.

She felt a slight chill as the door to the shower opened and then the heat of Logan standing behind her. The warm breath on her neck made her nipples tighten and her abdomen quiver.

"Didn't want to miss out on the chance to see you all slippery with soap like I did last night. I hope you don't mind," he said huskily.

Did she? He'd already seen her naked and gotten up close and personal with her pussy, but taking a shower with him seemed more intimate, hinting at a relationship between the two of them. "Shower's big enough for the both of us."

His hand skated down the length of her spine and cupped her bottom. "Shower's big enough for both of us and two more." He nipped her ear. "Yeah, you thought I didn't notice how excited you got when I told you about how much I enjoyed sharing a woman with my friends? Your pulse was hammering at the side of your neck like a frightened little bird. But the only thing you were frightened of was how I'd react if I knew how much you wanted it."

She opened her eyes. "You told Sawyer you wouldn't share me."

"I wouldn't. Not with him. Sawyer's needs are too dark for you. And frankly, I wasn't sure if sharing would be something you'd be into."

Her breathing hitched. "Will it hurt to have two cocks inside at the same time?"

"Not if I start preparing you for it," he said roughly, his voice sounding as if his throat had been rubbed with sandpaper. "Turn to face me."

Biting her lip, she spun around and, dizzy from arousal, rested her hands on his chest for support. Rivulets of water ran down between his flat brown nipples, enticing her to lick. But before she could follow through, he moved, pulling two of the suction cups off the mirror and positioning them lower. Confused by his actions, she was speechless when he grabbed one of her hands and slipped it into the ring hanging from the suction cup then tightened the ring, securing her to it. He repeated the process with her other hand, so both arms were raised slightly above her head and she was facing the mirror.

Now the suction cups made sense.

Shower bondage.

He seized a small tube beside the shampoo on the shelf and kneeled behind her, one of his hands sliding around her to the front where he quickly pulled back the hood of her clitoris to expose the bundle of nerves. Using tiny circular motions, he rubbed it while repeatedly sinking his teeth into the flesh of her ass.

Sparks of heat lit up her pussy and had her squirming in place.

Staring at herself in the mirror, she watched as a woman she barely recognized moaned and begged for more. Beads of water streamed down her pink flushed cheeks, and her eyes were glazed over as if she was drugged.

He shifted his hand, plunging his fingers into her pussy as his thumb strummed her clit. "You want to know what it's like to have more than one cock pumping away inside of you? Well, I'm about to give you an exclusive sneak peek to get you ready for it. See, right now, I've got two of my fingers in you. Your pussy's clamping down on them, sucking them in, with no resistance. But as you learned on the plane, my cock's a lot wider than two fingers, so I'm gonna have to add one more." There was a pinch of pain as his third finger joined the others, stretching her walls, but the pleasurable waves of heat rolling through her quickly numbed the sting. "Now pretend that's my cock inside you right now, fucking you. Owning you. Feels good, doesn't it?"

"Yes," she managed to croak out. "It feels better than good."

"Ever have anyone play with your ass?" he asked darkly.

"No." A couple of guys had asked, claiming they could make her come that way, but she'd never trusted anyone to make it pleasurable for her. Until Logan. She had no doubts that he'd not only make it pleasurable, he'd set her on fire from the inside.

The fingers of his other hand skimmed over her crack. "If you want to stop, use your safe word. Tell me what it is."

"Family," she said breathlessly.

She looked down at him and saw him squirt gel from the tube he'd grabbed earlier onto the pads of two of his fingers.

"Lube. One of the most important ingredients for successful anal sex." He pressed a cold fingertip between the cheeks of her butt. "Sawyer probably stocks it by the truckload in this place."

The tip pushed into her, the pinching feeling foreign to her, but not overtly painful. He swirled it inside her, before slowly moving it back and forth in tandem with the ones in her pussy.

She concentrated on breathing and relaxing her muscles to allow him farther inside. He must have sensed it because not a moment later, he pushed his finger all the way into her. She emitted a tiny squeak at the weird sensation of having something in her backside. But when he dragged it almost all the way out and then plunged it back inside again, her forehead thunked against the mirror and the word *more* fell from her lips.

"You are so fucking sexy," Logan said, inserting a second digit in her ass.

The addition had her going on her toes. She was so full of him, she couldn't think of anything but how incredible it felt to be stretched and filled to capacity.

He wasn't especially gentle as he fucked her pussy and her ass with his fingers and stroked his thumb over her clit. And she didn't want him to be. He was taking her. Owning her body with every part of himself. Proving he was in control, and there was nothing short of saying her safe word that would stop him from his domination over her.

Her lips were sealed other than to cry out his name over and over.

Her muscles tightened, her legs shaking like a newborn baby foal's, and liquid heat bubbled in her core. Everything inside her tensed. Her breathing stalled in her chest. Her eyes squeezed shut. And then the heat boiled over, waves of contractions clamping down on Logan's fingers of both hands.

Slowly, Logan withdrew his fingers. He pressed tiny kisses up her spine until he stood once more and washed his hands. He removed her wrists from the cuffs and kissed the inside of each of her wrists before lightly massaging both of them and her shoulders.

He turned her around and kissed her softly on the lips.

Her gaze fell to his erect cock. With a grin, she wrapped her hand around it, reveling in Logan's groan.

"You don't have to—"

"Shh. I know. I want to," she whispered, looking up at him.

His eyes were closed and his face pinched in concentration. "Won't take long."

One hand worked his cock, twisting and rubbing as she found all the spots that made him moan, while the other massaged his balls.

It took only two minutes before his cock pulsed and twitched. He threw his head back, the cords of his neck straining. "Rachel."

Streams of come spilled over her hand. She marveled at the sexual abandonment on Logan's face as his body shook from climax. He was so dominant. So powerful. But for a few precious moments, he'd trusted her enough to transfer his power over to her. She'd held it in her hands.

His eyes opened and he smiled.

And that was it.

She was a goner.

Forget falling.

She'd fallen.

Head over heels, face-first, no hands fallen in love with the man. He understood her like no one else. When she was in his arms, the rest of the world fell away and her mind quieted. She loved his intellect and his bravery, but it was the way he made her feel as if she was the most important person in the world to him that had stolen her heart.

She returned his smile.

They had a couple more days together, and she'd enjoy every moment of them to the fullest. And when it inevitably ended and he shattered her heart into a million of pieces, she'd move to New York and start a new life for herself there.

Where once again, she'd be all alone.

Chapter Seventeen

THE SENATOR BOARDED the private plane and, with a curt nod, greeted the flight attendant before taking his usual seat by the window. Within a minute of his arrival, he had a scotch on the rocks in his hand and three different newspapers on the table in front of him. His back throbbed mercilessly from his lover's latest beating, but when he read the headline of the *New York Times*, an icy pain sliced his chest.

His men had failed again.

How many times had his father told him a man was only as good as those who served under him? It had been beaten into him, both figuratively and literally, since he was a boy. That's why he'd done his research before choosing two of the FBI's best and most easily corruptible agents. Even with his money and power, it wasn't fucking easy to access the type of records he needed to make his choice. It took years to quietly research the best matches for the job at hand.

Seymour Fink had been classified as a genius in second grade when state tests showed he could both read and do math on a tenth-grade level. Amazing in itself but even more amazing by the fact that he came from the poorest section of Philadelphia and was being raised by his heroin-addicted single mother. Unfortunately, his mother's neglect resulted in poor hygiene and malnutrition, a sad combination for a painfully thin child that resulted in numerous broken bones and missing teeth after daily beatings by school bullies. By the time the state finally took the child out of the home, he'd broken nearly every bone in his body.

Eventually, he was adopted by a wealthy couple who saw the potential in him, and from that point on he was given every opportunity. He'd graduated from Harvard at twenty in chemical engineering and from Cambridge at twenty-four with a dual degree in public health and chemistry. His knowledge of biological agents led him to help the government write policies on how to protect our country from bioterrorism. His adopted parents had encouraged him to become a college professor or a politician, but instead he'd applied to the FBI. By all intents and purposes, there was nothing on the surface to suggest he would betray his country.

But everyone had a weakness to exploit, and Fink's was his birth mother. For years, he siphoned off money from his adoptive parents to fund his mother's drug habit—even going as far as supplying it to her. What drove a man so brilliant to act so foolishly? He didn't only endanger his career and his freedom, but the relationship with those who had loved and supported him throughout the years. And all the while, he'd been stealing from them. A man like that would do anything to protect his birth mother. If he went to jail, who would care for her? No one. She would die.

It was that easy. A threat here and there. A promise that should anything happen to Fink, he would ensure his mother received enough money to support her addiction. And the genius belonged to him.

On the other hand, Evans's file was an enigma to him. A challenge. The man was a brute, an ex-football player and an ex-cop with a degree in criminal justice. He was above average in intelligence and had grown up in the suburbs, supposedly loved by all those around him. By all accounts, his background was perfect. *Everything* about the man seemed perfect on paper. Which was why he knew the man harbored secrets. After following him for two nights, he discovered his predilection for roughing up hookers during sex. Armed with the information, he'd gone to blackmail him only to discover the man didn't need to be blackmailed. He'd voluntarily signed up for the job.

What they were doing was for the good of this country. Would people die? As in any war, it was certainly possible. But his plan would strengthen this country against the potential of terrorist attacks that could wipe out Western civilization as they knew it. Instead of thousands of dying, hundreds of thousands would die. His pleas had fallen on deaf ears for decades, and now, with the country in financial and international turmoil, it was time to correct its mistakes.

The fact that he'd become even wealthier than his parents was a bonus.

In just a few months, he'd never have to bow down to his family's whims again. He'd prove that he was a real man who would no longer be manipulated by them in their plays for power and wealth. It was his turn to shine while they and his brother could retreat into the darkness where they'd stuck him all these years.

It would be his turn to run for president, and there wasn't a single candidate who would be able to defeat him.

Only a few of his most trusted allies knew of his plan. Everything would be as perfect as Evans's employment file if they could just eliminate that lawyer and reporter. They were like those no-see-ums, insignificant and annoying, but they'd already proved smarter than he'd given them credit for.

Evidence had been planted to ensure no one would look any further than the two of them for Rinaldi's murder. His first choice was for the two of them to be put down before they could talk to anyone. But if that wasn't possible, he would also have a plan in place in case they were arrested.

The flight attendant appeared before him, her shirt now unbuttoned to expose the swells of her generous tits. "The captain would like to inform you we'll be taking off now, and that he anticipates a smooth flight to Las Vegas, sir."

Watching her take her seat, he took a sip of his scotch and considered his options. Logan Bradford and Rachel Dawson could hide for now, but when the moment was right, they'd play right into his hands.

First stop—Las Vegas.

Next stop—the White House.

Chapter Eighteen

As Rachel typed on the laptop that Sawyer had dropped off and nibbled on her last square of chocolate, she sent up a silent prayer of thanks for the inventions of computers and the cocoa plant. Since her last orgasm, she'd been ravenous and making her way through every type of junk food in the vending machine.

The recognition of her feelings for Logan had scared her spitless, and without her usual rocky road ice cream to soothe her, she'd just have to make do with chocolate bars.

With his lips tilted up in a grin, Logan watched her lick her fingers clean of the chocolate. "Hungry?"

She scrolled down the page on viral hemorrhagic fevers until she found the one specifically on the Leopold virus. A pang of satiety hit her stomach. "Not anymore."

As she read how the virus ravaged the body, she couldn't understand how anyone would be so cruel as to intentionally release it. Did Evans and Fink have a grudge against Senator Hutton or one of the persons attending Friday's speech at the Tuscany? Were they acting alone? And what did it have to do with Rinaldi? She played with the idea that maybe he had been behind it. He was sadistic enough to enjoy the tremendous amount of pain and grief that this would inflict. He'd go from a serial killer to the largest mass murderer the world had ever known. She and Logan needed to find the link between those agents and Rinaldi.

Nausea swirled through her. After reading this, she was regretting the candy and chips she'd just finished. "According to the CDC, they're not certain if Leopold is contagious before the symptoms start. That means every exposed person could potentially infect everyone in their path until they realize they're sick and are isolated in the hospital." She closed the laptop, not wanting to read any more. It was like a best-selling horror book or a Hollywood blockbuster. "Worst-case scenario, the wealthy men and women who attend Senator Hutton's speech get on airplanes and fly across every continent on the planet, killing millions of people before we can convince the government that it happened."

Logan threw his arm over her shoulders and tugged her into him, kissing the top of her head. "We won't let that happen."

The weight of the world was on their shoulders, and she was glad she didn't have to carry the burden alone. If she had to do it with anyone, Logan was the man she wanted beside her. And above her. And behind her…

Logan's new cell phone rang, playing a popular Taylor Swift song. She laughed. No wonder Sawyer was so eager to make sure Logan chose that particular phone when he'd dropped them off earlier. She picked up her new phone off the nightstand and checked the settings to see what song Sawyer had chosen for her. Frowning as she listened, she wondered why he'd selected Kelly Clarkson's "Miss Independent."

He ended the call and slipped his phone into his pocket. "The guys are here." Frowning, he ran his fingers through her hair and gave her a side-glance. "I'm not sure how to prepare you for them. They're unique."

After meeting Sawyer and hearing about their propensity for sharing women, she wouldn't have expected any less. "I'm sure if they're your friends, I'll like them."

Logan picked at some fuzzy lint on her shorts, the back of his wrist brushing against the skin of her thigh. "We went through a lot together in the army. Experiences like that can either create lifelong bonds or destroy friendships completely. I was lucky to work beside men whom I not only call my friends, but consider my brothers."

She would've expected a man with four navy SEAL brothers to have spent his life in the military. "You mentioned something in the car when I asked you about why you left. You said you and the army weren't a good fit. What did you mean by that?"

His lips pressed into a thin line. "I have a hard time blindly following orders."

Mockingly, her hand flew to her chest. "No. I'm shocked."

He gave her a smile, but it quickly disappeared. "The guys and I worked in intelligence. We came across some sketchy information and agreed it was probably a setup. My commanding officer felt differently and sent in some men to do a rescue op. Turns out we were both right. The rebels actually did have an American relief worker, a girl who couldn't have been older than twenty, as a hostage. But when the soldiers entered the home where they were holding her, it triggered a bomb and a planned attack."

He paused, the air heavy with grief and the memory of spilled blood. Her heart ached as if she had been there in Afghanistan with him. She wanted to hold him, comfort him, but she knew the best thing she could do for him now was to just listen and allow him to finish.

His hands curled into fists. "Twelve men lost their lives because of the information we gave to our commander. Twelve men lost their lives because they didn't have the right to disobey orders. Twelve men died because there was nothing I could do to stop it." He pushed off of the bed and paced the room. "My commanding officer was a good man. He didn't rush the soldiers into the house because he wanted glory or because he was an asshole. He disregarded the risk because there was a woman in trouble and he couldn't handle the thought of her suffering. He wanted to be her hero. Instead, he was her executioner. And his own."

Tears burned behind her eyelids, but she blinked them back and shifted her position on the bed, throwing her legs over the edge of the mattress. "I'm sorry that happened to you."

He stopped pacing and turned to her, his brows furrowed. "Thank you, but you don't need to feel sorry for me. I survived." He sat on the bed next to her and held her hand. "But it changed me. That's when I began to need control over every aspect of my life, including sex. The guys you're about to meet are a lot like me. Control…it's important to all of us. Maybe that's why we all became hackers. We couldn't handle having something out of our control." He hefted her to her feet. "Come on. I'd like to introduce you to them."

Sawyer was waiting for them in the hallway and led them past the guest rooms to an office at the opposite side of the hotel. "Welcome to Tech Central," Sawyer said, motioning Rachel and Logan into the room with a sweeping gesture.

Immediately, she discovered the room was aptly named. While the room wasn't large, every part of it was overrun by wires and gadgets, most of them unidentifiable to her. On the walls hung multiple giant screens, all of them seemingly connected to the computers and smaller monitors set at various points in the room. With all its lights and switches, the space reminded her of the control room at her news station if it were combined with the cockpit of an airplane. There were baskets filled with cell phones and others filled with what appeared to be radios and walkie-talkies. And she had no idea what to make of the three tall metal units with lights running up and down the front of them.

Sawyer must have read her confusion. He walked to the odd units and rested his hand on top of one. "In layman's terms, these are our own private servers, complete with unique security programs to cloak our IP address. We can go anywhere on the web, including the Dark Web, without being traced or tracked."

She was familiar with the Dark Web from a high-profile legal case in which a Michigan high school senior had gotten arrested for running a teenage prostitution ring he'd staffed with girls who went to his school. He'd used his computer skills to run a business on a "hidden" part of the Internet.

Sawyer pointed at the baskets. "We've got your typical burner phones, signal jammers, bug detectors, key loggers, frame grabbers, open-source software defined radios...you know, everything you'd expect."

Wide-eyed, she slid a glance at Logan. To her, it was as if Sawyer was speaking another language, but Logan nodded enthusiastically, unfazed and seemingly impressed by Sawyer's toys.

Three men walked in, stealing what little space was left in the room, as well as all the oxygen from her lungs.

Dear God, did all hackers look like this?

Realizing that her jaw had dropped open wide enough to catch flies, she quickly closed it. As soon as the guys spotted Logan, they rushed him, shaking his hand in greeting and smacking him on the back.

Watching with great interest from the sidelines, she observed the group of friends interacting as they quickly caught up with one another, using so much profanity she felt as if she needed another shower.

At five foot seven, she wasn't used to feeling so small, but all of them towered over her. They were all breathtakingly handsome, although each in his own way. The amount of testosterone in the room was overwhelming.

She folded her arms in front of her to cover the proof of how these men affected her. Her mind flew to her earlier conversation with Logan about their propensity for sharing women. She couldn't imagine a woman alive who would turn down the opportunity to have all those hands on her. No wonder they stuck to the combination of two guys, one woman.

Any more and the woman would spontaneously combust.

Was she seriously considering having a ménage à trois with Logan and one of his friends? Her gaze landed on the straining biceps of the biggest of the men, and she smiled.

Oh yeah, she was.

Since Logan had shared his feelings for her back in Florida, she'd been cautiously optimistic that they might actually have a shot. But either way, she was going to greedily consume every chance she got with him, including sharing all his kinks.

After a few minutes, Logan crooked his finger at her. "Guys, this is Rachel Dawson." When she joined his side, he slipped his arm around her waist and nodded his chin in the direction of one of the men. "This here is Eddie 'Oz' Ackerman."

"Call me Oz," he said, his beaded dreadlocks swaying as he took her hand. With skin as dark as her favorite chocolate and teeth so bright and straight she wondered if they were fake, he leaned forward as if about to tell her a secret. "So are you two fucking? Because if you aren't, I call dibs."

Logan's arm tightened around her. "You'll have to excuse him. Oz was dropped on his head when he was a baby."

A man who reminded her of Vin Diesel pounded Oz on the shoulder a couple of times. "And he liked it so much, he became a Hollywood stunt man just so he could get dropped on his head daily."

After the roar of laugher died down, Sawyer pointed to Logan's possessive hand on her hip. "As you can see, Logan's already made his claim on the lovely Ms. Dawson."

"Our loss," said the Vin Diesel look-alike. He pushed Oz away and held out his hand to her. "Hunter Garrett. Sorry we're meeting under these circumstances."

The biggest and most imposing of the bunch, Hunter was surprisingly friendly. The massive biceps she'd been admiring earlier seemed even larger up close, and the rest of him was just as muscular. Looking as if he could bench-press a car, he had a full sleeve of tattoos decorating both his arms, and piercings on his tongue, lip, and eyebrow.

She wondered where else he was pierced.

"And I'm Rowan Kimball," said the last man quietly, not looking at her or offering his hand, but drumming a beat on his thigh. He didn't seem rude, but possibly a bit shy. Although a man with his thick black hair and stunning blue-gray eyes had no reason to be. His face was all sharp angles with high cheekbones she would kill for.

"I've accessed Senator Hutton's private security company's schedule as well as its details on the logistics of his speech," he said as he ambled to one of the computers and sat down. He typed furiously and then the monitor in front of him lit up with information.

She walked up behind him to get a better look at the screen. "Wait, you're telling me you're good enough that you could hack into a security company's records?"

"Honey, there ain't nothing we can't hack," Oz said, taking a seat behind a different monitor. "If there was a computer in your panties, we could be in and out of there without you ever noticing."

Hunter chuffed out a laugh. "Dude, do not speak for all of us. Believe me, if I was ever in her panties, she'd know it."

She didn't doubt that any one of those men would definitely leave his carbon footprint behind if he got anywhere near her panties. "No one is going near my panties," she said without conviction.

Logan's hands wrapped around her waist as he bumped into her from behind, not so subtly reminding her there was one man who would definitely be going near her panties later. "Can we move on from Rachel's panties and move on to what you've all learned?"

Rowan's screen lit up with a timeline of the senator's schedule. "Senator Hutton is arriving tomorrow evening. He's staying in a private donor's home in Lake Las Vegas, and then on Friday at one, he's speaking about his bill to increase funding for anti-bioterrorism to a room filled with his wealthiest donors, in the Tuscan Theater at the Tuscany Hotel."

"That would be the perfect place for Evans and Fink to release Leopold," Logan said excitedly. "Oz, can you access the blueprints of the hotel?"

Oz snorted. "Can I?" He shook his head dramatically and sighed as his fingers went to work, flying across the keyboard. "You insult me."

In awe, Rachel watched as Oz brought up the Clark County Buildings Division's internal server and accessed the blueprints with as much ease as she checked her e-mail. Logan hadn't been kidding when he said they were the best hackers in the world. She'd been impressed by Logan's ability to hack the cruise lines, but these guys made hacking look like child's play.

Staring intently at the blueprints, she located the theater that was situated in the middle of the hotel, near the largest table games room in the casino and a wedding chapel.

Entertainers performing in the theater wouldn't exactly use the same entrances as the rest of the hotel and casino patrons. They would have their own separate entrance.

"Rowan, does the senator's security company note which entrance he's using at the hotel?" she asked.

Rowan scrolled down the page, stopping on detailed notes about the logistics of the senator's arrival and departure from the theater. "BH22E. They must have used a code."

Hunter tsked. "Rowan, Rowan. It is indeed a code, but not a good one. BH stands for 'back of the house,' the area of the casino the public never gets to see." He moved over to stand beside Oz and flashed Rachel a smile. "I'm more than a pretty face." Turning to Oz, he pointed at the blueprints. "Oz, enlarge the back of the house for us." Once he did, Hunter shook his finger. "There. The top right, see the number twenty-two? It's on the east side of the building. Back of the house, door twenty-two, on the east side. If you ask me, the senator is overpaying his security team."

Rachel had a feeling the security team members were probably quite competent when it came to doing their jobs. There was no way they could have prepared to come up against three hackers with these abilities. She hadn't even known it was possible to break into companies' private servers.

"Once they bring the senator inside, he'll take an elevator to the bottom floor of the hotel and walk through the catacombs to get to a private elevator that goes directly to the backstage of the theater," Rowan said, quickly summarizing the copious notes.

She glanced over her shoulder at Logan. "If Evans and Fink don't want anyone to trace the virus back to them, they can't be seen walking around with the tank in their arms. How are they going to get it into the theater?"

His mouth pursed and lines etched his forehead as he considered her question. Then a glint came into his eyes. "They don't ever have to set foot into the theater. They're going to release it through the air vents. Oz, find the mechanical room."

Oz quickly pulled up the plans of the hotel's lower level.

"There," said Logan, pointing at the screen. "The entrance to the room is almost directly below the theater. As FBI, they'd have easy access to the same blueprints we have. They just have to find the duct that leads to the theater."

Sawyer tapped his temple. "So if I were these agents, I'd follow closely behind the rest of the security team and access the hotel through the same door. But instead of taking the elevator down to the catacombs, I'd go to the basement level, which houses some offices and the maintenance of the hotel."

Exhilaration filled her. This is what she loved to do. Figure out how all the pieces of a puzzle fit together. "No one on the hotel's staff would blink twice if FBI agents checked out the security of the basement below the theater." She bit her lip, stumbling into a glaring roadblock. "But how are we going to get access to the basement of the Tuscany? The minute we step into that hotel, we'll be recognized."

Oz burst into hysterical laughter, slapping his knee.

"Why is he laughing?" she asked.

Sawyer sidled up beside her. "Because this place has every costume you can think of to help you conceal your identity." He grinned wickedly. "Role play is a popular kink offered at Paradise Found."

The room's temperature seemed to increase ten degrees. She gulped, wondering if Logan would ever be up for wearing his army uniform for her. "Got any creds that will help us pass as part of the senator's security team?" she asked.

"We can not only create them," Oz said, "but have the security company's records show you're part of the team." He spread his arms out wide. "Never doubt the all-powerful Oz."

Rowan scratched his head. "Did you guys think maybe you could just call anonymously and warn the senator?"

She wished it was that easy. "Like he'd believe us? Besides, it wouldn't stop the plan. Only postpone or alter it. At least now, we know roughly when and where it's occurring. This could be our only opportunity to stop it."

They needed something to prove Evans and Fink were dirty. But what? She frowned. If the agents were working for someone else, they would've been paid. "A trail," she said out loud. "We need to find out if Evans and Fink have received any large sums of money recently. How do we do that?"

Logan rested his chin on her shoulder. "The guys can access their US bank accounts, but it will take some time for them to uncover any overseas accounts, especially if they've used an international corporation to cover their tracks."

"But we can do it," Rowan said. "I'll work on it tonight while you guys are in the club."

Logan picked his head up. "Oh, we're not—"

"That would be great, Rowan. Thanks," she said, interrupting. She wanted to see what went on in the club. "Hey, Sawyer? Do you think you could find us some masks? I think I'd like to take you up on your offer and check out Paradise Found. After all, we are in Vegas. And what happens here..."

"Stays here?" Logan asked seriously.

His question deserved a serious and truthful answer. She smiled. "I hope not."

Chapter Nineteen

RACHEL MUST HAVE lost her mind somewhere between Florida and Nevada. That was the only explanation of why, in addition to a black mask that covered the upper portion of her face, she was wearing only a black lace shelf bra and matching thong—in public.

How far she had come from a few days ago at Benediction in her pants and a conservative blouse when she'd agreed to allow Logan to bind her with his ropes over her clothes.

Sawyer had begged Logan to show off his Shibari skills tonight in the club. Now she was practically naked on a stage inside Paradise Found and getting ready for Logan to bind her in front of an audience.

She may have spent only a short time inside the dungeon of Benediction, but that was all she needed to understand the differences between that club and this one.

Benediction catered to the wealthy, its patrons paying thousands of dollars for the privilege of belonging to a club where other members of high society could play with like-minded sexually adventurous people without having to worry about being outed for their predilections for kinky sex. Those who scened at Benediction did so in luxurious surroundings, with expensive equipment and state-of-the-art security. They had gorgeous locker rooms that rivaled a high-end spa, fantasy rooms, and free alcohol for those who weren't participating in any BDSM scenes.

Paradise Found, on the other hand, was more like a typical nightclub, although no alcohol was sold or permitted. The music was so loud she could feel the vibrations of the bass thumping against her chest, and half-naked bodies crowded the dance floor, bumping and grinding to the electronic beat, the air laden with the scent of sweat. Only when her gaze wandered to the other areas did she spot the similarities between the two sex clubs.

Along the outer fringes of the room were beds on platforms, almost all of them in use with various pairings and combinations of men and women having sex right out in the open for everyone to see. Those who didn't have access to beds utilized couches, chairs, benches, and even the floor. There was one guy being flogged and a woman bent over a bench being spanked, but the kink here seemed to be more about public sex and ménage.

Her stomach churned from nerves and her heart pounded so wildly, she had to take deep breaths in order to get enough oxygen into her lungs to counter the dizziness.

But her apprehension had nothing to do with her embarrassment over her body. She was comfortable in her skin, and besides, no one could identify her behind her mask. Except for Logan's friends, the people in Paradise Found were strangers whom she'd never see again. No, the nervous knots in her belly had to do with the amount of control she was handing over to Logan.

Of course she trusted him. She wouldn't have agreed to this if she didn't. But trust was something new to her, and everything was happening so fast. It was as if she was a caterpillar in a chrysalis about to be reborn into a butterfly. And that terrified her because while butterflies were beautiful and free to fly, they had a short life span. Every moment spent with Logan, she was falling deeper and harder for him. Soon—if not already—it would be too late to save herself from completely metamorphosing.

And then what would become of her if he changed his mind and left her?

For years, she'd prided herself on relying on no one. She was a tough career woman who didn't need or want a man in her life. But Logan had her rethinking everything she believed about herself.

Shutting out the chance to find love was the act of a coward. She'd thought she was so brave because she could face down a serial killer during an interview and help stop a dog-fighting operation, but the real truth was she was never in any real danger with the armed guards beside her and cameras filming live. It wasn't until she'd been confronted with watching a man die a violent death that she'd learned what it was to truly fear for her life.

Before Logan, the only real risk she'd ever taken was leaving her family behind and starting a new life all on her own. But fear kept her from reestablishing a relationship with them. Fear kept her from letting go during sex and being able to experience orgasm.

She was tired of being a coward.

Which was why she had readily agreed to do a Shibari suspension scene with Logan for one hundred strangers. Trusting him with her body was easy. It was the submission that terrified her. When he dominated her, he knocked down all the barriers she'd built to protect herself from the fear of losing control. It was in those moments her heart was vulnerable to him. But with each passing day, he'd managed to chip away the layers of concrete encasing it until only a small piece of the protection remained.

Tonight he might penetrate that last layer and own her heart completely. He would uncover the naïve little girl she had buried and forgotten when she'd become Rachel Dawson, the girl who had grown up believing a wife had no choice but to obey her husband. As terrified as that idea made her, it also filled her with hope that she may finally have met a man who wouldn't stifle her. Who would support her dreams and goals as if they were his own.

Wearing only jeans, Logan stood behind her, the hairs of his chest tickling her spine and his erection bumping against her lower back. His hands soothingly brushed up and down her arms. "Are you ready?"

He only meant to ask whether she was prepared for the scene, but to her, the question meant so much more.

She nodded and blew out a breath. "I am. I really am."

He stepped away from her to pick up the hemp rope and a couple of other items, his whole demeanor changing from the playful man to the dominant one, a man who pushed her boundaries to the edge. He held himself differently and became someone taller, more formidable. He'd accept nothing less than complete and total submission from her.

It was a gift she wanted to give and wanted to continue to give for as long as he'd have her.

Earlier this evening, after dinner, he'd spoken at length about what would happen tonight during the scene, and they had gone over her limits. Because there was suspension involved, he wouldn't gag her, the ability to communicate too important during this complicated scene. He'd tie her in a Japanese bondage sideways suspension called *Yoko Tsuri*.

The control freak in her wanted to watch every single knot he made along her body, but to surrender more freely, she kept her eyes focused ahead of her, ignoring the people, including Sawyer, watching the bondage scene with great interest.

Logan planted a kiss on her shoulder as he unhooked her bra and exposed her breasts. Her nipples puckered, caressed by the air. His lips disappeared, replaced by the soft whisper of the rope along her spine. Then with shocking ease, he ripped away her panties, leaving her completely bare. "Grab your ankles."

She shivered at his words, as well as the knowledge of what was to come. She bent forward and waited, the anticipation and the position making her light-headed. Cool liquid dripped between the cheeks of her butt, and then Logan began pushing a butt plug into her.

He'd promised it would not only help prepare her for being taken by two men, but also keep her on edge during the scene. She inhaled through her nose and exhaled through her mouth, relaxing her muscles to allow it in. The odd sensation of fullness was similar to his fingers, only the rigid plastic plug was less forgiving. He continued to push the plug into her, stretching her wide until finally seating it completely.

His hand smacked her ass, moving the plug inside her and sending a bolt of pleasure to her pussy. "Stand straight."

Once she stood, Logan tugged her arms behind her, arching her spine and pushing out her chest as if proudly displaying her breasts to the world. Her wrists were bound to the small of her back. On instinct, she tried to move them, but the rope held her immobile.

Rather than panic, she smiled, her heart rate slowing upon the realization that, short of a safe word and the limits they had negotiated earlier, she no longer had any control on this stage. Her eyelids grew heavy, and a warmth settled into her limbs. His ropes continued to slide around her upper torso like a lover's embrace, creating the cocoon for her metamorphosis.

She breathed steadily as he went to work binding her body, her gaze raking over the busy beds across the club. Although public sex wasn't something she wanted to try, at least at this point, she appreciated the buffet of scenes laid out in front of her, especially the bed with a redheaded woman kneeling between two men, one with smooth dark skin and the other olive-toned, each a beautiful contrast against her alabaster skin.

Rachel's gaze homed in on the bliss on the woman's face and the sleepy arousal in her eyes that Rachel could see all the way from the stage. The realization that soon she could be that woman sent an excited chill coasting down her arms. As the threesome shifted on the bed, the faces of the men caught her attention.

Oz and Rowan.

She could tell this wasn't the first time they'd made love to a woman together, their bodies moving with certainty and precision as they positioned the redhead onto all fours, Rowan behind her and Oz in front. Rowan lined up his cock to her entrance and pushed himself into her fully, one hand holding the end of the woman's braid and the other gripping her hip. His thrusts drove the woman forward, each one propelling her mouth onto Oz's cock. Oz cradled the woman's face in his hands as if she was a treasure, a complete dichotomy to the brutal force Rowan used in fucking her.

After meeting Logan's friends, she would've never guessed quiet Rowan would take the lead in a ménage. In Tech Central, he hadn't appeared to have a dominant bone in his body, but the Rowan in Paradise Found was just as dominant as the man currently looping rope around her waist.

Logan crouched in front of her, placing his hands on her thighs. "Part your legs for me."

A quick buzz hit her clit, jarring her and stealing her breath with its intensity. She looked down just as Logan pushed a silver egg-shaped vibrator into her pussy.

The vibrations weren't strong enough to propel her to climax, but they would certainly keep her primed and ready for whatever he had prepared for her later. The pulse in her neck beat to the frenzied rhythm of the music.

Rope wound around her thighs, and her attention flew back to Rowan, Oz, and the redhead. They had switched positions, the woman now on her side with one leg resting on Rowan's shoulder as he plowed into her relentlessly while Oz ate her pussy.

Rachel shuddered, realizing there was no way Oz could avoid Rowan's cock. Did that mean they were bi? Logan had said he personally wasn't, but he hadn't revealed his friends' sexual preferences other than they chose to share women.

Her own pussy clenched at the fantasy of these dominant men submitting to one another. What she wouldn't give to see Oz make use of his big mouth for sucking Rowan off.

Her legs shook as the first stirring of orgasm began and her wetness dripped down her thigh. She breathed through it, controlling her arousal. She'd promised Logan when they'd negotiated that she wouldn't come without his permission tonight, and she didn't want to disappoint him.

Logan's lips swept up her neck until he reached her ear. "Are you getting turned on by the scene or by watching my friends fuck that woman?"

She gasped, wondering how he knew. While the ropes along with the plug and vibrator got her hot, she had to admit it was the visual that was pushing her toward climax. Would he be upset if he learned the truth?

She looked him in the eyes. "Both."

A smug grin crossed his face. "Thank you for being honest with me, Tiger. Because now I can be honest with you. I set it up tonight because I wanted you to witness what it will be like for you when you're in between me and one of my friends. Check out that woman's face. See the ecstasy on it? That's what I want to see on your face if or when you're ready."

He tangled his fingers into her hair and pulled her neck back. "I'm going to suspend you from the ceiling now so that you and that woman will both be on your sides, facing one another. Do you need me to adjust any of the ropes? Any tingling or buzzing in your extremities?"

"No buzzing except for the ones inside my pussy, Soldier Boy."

"Then hold on because you're about to go on a ride," he said gruffly.

Her feet suddenly left the ground, and she was tipped on her side facing the clapping audience. Her eyes searched out the redhead as Logan bent forward and affixed his talented mouth to her clit, swaying her back and forth and side to side. She wanted to squirm away, the sensation like a match lighting her pussy on fire.

Her inner walls fluttered, her body shaking uncontrollably. Between the fullness in her ass, the vibration in her pussy, his tongue lapping at her clit, the rope pressing on her skin, and the sight of Rowan and Oz coming on the redhead's skin, rope after rope of their ejaculate mixing together, she couldn't hold back her climax for long.

The room spun around and around.

"Please," she begged, too far gone to say the words. She threw her head back, Logan's name echoing in her mind over and over.

He lifted his mouth away from her pussy long enough to give his permission. "Come for me, Rachel. Let go."

He sucked her clit into his mouth and she detonated, spasms not only racking her pussy, but her entire body as heat consumed her.

Shaking from the aftershocks, she would've sagged in exhaustion if the rope wasn't holding her in place. She closed her eyes as Logan lowered her to the floor and began the process of removing ropes and toys from her body. Before long, she was back in the air, this time in Logan's arms as he carried her off the stage and out of the club.

She sighed and snuggled into his chest. "Where are we going? I thought I was going to get to use my mouth on you."

He unlocked their hotel room door and strode inside.

Logan tossed her down onto the bed, her backside bouncing off the soft mattress, and he climbed over her, pinning her arms over her head. He ripped off his mask then hers. "I changed my mind. I want to make love to you without any ropes. Without an audience. Without any embellishments. Just you and me. My cock. Your pussy. Are you on birth control?"

"Yes."

He looked deep into her eyes. "I'm clean. I don't want any barrier between us. You okay with that?"

"I trust you."

He kissed her, making love to her with his mouth and giving her a taste of what was to come. A few short minutes later, he tore his lips away and jumped to his feet. He divested himself of his pants and crawled back onto the bed in between her waiting thighs. "I'm sorry I can't give you more foreplay right now, but if I don't get inside of you in less than ten seconds, I'm going to explode."

She reached down to caress his stubbled cheek. "Then quit talking and fuck me already, Soldier Boy."

He nipped her inner thigh and then kissed the spot. "Haven't you figured it out already? I like to do both at the same time."

He rose up above her, lifting her leg and resting her ankle on his shoulder. "The ropes helped you learn how to relax in order for you to learn how submit to me, but you don't need them anymore. You belong to me, Tiger. And it's time I prove it to you."

She smiled, knowing it was true. "Give me all you got."

He notched his cock to her opening and, on a groan, thrust inside her. "I'd go on the run for the rest of my life to stay inside this pussy. You were made to take my cock, Rach." He pulled back before slamming back inside her, his pelvis rubbing against her clit. "So take it. Take me. All of me."

Although Logan dominated her with his cock, he was also out of control, lost to the world where only they existed. The cords of his neck bulged as he threw back his head with a snarl on his face. Chasing his own release, he was primal, consumed by the friction and heat inside her pussy. In this moment, he belonged to her as much as she belonged to him.

With his hand on her ankle, he lifted her leg off his shoulder and spread her wider. The new angle allowed his cock to hit that magic spot that she hadn't known existed until him. Her body trembled harder with every thrust. The added swivel of his hips drove her higher and higher until she could no longer see the ground.

"I feel your pussy tightening on my cock," he said, his eyes squeezed shut in concentration. "It's time to let go, Rachel. I want to feel you let go. And then I'm going to come so hard inside that tight pussy of yours, I'm going to fill you up."

She couldn't deny him.

From inside out, her body tensed as if frozen in time, and then everything exploded into fireworks of heat, waves of pleasure rolling over her.

"You're clamping down on my dick so hard, I can't hold back any longer. Feel what you do to me, Rach. Feel how much…" His motions frenzied and a guttural cry roared from his chest. He stilled, his dick jerking and bathing her with his come.

He collapsed on top of her, laying his head on her chest as if listening for her heartbeat. She swept her hand over the top of his head and down his neck, over and over, embracing an intimacy she'd never experienced.

Sure she'd fucked before. But tonight was the first time she'd ever made love.

Chapter Twenty

NAKED AND ON his knees on the marble floor, the Senator prayed at the altar of his lover, his arms secured behind him by thin bands of steel that dug into the flesh of his wrists and sent warm trickles of blood down his fingers and onto his back. They had completed the rest of the three-hour-long ritual that would purify his soul and prepare him for today's event.

His parents and brother still knew nothing of the plan, not because they would try to stop him but because of plausible deniability. Their concern for the life of their youngest son had to appear genuine when they learned he'd been infected with the deadly Leopold virus. Of course even then, they wouldn't truly give a damn about him other than they'd lose their chance to rule the country for another eight years. Once he explained to them how he'd orchestrated the whole thing, they'd finally accept him as a worthy equal in their family.

His lover squeezed the vise around his cock and balls tighter, stopping only when the cry of surrender ripped from his throat. If he hadn't been sterilized as a child as punishment when he'd lost his sixth-grade election to become class president to a girl, this torture would have likely done the trick. But he didn't care. He was flying high on endorphins, the hot rush of expectation simmering through the blood in his veins.

He couldn't have planned it better. Since Evans and Fink had fucked it up, he'd acted presidential and had adjusted the plan accordingly. What were two more murders in the scheme of things? The two were nothing, weaklings who in Darwin's evolutionary scale would fall below the canines. They were followers, their sole existence perpetuated on their ability to serve the alpha. Since his birth, he had been treated like the omega, but it was time to show everyone he was the alpha in his family. With his wife by his side, they'd return the country to better times, when the international communities didn't just respect the United States, but feared it.

Dropping the atomic bombs in Japan had been one of the bravest acts of the US government since the Civil War. It'd shown the world it wasn't afraid to take bold risks in order to ensure the safety of the American people. He shared the same vision as those men, yearned for a time when the rest of the world looked to the United States for guidance. With the Leopold virus and its patented cure in its grasp, the country would be in the position to threaten its enemies and protect its allies, all the while, secretly making him and his wife, Sari, rich beyond their wildest dreams. Since none of their stock holdings or the Antiguan accounts were in their names, the money would be virtually untraceable thanks to modern technology and a simple ATM card. Besides, who would believe the country's hero could be responsible for releasing a hemorrhagic fever virus? And exposing himself to it?

Most men might be scared of a virus with an 80 percent mortality rate, but then again, they hadn't suffered through fifty-eight years of torture. This wouldn't be the first time he'd be laid up bleeding from every orifice, pain suffusing his joints and muscles. However, it would be the first time he'd received medical attention for it. There was a slight risk the hospital would question his multitude of healed and unhealed injuries, but his wife knew to pay them well for their silence.

As his lover commenced the next portion of the torture and the scream tore from his throat, he came violently, ejaculate splashing the floor and mixing with his blood. He bowed his head in a prayer of thanks and waited silently for the torture to end.

More blood would be shed this afternoon.

He couldn't wait.

Chapter Twenty-One

"So once you get into the mechanical room, you're just going to what exactly?" Oz asked, munching on Rachel's new addiction, chocolate-covered potato chips. "Walk off with the tank and…?"

She looked at Logan and shrugged. "As long as we stop the virus from releasing, the rest we'll play by ear."

They had spent the past three hours going over every step of tomorrow's operation to save the world. While Logan's friends wanted to come with them to the Tuscany Hotel, they all agreed that they'd need to stay behind to provide any necessary intel and serve as the second line of defense should anything go wrong. The fact was she and Logan didn't want to draw them into it any more than they already had. They'd already broken several federal and state laws that would put them behind bars for the rest of their lives. If things got ugly tomorrow, she and Logan didn't want the guys' lives on their consciences.

"Any luck finding out if Evans and Fink have gotten any large deposits of money in the past few months?" she asked Rowan.

Every time she looked at him or Oz, her cheeks heated. Last night's memory of them was burned onto her retinas. Even though they knew she'd watched them, Oz remained the same smart-ass as yesterday and Rowan was just as reserved. It was hard to believe only hours before, Oz's tongue had been on Rowan's cock while today the two of them barely interacted except to discuss something technological.

"I did find something," Rowan said flatly. "Fink's mother has received a deposit of just under ten thousand dollars every week for the past five weeks from an Antiguan bank. The foreign account is registered to a dummy Antiguan corporation that was set up to shelter its multiple clients by keeping their names off of it, and unfortunately, the list of who those clients are isn't kept online."

She sighed. "So it's impossible to trace."

"No, not impossible," Rowan said. "Just more difficult. I need more time, but I'll be able to get you that information."

"Why did you even think to look at his mother's bank account?" Logan asked, his shoulder knocking into hers as they sat next to each other on the small couch in the corner of the room.

Rowan turned to them. "When I didn't find any deposits into his account, I checked his closest relatives. Sometimes people hide money in their spouses' accounts, and since Fink doesn't have a spouse, I checked his next of kin, which was his mother."

"Maybe the money his mother is receiving is legitimate," she offered. It was unusual but not unheard of. Maybe it was some kind of investment that was finally paying off.

Rowan avoided looking in her eyes, choosing to keep his gaze on Logan. "Probably not. Before the deposits, she had less than twenty dollars in her account. Her police records show multiple arrests and short prison sentences for drug possession and intent to distribute. She's a junky and, from the looks of it, a bad one."

She shot up from the couch. "You can get into the police reports?" At the rise of his brow, she switched tactics. Of course he could; the man had already proved his hacking talents. "I mean, *since* you can get into the police reports, would you mind pulling up the one on Logan and me? I want to know what evidence they're using to support their claims that Logan killed Rinaldi."

They couldn't have any evidence since Logan hadn't committed the crime, right? Everything she'd heard on the news so far was mere conjecture about his motive for wanting Rinaldi dead. Nothing had been released about the evidence.

She paced the room as Rowan worked his magic. It wasn't more than a couple of minutes later that Rowan pulled up the report.

"Here it is," he said. "According to this, the Beretta M9 pistol used to shoot Anthony Rinaldi was registered to Logan Bradford."

Logan jumped up from the couch. "No way. Yes, I used the Beretta M9 in the army, but I have a Glock now. There's no way that gun was registered to me."

She joined Logan's side and rubbed the back of his neck in reassurance. "Obviously, once Evans and Fink had someone to pin Rinaldi's murder on, they doctored the records. Any fingerprints on the gun?"

Rowan scrolled down the screen. "Wiped clean. They also didn't find any of Logan's prints at the scene of the crime."

"But of course, they did find Evans's and Fink's," Hunter pointed out. "What does it say about why the agents were there?"

Rowan paused, reading. "Evans and Fink were assigned to follow Rinaldi once he was released from prison to see who he communicated with. According to the report, Rinaldi went home and discovered his wife and his children had gone into hiding. Evans and Fink observed through a telescope as Rinaldi went on a rampage through his house and broke down. An hour later, he snorted three lines of what was later confirmed as a potentially fatal combination of exceptionally pure cocaine and heroin and got into his car, driving west and parking in front of Cole DeMarco's home. Evans and Fink couldn't pass the gate, and since they were to remain out of sight, they parked farther down the street, keeping their eye on Rinaldi's car."

“That explains why Rinaldi was walking funny,” she said to Logan. “He was drugged.”

“How does a guy who had been in prison for months get drugs that fast?” Logan asked, moving to stand in front of her.

She smiled, the thrill of putting together the pieces of a story a high she never got tired of. “Two corrupt FBI agents give it to him as a coming-home present. They must have known he used. It would have been in his records. And after going without drugs for months, he wouldn’t turn them down.”

Logan nodded. “The drugs were supposed to kill him. When they didn’t, Evans and Fink had to come up with a different plan. But why did Rinaldi come to Benediction?”

It was a good question and something that had bothered her since that night. The man had just gotten out of prison. Had he really come to Benediction just to gloat about his release? The report stated he’d broken down upon finding his family gone. That had to mean something.

“One thing you could always say about Rinaldi was he loved his wife and kids,” she pointed out. “He never would’ve placed them at risk of becoming sick with the Leopold virus. With them gone and out of his control, he couldn’t guarantee their safety. What if in that moment he changed his mind and decided he wanted to back out of the plan? Who would he go to for help? Not the FBI, who were already involved. Who would believe a man like him?”

Understanding dawned in Logan's eyes. "You think he was coming to convince Cole to help him?" He gritted his teeth. "Only we never let him get the chance."

She laid her hand on his cheek. "Bullshit. He had the chance. He just didn't take it. The man was a psychopath. Who even knows if he remembered why he came to Benediction in the first place. He was hopped up on a high dose of cocaine and heroin, and he wasn't sane to begin with. You did the right thing by throwing him off of Benediction's premises."

Logan nodded as he scratched the back of his neck, but she could tell he shouldered some of the blame for the events that followed Rinaldi's appearance at Benediction.

"Didn't Cole's video cameras catch the murder?" Logan asked Rowan.

"Unfortunately, according to the report, he's got videos set up on the area in front of his gate, but not the patch of road where the murder occurred," Rowan said. "The video shows him leaving and both of you following, then you disappear from the feeds for a good five minutes, during the time when the murder took place."

"When we were behind the bushes," she muttered.

Rowan continued, speaking over her. "The camera picks you up again when you ran up the driveway and back into Cole's house."

Logan clenched his hands. "So there's nothing on the tapes to help exonerate us."

"It's worse," Rowan said. "Evans and Fink claim they witnessed it all, but didn't get there in time to save Rinaldi."

"Son of a bitch," Logan shouted, startling her by punching the wall.

"Shh." She rubbed his back. "Don't worry. We're going to stop them and prove we didn't do it. Trust me."

After a large exhale, Logan turned around. "Isn't that my line?"

She gave him a smile she didn't quite feel at the moment. "I thought I'd borrow it. Hope you don't mind."

"I don't." He bent and whispered in her ear. "How you feeling by the way? Sore?"

Arousal blasted through her. Heck yeah, she was sore. And she loved it.

She opened her mouth to reply when Oz interrupted. "Hey, guys. Did you know you have an attorney who held a press conference in defense of you two?"

Oz put the news article up on one of the larger monitors.

"Holy shit," Rachel said. "It's Kate."

She wasn't sure why she was surprised. It wasn't the first time Kate had proved how far she would go to help out those she cared about.

"She's my law partner," Logan explained to his friends, his eyes never leaving hers and conveying everything he didn't say. *And nothing more.*

"And my best friend," she added, giving Logan a real smile that this time she felt all the way into her bones.

"Well, she's fighting to clear your names," Oz said. "Already got the charges dropped for the dog kidnapping and the gas station robberies." He whistled. "That girl is fine."

"She's taken," Rachel said, thinking of Kate lighting up every time she spoke about Jaxon. "Very taken."

Sawyer stood from his chair. "Who's that woman standing behind her?"

She squinted, barely making out the figure in the background. "That's Lisa. Another one of my friends. She's a publicist, so she helps coordinate press conferences for Kate and Logan when necessary. Why?"

Sawyer stared intently at the photograph. "She looks familiar. How long have you known her?"

She bit her lip, thinking back to when she first met her through Kate. "Not too long. She was a legal secretary at the firm where Logan and Kate interned their third year of law school. Kind of mousy, but she's a spitfire when she needs to be. I'd hook you up, but she's not into kink. Like at all. I don't even think she dates."

None of her friends were an open book, with the exception of Gracie, which was probably why she felt comfortable with them. They all had their secrets, and they didn't need to share every detail about their lives with one another. But Lisa didn't volunteer anything about herself. She was almost as good as Rachel when it came to deflecting personal questions. In fact, Rachel didn't know much about the woman's life before she'd worked at the law firm. But it wasn't as if they knew about how Rachel had been raised either.

Sawyer raked his fingers into his hair and blew out a breath. "Fuck. I need…" Without saying anything more, he strode out of the room.

"What's with him?" Hunter asked, stealing the bag of chips from Oz's hands.

Oz frowned. "No idea."

She guessed their meeting was over. It was just as well. They were ready for tomorrow—or, at least, as ready as they could be. She could think of a dozen things she'd rather be doing with her mouth right now than talking.

As if reading her mind, Logan pushed an errant hair behind her ear before whispering into it. "So, one more night in this place. Got any idea of how you'd like to spend it?"

He was going to make her say the words.

She looked into his eyes, her heart suddenly pounding so hard she wouldn't be surprised if the other guys could hear it. "You said when I was ready, you'd show me what it was like to be fucked by two men. Well, I'm ready for it. Tonight. With you."

Chapter Twenty-Two

"ARE YOU SURE you want this?" Logan asked her once again. "You can change your mind at any time."

They were in their hotel room, she and Logan lying naked under the covers of the bed, on their sides facing each other, after having taken a nap. *A nap.* In less than a few days, she'd gone from sleeping two hours a night to a full night's sleep plus a three-hour nap. She sure was making up for lost time. She had an insatiable appetite for more than junk food now. Sex and sleep had become her new addictions, in that order.

In ten minutes, someone would knock on their door. She didn't know who because Logan had set it up after their meeting. He promised his friend would be discreet, but it wasn't as if the other guys weren't going to figure it out. When one of the guys didn't show up to Paradise Found, the others were bound to put two and two together.

She threw her leg over his, hooking his ankle with her foot, and ran her hand over his chest. "I'm sure. I want to know what it's like to completely lose control. One thing I have learned this week is that life is unpredictable. I've played it safe for so long, scared to truly lose myself, but what I realize now is that I'm the same girl I was when I left my parents' house at eighteen. I was so afraid to lose control of my life again that I never started living it. Anything can happen, and I don't want to spend another night wondering what it feels like to make love with two men. Plenty of women have the fantasy, but far too few of them make it a reality. I don't want to be one of those women. I want to live the fantasy."

She couldn't do it back in Michigan. Here in Vegas, where sinning was not only acceptable but encouraged, she could live out the fantasy she never imagined would ever become a reality. With Logan, she felt safe to explore her sexuality. He didn't chastise her for craving a sexual act that most of the world would consider deviant. Instead, he made plans to give it to her.

She never would've guessed he was such a dirty, kinky man or that she would like it so damned much. They had all of the country's law enforcement looking to arrest them and at least two men who wanted them dead, and she'd never been so happy in her entire life. She didn't want to stop and analyze why or think about what would happen when it was finally resolved and they returned to their real lives.

A quiet knock fell on the door.

This was it.

Nervous excitement buzzed through her. She sat up and combed her hair with her fingers while Logan rolled out of bed to answer the door. She didn't know why she was bothering to fix her hair when it was just going to get messed up soon anyway.

Logan slowly pulled open the door, revealing Hunter standing behind it. As he walked in, Rachel instinctively pulled up the sheet to cover her breasts.

He tossed her a chocolate bar. "My momma raised me right. Figured it was only polite to bring a girl candy before I fucked her."

She stared at the chocolate before flicking her gaze up to Hunter. And she laughed. With that one smooth move, he'd eased the awkwardness. His eyes sparkled and a grin pulled at his lips, the hoop at the corner catching her eye.

"Thank you for the candy," she said, smiling, tearing open the wrapper. She'd never turn down chocolate.

Unabashedly naked, Logan strode back to the bed and sat beside her, not bothering to cover himself. Hunter didn't pause before sitting on the edge of the mattress on her side of the bed, twisting himself toward Logan.

For a couple of minutes, the men talked about baseball while she scarfed down the candy bar. It would almost pass for normal had two of the three of them not been naked. She understood they wanted her to feel comfortable about the threesome, but this was ridiculous.

She crumpled the wrapper into a ball and shot it across the room toward the trash. Damn, she missed. She dropped the sheet, exposing her breasts. Enough of the small talk. "If someone doesn't touch me soon, I'm going to have to take care of it myself."

Logan smirked as he brushed her arm with his knuckles. "No you won't. You love the anticipation. The idea that you don't know what's going to happen next. Whose cock you're going to have in your ass and whose will go in your pussy."

Starting with her calf, Hunter stroked his hand over her covered leg, resting it on her upper thigh. "You want me to go at any time, you just say the word."

She squirmed, her pussy already growing wet from their touches. "I don't want you to go. I want this. Both of you. And I don't want to wait any longer." She turned her head to Logan and begged him with her eyes. "Please don't make me wait any longer."

He cradled the back of her head in his hand and pulled her into him, his lips crashing over hers. His tongue excitedly plunged and retreated, over and over, mimicking what she'd like him to do with his cock. She felt Hunter's heat at her back. His hand curled around her to palm her breast and swipe his thumb over her nipple.

A moan fell from her lips into Logan's mouth. He kissed her harder, his teeth banging against her own. His free hand drifted to her other breast, his actions mirroring Hunter's.

She nipped Logan's lip hard enough to draw blood, impatient and desperate for more of their touches.

He pulled away with a devilish grin, rubbing his lip where she'd bitten him. "I guess you're pretty eager." His gaze bounced to Hunter. "Get undressed."

She watched as Hunter stood and whipped his shirt off in one swift motion. His body was a work of art. She'd known about the tattoos covering his arms, but without his shirt, she got to appreciate them, her gaze lingering on his bulging biceps. His muscled chest was decorated by the black outline of a dragon shooting red fire from its mouth, and small hoops hung from both of Hunter's nipples.

His shorts fell to floor, revealing everything he'd been packing behind them.

Her eyes widened and her jaw dropped open.

His dick was pierced.

He chuckled. "Get that reaction a lot."

"Does it hurt you?" she asked, a blush creeping out over her chest at being caught ogling his cock.

He set one knee on the bed, his cock jutting out as if begging for her mouth. "It did when I first got it, but I like pain, so it didn't bother me."

She swallowed. "And it won't hurt me?"

He leaned forward and stuck out his tongue, showing her the metal ball on it. "My piercings will only enhance your pleasure."

She wondered how two men could make love to one woman when both of them were dominant. But in ordering Hunter to remove his clothes, Logan had made it clear that tonight, he was taking the lead. Did it always work that way for them? Or was Logan in charge because she belonged to him?

"Lie on your back," Logan said, his hand on her nape.

The minute her head hit the pillow, both men's heads descended, each of them taking a nipple into his mouth.

Her spine arched, a moan escaping from her lips. Her eyes wanted to close, but she forced them to remain open, dropping her gaze to the tops of the guys' heads and watching them bob as the men worked their magic on her breasts.

Logan used a harder suction to draw it fully into the cavern of his hot mouth. Hunter teased it with his tongue, rolling his piercing over her pebbled tip. Heat blasted to her pussy, waking an arousal she hadn't known existed. She'd gone from not being able to come to thinking she might come just from having their mouths on her nipples.

But before she could test that theory, Hunter slid down her torso, settling between her thighs and parting her legs, spreading her pussy open. He didn't waste time getting to work, his tongue lapping at her clitoris like a cat drinking milk. Using his broad shoulders to push her thighs apart even more, he shifted his tongue, teasing the metal ball back and forth on her clit and slipping his fingers inside her wet channel with ease.

When he crooked his fingers, finding her G-spot as quickly as Logan had, her legs began shaking and her head tossed side to side on the pillow, the overload of sensations and the tension coiling in her pussy too much for her to process.

She hoped she wasn't supposed to ask for permission to come because she had absolutely no control over her body. She was a puppet and they held her strings, making her limbs dance and her spine bow off the bed through their ministrations. Nonsensical cries and pleas ripped from her throat. She tried to close her legs, the raging storm between them too overwhelming, but Hunter held her still with his large hands wrapped around her thighs.

Logan played with her nipples, his tongue swirling around one while his fingers pinched and rolled the other. When his other hand covered her throat like a collar in a display of possession, she detonated, the tension unraveling like a spool of thread sending waves of heat spreading throughout her body.

Hunter and Logan allowed her a moment to recover before turning her on her side. She heard the sound of a cap lifting and the squirt of liquid.

"Relax and let me in," crooned Logan, his fingers coating her crack with cool lube. "I'm going to get you ready to take us both. You still with us?"

She swallowed, her lips tingling as if she hadn't used them in ages. "I'm with you."

His finger rubbed between her cheeks, lighting up nerves that had rarely been touched. She was too far gone to care about propriety. Nothing tonight was polite. It was deliciously deviant, and if it felt good, she wasn't going to worry about it.

She'd come full circle from that night at Benediction when she'd intended to do an exposé on BDSM. At that time, *safe*, *sane*, and *consensual* were just a bunch of words with no personal meaning for her. Now she understood, not through the experiences of her friends but through her own.

It was freeing, as if the invisible chains that had been wrapped around her heart and had prevented her from living her life to the fullest all these years had suddenly been removed. No one else had the right to tell her how to think…how to act…how to *feel*…so long as it was all safe, sane, and consensual.

She tossed her head back as Logan's fingers entered her back passage, plunging and retreating with rhythmic intent. Just like before, she wanted to escape the odd sensation as much as she wanted more of it. She tried to relax, but her hips moved on their own volition, gyrating back and forth onto his fingers.

"Hunter, why don't you get her pussy ready to take you while I work on her ass?" Logan asked in a way that sounded more like an order rather than a question.

"My pleasure, brother," murmured Hunter, raising her leg up into the air and plunging his fingers inside her needy cunt.

"Oh, fuck," she cried, filled by the fingers of both men. This was nothing like before when Logan had fucked her with his fingers in both passages. Much like their personalities, each of the men had his own way of touching her. Hunter explored the depths of her cunt with precision and force while Logan's touch was more reverent and gentle. "I need…"

Logan sunk his teeth into the flesh of her ass. "Soon, Tiger. When you can take four of Hunter's fingers and three of mine at the same time, we'll replace them with our cocks. You're almost ready."

Her toes curled. She already felt filled to capacity. How could she take any more? Maybe her body wasn't built to accommodate two men inside her.

She couldn't do it, but she wanted to. Oh, how she wanted to.

As her mind warred with itself, the men stretched her with their additional fingers, proving their mastery over her body.

It didn't feel good and it didn't feel bad.

It just felt.

Logan withdrew his fingers and cleaned them with an anti-bacterial wipe. Then he snagged two condoms, tossing one to his friend before tearing the wrapper of the other. "Hunter, get on your back and put the condom on." Logan lifted her limp and shaking body into his arms as Hunter positioned himself in the center of the bed with his head on the pillow and carefully unrolled the rubber down his length. "Climb up and sink down on his cock, Tiger. Let him feel how hot he's made you."

She didn't hesitate, her empty pussy throbbing with the need to be filled again. Straddling Hunter, she gripped the base of his cock and lined it up with her opening before lowering herself onto him.

He wasn't as wide as Logan, but he was longer, his tip practically bumping against her cervix. Experimenting, she rode his cock almost all the way up before slamming back down on him and emitting a cry of pleasure when his piercing rubbed over her G-spot.

Logan came behind her, his chest against her back. "I need you to bend forward and rest your chest on Hunter's. You can hold on to his shoulders if you need to."

She was never more thankful that she'd taken all those Pilates. With Hunter's dick inside her pussy, she folded her upper body, wrapping her hands around those biceps of Hunter's she'd been dying to grab.

Hunter smoothed his hand over her hair. "Rachel, you are one sexy woman. I'm so fucking fortunate that your boyfriend chose me to share this with you."

Logan's hand pressed down on the middle of her back a second before she felt the head of his dick at her back opening. "Relax and let me in, Tiger."

Inch by inch, he pushed his cock into her ass. She moaned, trapped between the two men as they softly rocked back and forth, comforting her with words of praise. It didn't really hurt, but it was uncomfortable, and she wasn't sure if she enjoyed the sensation of dual penetration.

Then Logan seated himself fully inside her and began fucking her ass with an almost brutal intensity. Her mind went blank as a delicious heat spread throughout her body. It didn't take long before all the discomfort disappeared, leaving behind only white-hot pleasure.

She threw her head back. "More."

Logan's hands went to her waist and Hunter's to her hips. With a perfect rhythm that proved they had done this before together, they raised her up and down on Hunter's dick as Logan thrust in and out of her ass.

Having no control over the movements of her body, she was like a rag doll being tossed around by a wild dog. She was completely helpless at the whim of these two strong men. Having an orgasm wasn't her choice. Hunter and Logan demanded it of her.

A tremor worked its way down her spine until her entire body shook, and her heart beat and her pulse skyrocketed. Her climax didn't build. It simply crashed over her again and again, not giving her any time to recover before another one hit, until she wasn't sure if she had come multiple times or once continuously.

With his eyes shut and a grimace on his face, Hunter roared as he came. Breathing heavy, he stopped pumping, his dick twitching inside her as his come shot into the condom. A moment later, Logan leaned over her and bit her shoulder as he came too, his body collapsing on top of her back.

Hot and sweaty, she basked in the afterglow of the most incredible fuck of her life. Logan and Hunter had shown her pleasure beyond her wildest dreams, turning her fantasy into a memory she'd never forget as long as she lived. She sighed, too content to move out of the warm cocoon of their erotic threesome.

But all too soon, they shifted out of their position on the bed, laying her head on the pillow. A damp towel cleaned her between her thighs and her backside before the covers were drawn up over her. She heard Hunter and Logan murmuring quietly to one another and then the snick of the door closing.

Although her eyes were shut, she sensed that night had fallen, plunging their room in total darkness. Logan slipped under the blankets with her and curled around her, his arm thrown across her middle.

Just as she couldn't fight her orgasm, she couldn't fight against the need for sleep.

She was done fighting.

After all, it was impossible to win against the inevitable.

Chapter Twenty-Three

RACHEL WAS HAVING the best dream ever. Logan was between her legs, licking at her clitoris with a warm, damp tongue that hit every nerve ending as if they were completely exposed. Her inner walls fluttered as a feeling like warm maple syrup flowed through her pussy. She ordered the tongue to go faster and clenched her vaginal muscles, trying to bring herself to a climax, but it wasn't enough to push her over.

It was a slow and steady build, her body trembling as the kindling went aflame and the heat built in her pelvis. She tried to close her legs and trap the wicked tongue between her thighs, but when the leg muscles contracted without success, she realized she was immobile.

Her eyes shot open.

Somehow without waking her, Logan had bound her wrists and ankles to the bed with rope, leaving her spread-eagle and open to his ministrations. He gazed up at her with heat in his eyes while he slowly slid his tongue up her slit and over her distended clitoris.

Although she was burning, chills racked her body as Logan dragged her over the edge and into climax.

Logan kissed her thigh then began releasing her from the binding. "Good morning. Sleep well?"

She smiled sleepily. "I did. But my wake-up call was even better."

"It's time to get ready," he said, massaging her wrists with his thumbs. "About an hour ago, Sawyer brought by our suits plus our IDs to get us into the hotel as part of Senator Hutton's security team. You slept right through it."

She didn't doubt it. She'd probably slept more than eight hours straight through the night, and she was still exhausted. "You and Hunter wore me out last night."

"Did you enjoy it?"

She rolled her eyes. "Uh, yeah, Soldier Boy. I think my three orgasms proved it. But…"

"But?"

Apprehensive to admit the truth, she sat up and turned to him. "I don't regret it, but it's not something I'd like to do again. I know it's your kink—"

He cupped her face in his hands. "You're my kink. And if you're not into it, then I'm not into it. Besides, I don't want to share you again. I was a bit jealous of Hunter last night. From now on, it's just you and me. That okay with you, Tiger?"

She threw her arms around his neck and pulled him in for a kiss. She'd give almost anything to make love with him again this morning, but they didn't have enough time. If everything went according to their plans, they'd have the rest of their lives to make love.

And she couldn't wait for the rest of their lives to begin.

After showering and getting dressed, she and Logan met the guys in the kitchen to go over everything one last time. Nervous around Hunter because of last night, she was put immediately at ease when he acted as if the whole thing had never occurred. She felt as though she was one of the guys as they studied the hotel's blueprints one more time and reviewed their plan for accessing the mechanical room.

To keep Rachel and Logan from being recognized, Sawyer had helped them alter their appearances. Already in a conservative navy suit to match those of the security agency, Rachel wore horn-rimmed glasses with thick lenses and covered up her long black hair with a honey-blond wig that had been cut into a blunt bob. For Logan, Sawyer had dyed his hair, turning him into a carrot top, and then applied scarring liquid to his face, creating several thin scars that marred his cheeks. While they didn't look drastically different, it was enough that they shouldn't immediately be recognizable.

At ten in the morning, she and Logan took Sawyer's car and headed to the Tuscany Hotel and Casino. Although they had driven by the strip when they'd first arrived in Las Vegas, they hadn't gotten close enough to give her a true representation of just how large the hotels actually were.

The newest hotel and casino on the strip, Tuscany, was no exception. She'd read up about the hotel, needing to know everything about it before today.

She'd never been to Italy, but if it looked anything like this, she'd make sure to add a trip there to her bucket list. Set on rolling hills of grass, the hotel was created to look like a Tuscan stone villa. Hundreds of Italian cypress trees lined the driveway that led from the street up to the main entrance, and each warm-toned stone that went into building the road and the hotel was imported directly from Tuscany. Olive trees grew on the grass, their limbs tangling together.

It took millions and millions of dollars each month to maintain a landscape that didn't belong in the desert. The investors had taken a real gamble with this property, but according to their latest financials, it was paying off handsomely for them. It was the "it" place to stay on the strip these days, which was probably why Senator Hutton had chosen it for his speech.

Sweltering in the desert heat, Logan and Rachel had spent the past hour staking out the hotel, watching Senator Hutton and his staff arrive. They were dressed identically in navy pantsuits with white shirts, the only difference being Logan wore a tie. Copying the agents of the security firm, they'd clipped their IDs to the lapel of their jackets.

Sawyer had also set them up with guns, items that made her uncomfortable and comfortable at the same time. She didn't have a lot of experience with them, other than going to the range with Kate a few times, so she really hoped she wouldn't have to use hers. Unlike the seasoned Kate, she'd managed to hit the paper target only about half the time and had never hit the bull's-eye. If a situation arose requiring her to use the gun, Rachel figured she was more likely to shoot herself in the foot than the target.

Senator Hutton's speech was scheduled to begin in thirty minutes. She and Logan had waited outside to watch the senator and his security detail arrive and enter the hotel, but they hadn't spotted Evans or Fink so far. It was possible they were already in the mechanical room, waiting for the senator's arrival. It would be so easy if she could just call the Feds and tell them what Evans and Fink were up to, but as shown by everything they had gotten away with so far, they'd probably just pin the appearance of the tank with the virus on them.

And she was done being framed for crimes she hadn't committed.

More than ready to end this thing and desperate for air-conditioning, she walked confidently toward the BH22E entrance, her spine straight and her eyes forward as if she had every right to be here.

Logan pounded on the door, and a Tuscany security employee answered.

"We're here with Banks Security," Logan said.

The man's eyes narrowed. "Identification."

"Here you go," she said in a fake southern accent, ignoring Logan's sideways glance as she unclipped her ID and gave it to the guard.

He examined it for a long minute then returned it to her, then checked out Logan's next. With a nod, he handed it back. "The rest of your team already took the senator down to the bottom level."

She metaphorically breathed a sigh of relief that their fake IDs had worked. One giant hurdle passed. Within a few minutes, they'd have access to the mechanical room.

"We were just scoping the outside of the hotel for anything out of the ordinary," she said, wanting to give an explanation as to why they hadn't shown up with the others so he wouldn't be suspicious. Of course, it only made her sound *more* suspicious. "All clear."

Logan stepped inside, most likely to keep her from saying anything else. "Now we'll just take the elevator and meet them at the theater."

"Elevator's broken," the guard said. "Maintenance is repairing it now, but as I told your comrades, it will be working by the time the senator finishes his speech."

She wouldn't panic. This was why they had the guys on standby. She and Logan were each wired for communication to and from them.

Not blinking, Logan stayed cool. "So which way do we go?"

The guard pointed. "You'll have to follow the hallway through the double doors, which will take you into the back of the house by the offices. You can use that elevator to the tunnels that lead to the theater. As I told your friends earlier, we've emptied the offices of all employees except for those executives who have already gone through security clearance with your firm. A couple of your guys have stayed behind on the off-chance anyone should try to follow the senator."

Her stomach dropped to the concrete floor. There's no way they could go that way if anyone from Banks Security was stationed there. They'd know right away she and Logan weren't part of their company.

"Great," Logan said, his expression neutral.

Waiting until they were out of earshot of the guard, she remained silent as they began making their way down the hallway.

"Hunter," Logan said quietly, "tell me there's another elevator that will take us down to the mechanical room."

Hunter's voice replied in her ear. "There is, but you're not going to like it. It's just off one of the hotel's kitchens. Plenty of witnesses, but if you act like you're supposed to be there, no one should bother you."

It wasn't great, but it was better than the alternative.

"Which way?" Logan asked.

"Before you get to the double doors, make a left," Hunter said. "No, I mean a right."

As she spotted the hallway Hunter had spoken of, Logan stopped. "Which is it, Hunter?"

"It's your right. Sorry," Hunter muttered.

They turned right down the hallway, walking for what seemed like forever. Where the hell was it? Finally, after a few minutes, they heard the sounds of dishes clinking and people speaking. Off to their left were swinging doors that would lead them to the kitchen, but she still didn't see any elevator.

"Hunter, we're just off the hotel kitchen and there's no elevator," Logan said through gritted teeth.

"Yeah, about that," Hunter said, guilt evident in his voice. "You have to cut through. The elevator's off the other side of the kitchen."

Logan pinched the bridge of his nose between his fingers. Then he dropped his arms and turned to her. "Ready to do a little more acting?"

She smiled. "Ready. I'm sure it will be a piece of cake."

She pushed her way through the swinging doors, Logan right behind her. Holding her breath but trying to act as though they belonged, she walked with her head held high and her gaze straight toward the opposite door.

Everyone in the kitchen wore the hotel's uniform of black pants and a burgundy blazer, so the movement of someone dressed in all black caught her attention. Her neck itched from the intuition of danger. She snapped her gaze toward the side of the room and spotted Fink headed toward the same door as she and Logan.

"Logan!" she cried as Fink whipped out his gun. "Run!"

They fled through the kitchen. Logan swerved away from her, bumping into a man carrying a stack of dishes. As the plates crashed onto the floor, she realized he'd done it intentionally to block Fink from catching up to them.

Logan grabbed her hand. "Guys, you need to find us a way out of here. We just bumped into Agent Fink, and he's got a gun."

Oz's voice sounded in her ear. "You need to go into the casino. The guy can't afford to shoot you in there."

"I'll find you another way down to the basement level," said Hunter.

They raced down the hallway toward a door she prayed would take them out into the public. Logan threw it open and they ran out into the busy casino, greeted by bright lights and the ringing of slot machines. The casino stayed within the theme of Tuscany, Italy, appearing as if it were set in the middle of a vineyard, with vines wrapped around columns and pictures of grapes on the carpet. Another time, she would've loved to inhale the ambiance of the room. Right now, though, the only thing she could concentrate on was finding somewhere they could hide from Fink.

"Come on," Logan said, tugging her toward the right, into a crowd of businessmen.

"Well, I guess Evans and Fink know we're here," she said, catching her breath. She checked over her shoulder, relieved to see the FBI agent headed in the opposite way. "Where are we going?"

"Tuscany Wedding Chapel," Oz said.

Logan growled. "Oz, now's not the time to joke—"

"There's an elevator in there that will take you to the basement. It's located in the back of the chapel."

She stopped, looking around for a sign for the wedding chapel. Above them, an arrow pointed for them to go left for both the chapel and the theater.

When they'd studied the blueprints, she had noticed that the chapel was right next to where the senator would be speaking. That meant the area was going to be swarming with security.

"There," she said, pointing toward the back of the room. "That way."

She walked quickly, knowing running would only draw more attention. She removed her ID and kept her head down as they approached the chapel. Logan opened the door and ushered her in.

A smiling little old lady with short gray hair and dressed in all pink stood behind a desk.

Logan strode to the desk. "Hi, I'm wondering if you can help me, see I—"

"Of course," the lady interrupted, her smile growing larger. "It's eight hundred and fifty dollars for the license, flowers, and ceremony. You two make a lovely couple. We have an opening right now if you'd like to follow me into the chapel."

"Cash okay?" Logan asked, shocking the hell out of Rachel when he pulled a wad of bills from his pocket. He whispered into her ear. "Sawyer gave me a bunch of cash in case we ran into any problems."

The woman put the cash into the register and handed them a marriage license. "Fill this out. I'll just go get everything ready for your ceremony. I'm Jane, and if you need anything, please let me know. After all, this is the biggest day of your lives and the Tuscany Hotel and Casino would like it to be one you'll cherish forever."

When Jane left, Rachel grabbed Logan by his arm and turned him toward her. "What are you doing?"

He took both her hands in his. "What does it look like I'm doing?" His lips tugged up into a grin. "I'm marrying you."

Marrying? Was he serious? She had never imagined herself getting married in Las Vegas. Hell, she'd never imagined getting married period. She wasn't one of those women who secretly hoarded bridal magazines.

She folded her arms across her chest. "I don't want to get married."

Logan laughed. "Relax, Rachel, it's just pretend." He picked up the pen and started filling out the application. "We won't file the license. But we need a way to get closer to the elevator."

Jane came barreling through the door and must have seen the apprehension on Rachel's face. "Oh, honey, don't be nervous. You make a beautiful bride."

Logan handed Rachel the pen, and she completed her section of the license.

She couldn't believe they were doing this. In a few minutes, they'd actually be married. Would it really be so bad? Yes, she'd never seen marriage as an option for herself, but then again, she'd never imagined trusting a man as she trusted Logan.

Never imagined she'd love the way rope felt on her naked skin.

Never imagined she'd make love to two men at once.

Never imagined herself falling in love.

But Logan had changed the impossible into the possible.

She signed her name beside Logan's, a bevy of butterflies taking flight in her belly.

Jane took the marriage license and thrust a bouquet of daisies into Rachel's hands. "If you'll follow me, everything is ready for your special day." She spun on her heels and led them through the doors of the chapel.

The chapel was much larger than she expected, with several rows of seats parted by a long aisle with a white runner that would take them to the front of the chapel. A man stood at the end of the runner, underneath a canopy adorned with grape vines. Pachelbel's Canon in D played over a speaker in the ceiling. Not having anyone to give her away, she and Logan strolled down the aisle together, stopping in front of the man who'd be marrying them.

The scent of alcohol permeated from him as he opened his binder. "Dearly beloved, we are gathered here today to join Logan Bartholomew Bradford and Rachel May Dawson in matrimony. Do you have the rings?"

Logan glanced at her. "Oh, we didn't—"

Jane smiled and presented a ring-sized box to Logan. "Right here."

Logan flipped it open and took out a simple gold wedding band.

The officiant nodded to Logan. "Put the ring on Rachel's finger and repeat after me. I give you this ring as an eternal symbol of my love and commitment."

Logan turned to face her, his expression as serious as she'd ever seen it. "I give you this ring as an eternal symbol of my love and commitment." He slipped the ring on her finger.

Jane handed a box to Rachel, and the officiant motioned to her with a wave of his hand. "Now you."

Her hands shaking, she opened the box, the gravity of the commitment hitting her. She took out the ring and grabbed Logan's hand. In that moment, everything felt right. "I give you this ring as an eternal symbol of my love and commitment."

"Would you like to say your own vows to one another or would you like to use ours?" the officiant asked.

Logan looked at her. "If you don't mind, we'd like to skip them."

The officiant chuckled. "Of course. Then by the power vested in me by the state of Nevada, I now pronounce you married. You may kiss the bride."

Logan gathered her into his arms and kissed her chastely. "I'll take the license," he said to the officiant after the man signed it.

Jane snatched it from the officiant. "Oh no, we file that for all our couples."

She glanced at Logan. If their marriage license was filed, did he really want to stay married? Did she? She'd always maintained she'd never marry. Never allow herself to be tied down. Yet in the past week, she'd done both. Literally. And she wasn't panicking. If she had to be married, there's no one she'd rather spend the rest of her life with than Logan. Would it be so bad if they tried to make it work?

Logan didn't look worried. If they decided not to stay married, maybe he could hack into the county's records and delete it.

"Do I have time for a break?" the officiant asked Jane. "I'm a bit parched, if you know what I mean."

Jane frowned. "I know exactly what you mean. Go, things are quiet right now with the senator's speech next door."

The officiant congratulated them before exiting the chapel for what Rachel guessed would be his liquid lunch. Now how could they get rid of Jane?

After shooting Logan a warning to get ready, Rachel fluttered her eyelids and let her body grow lax, crumbling to the floor.

Logan kneeled beside her, smoothing her hair off her face. "Rachel?"

Jane stood over her. "Is she all right?"

Rachel opened her eyes and faked grogginess. "I haven't eaten since this morning. I don't suppose I could trouble you for something to eat."

Jane's lips smashed together. Did she suspect she was lying?

The woman gave her a tight smile. "I'll tell you what. I'll just call the kitchen and see if they can deliver a burger for you."

Rachel sat up. "That would be great. I'll just stay here and wait." As soon as Jane left, she hopped to her feet. They rushed down a hall, passing the restrooms, until they finally made it to the elevator. She pressed the button to go down, cursing under her breath. What if they were too late to stop the release of the virus?

The elevator doors slid apart. She darted inside just as a hotel security guard arrived. He pointed his gun at Logan's chest. "Freeze."

Logan's held his hands in the air. "Go," he mouthed to her.

The doors shut and the elevator descended.

Even though they had just gotten married, she remained right where she'd always been.

Alone.

Chapter Twenty-Four

Her heart banging against her breastbone, Rachel stepped off the elevator. She looked to see if anyone was waiting for her in the hallway before speaking into the mike hidden on the inside of her shirt. "Guys, can you hear me?"

"Yeah, Rach. What the hell happened?" Oz asked in her earpiece.

"Security caught Logan before he could get on the elevator." She laughed nervously. "It's all up to me. And I have no idea where I'm going here." Not to mention, security knew she was down here. She had only seconds to get to the mechanical room.

"Okay," said Hunter smoothly. "I'm going to walk you through it. Sawyer's on his way to the hotel. You're actually close to where you need to be. The fifth door on your right is the mechanical room."

She shot down the hallway, counting doors along her way until she came to the fifth. She turned the knob and slipped inside, closing the door before anyone could see her. The dim room looked endless. "I'm in. What am I looking for?"

"You're looking for a tall piece of sheet metal. It's down about one hundred feet on your left," Hunter instructed.

The room was filled with different shapes and sizes of pipes, some in orange and some in white. She had no idea what the pipes were for.

She spotted the sheet metal in front of her. "I see it."

"Okay, good. Look around it for the tank. It might already be attached to the unit," Rowan said.

She circled the air supply unit, easily finding the tank. "It's here. And it's not attached. It's just leaning against the metal." Where were Fink and Evans? Was this a trap? Or what if she was too late and they'd already released it?

She bent down and grabbed it, surprised at how light it was.

"FBI," shouted a voice from behind her. "Put down the tank and lift up your hands where we can see them."

She spun around. Both agents aimed their guns at her.

Instantly, she knew she wasn't going to get out of this alive. But the reporter in her couldn't die without knowing the truth. "Just tell me why. Why are you going to release a virus that will kill thousands, if not millions of people?"

Her throat thickened with regret. It wasn't fair that she'd finally made the decision to live her life to the fullest and now she was going to die. She had so much to live for, and the thought of leaving Logan tore her heart into pieces. Would he mourn her? Would he know that she'd loved him?

Fink's hand trembled, a perfectly round burn on the middle of it. "A sacrifice for the greater good."

It didn't make sense. What did he mean by a sacrifice? "Why the senator? Why infect him?"

Fink opened his mouth to answer, but Evans interrupted before he could speak. "Why do anything? Money. Power. No one is going to stop us, especially not you or the currently detained Mr. Bradford."

Evans knew Logan was being held by hotel security and that he had her trapped. Her only chance was to keep him talking. "And Rinaldi? He changed his mind, didn't he? He wanted to stop you from releasing the virus."

Evans narrowed his gaze. "It didn't matter what he wanted. The minute he was released from prison, he was a dead man. You and your boyfriend made it too easy to pin the murder on you."

"Too bad we made it so hard to kill us, huh?"

Evans sneered, his eyes as black as midnight. "Originally, I was going to make your death quick and painless, but since you've given me so much trouble, I've changed my mind." He lowered his gun slightly. "I've decided to shoot your kneecaps first, so you can't escape. Maybe then I'll shoot you in the stomach so you'll slowly bleed out. And then of course, you'll become infected with the virus. By the time anyone figures out where the virus originated and finds you, you'll be long dead."

Fink's face turned white, and he brought his gun down to his side. "Evans, maybe we shouldn't do this."

"You know," Evan's said, "you're right." He spun toward Fink and shot him in the throat.

Blood sprayed, droplets hitting Rachel's cheeks. Surprise was etched on Fink's face as he covered his neck with his hand. Frozen in terror, she could do nothing but watch when Evans shot Fink again, this time in the head. Brain matter and blood splattered onto the air vents behind him as he slumped to the floor, the gun still in his hand.

The back of his skull had been completely blown off, and his eyes stared up at her as if pleading her to save him. Her stomach churned at the smell of blood, urine, and excrement. She fought the urge to wipe the blood off her face, keeping her hands up in the air. He may have been dirty, but he didn't deserve to die in such a horrific manner.

It was too late to save him.

But she'd be damned if it was too late for her.

Evans turned back to her, an evil smile on his face. "Now when they find your body with the canister it will look like you not only released the virus, but killed the FBI agent who tried to stop you." He kicked Fink in his stomach. "The stupid little man will die a hero, like he always wanted. But the real hero is the manufacturer of the vaccine that's going to save the lives of people all over the world. For a price, of course."

There was a vaccine? What did that have to do with Rinaldi? There had to be another player.

"That's who hired you? You're working for a pharmaceutical company?" she asked, catching a movement in the corner of her eye.

He tsked. "You're not as smart as you thought you were, Ms. Dawson."

When in Vegas…bluff. "Nope. I'm even smarter. Shoot him, Logan," she said, throwing a glance at her right.

Evans twisted to his left to see whom she was talking to. She whipped her gun out of her holster, aimed, and fired.

She didn't know where the bullet went. Prepared to shoot again, she pressed her finger on the trigger just as Evans rotated back to her.

A gunshot reverberated in the room. She reared back, expecting to have been shot. But there was no pain. No blood. She hadn't been shot. It had been her gun that had fired. Evans's mouth opened and blood poured out. She didn't wait for him to recover. She pointed and fired again, this time hitting him square in the chest. He fell over, his gun clattering to the floor.

Trembling, she lowered her arm.

It was over.

"FBI!" shouted a voice behind her. "Drop your weapon and put your hands on your head."

Her hands shook as though she had no control over them, and the gun clattered to the floor. She placed her hands on her head and turned to face the three agents pointing their weapons at her. A moment later, she was in handcuffs and being read her Miranda warnings.

Didn't they understand she had shot Evans in self-defense?

What if Sawyer's equipment didn't record Evans's confession?

Would anyone believe her?

Chapter Twenty-Five

SITTING ON A steel bench in a Las Vegas FBI holding cell, with dry blood caked on her skin and in her hair, Rachel had never wanted a shower more in her life. Since arriving at the Las Vegas FBI office, time had ticked by slower than a bunch of ducks crossing a busy street during rush hour. With nothing to do and no one to talk to, she replayed the day's gruesome scenes over and over in her mind. She couldn't shut them off, the images, sounds, and smells slamming into her again and again. Blood spilled violently and smelled rancid, and with it still on her body, she couldn't escape it. Curled in on herself, she shivered, her teeth chattering and her hands trembling.

Collecting evidence of Evans's and Fink's deaths, an FBI agent had clipped Rachel's fingernails, scraped her skin, photographed her, and fingerprinted her. Then they'd taken her bloody clothes, giving her scrubs to wear.

Immediately following her arrest, she'd exercised her Sixth Amendment right to counsel and had placed a call to Kate. She hadn't been surprised when Kate had told her she'd already heard from Logan and was searching for a couple of attorneys in Las Vegas to temporarily represent them. With her best friend on the phone, Rachel had to fight the urge to tell her everything that had happened between her and Logan this past week. But with no privacy and only a few minutes to speak on the phone, she had kept her mouth shut. Besides, she'd barely had the time to process it all herself.

She had killed a man.

It didn't matter that he had deserved it and that she had done it in self-defense. His blood would stain her hands for the rest of her life. But she wouldn't regret it. If she hadn't shot him, he wouldn't have just killed her. He would've released the virus and killed countless more. When they had arrested her, she had made it clear the gas canister contained a deadly virus, so that they wouldn't accidentally release it. Of course, they probably thought she and Logan were responsible for bringing the virus into the hotel.

The FBI was keeping her in a separate holding cell from Logan, so she hadn't seen him since the wedding chapel. She needed to feel his arms around her. Needed to know he was safe.

She tapped her nails on the bench. When would her attorney arrive? It was the middle of the night. Hours had passed and she'd yet to speak to anyone. Hadn't Sawyer given the FBI the recording of Evans's confession? Surely that should be enough to exonerate her and Logan of the crimes.

Squeaking footsteps sounded louder and louder, and then a female agent appeared at her cell. "Ms. Dawson, if you'll come with me. I'm going to take you to one of our interrogation rooms."

Her attorney must have finally arrived. Ready to explain her side of what happened, she followed the agent to a conference room and stepped inside. The agent didn't stay, closing the door behind her. Logan sat at the table, hunched over, exhaustion evident on his face.

"Logan," she said breathlessly, relieved to see him.

His head snapped up and their gazes locked. He shot to his feet as she flew across the room and into his open arms. Wrapping his arms around her, he hauled her to him. She closed her eyes and soaked him in, drawing upon his body's heat and inhaling his scent deep into her lungs. Laying her head on his chest, she listened to the steady beat of his heart. The chaos in her mind quieted and the trembling ceased.

Logan stroked her hair, a shudder racking his body. "Are you okay? I was so worried. They wouldn't tell me what had happened to you." He cupped her chin and tilted her face up to look at him. His eyes narrowed as he stepped back from her in a panic. "You're covered in blood."

"The blood isn't mine," she said, pulling him back to her and reassuring him with a gentle caress down his arm. "Evans killed Fink. And I—"

"Don't finish that sentence," he said, covering her lips with two of his fingers. "Don't say anything that they can use against you."

Right. Just because the FBI agents weren't in the room didn't mean they weren't recording them, just hoping they'd confess to the crime. Nodding that she understood, she kissed his fingertips.

He cradled her face in his hands, his eyelids growing hooded. "I was so worried about you. At the elevator, I hated sending you on your own like that. I couldn't take it again."

It wasn't the first time she'd thrown herself into the path of danger, and it wouldn't be the last. A touch of doubt niggled at her. How would he react when she was following a dangerous lead for a story? She pushed down her uncertainty, concentrating on the present. After all, when he was unable to do it himself, he'd urged her to continue their plan to stop Leopold's release. She placed her hands over his heart. "You and I both know I had to do it. There wasn't any other choice."

A muscle jumped in his jaw. "I know. But I couldn't handle it if anything happened to you." He rested his forehead against hers. "I lo—"

At the sound of the door swinging open, she turned. The agent who had processed her upon her arrival walked in along with the female agent who had brought her to this room, followed by a man she'd know anywhere.

"Senator Hutton," she said, holding the edge of the conference table in shock.

Only a couple of inches taller than her, with thinning white hair and a wrinkled face that gave away his advanced age, he still managed to hold an air of regality about him. He offered his hand. "Mr. Bradford. Ms. Dawson. I wanted to come and personally thank you for your heroic actions today."

Thank them? She glanced at Logan, who looked as surprised as she was to see him. After Logan shook the senator's hand, she did the same, noticing his manicured nails and learning he had a strong grip for an older person. "You believe us?"

Senator Hutton held her hand in his and covered it with his other, patting it in reassurance. "I do. The FBI received an audio recording from your friend Eddie Ackerman."

Confused, she looked at Logan for clarification.

"Oz," he mouthed.

She'd forgotten that wasn't his real name. Now that she knew him, she couldn't picture him as anything but Oz.

The senator continued. "They've listened to it and substantiated that it was indeed Agent Evans on the tape admitting to Rinaldi's murder and their attempt to release the Leopold virus. They've also verified the bullets that shot Fink came from Evans's gun."

The female agent took a step forward. "We're sorry for any inconvenience this situation may have caused you. You are free to go with the FBI's thanks and appreciation."

Logan stormed toward the agents, stopping right in front of them. "That's it? Two of your agents not only tried to pin a murder on us, but attempted to kill us." He turned and motioned at her. "Rachel saved the lives of thousands of people because of her heroic actions today. And all we get is an apology for the inconvenience and a thank-you from a couple of agents low on the totem pole?"

She joined Logan at his side, hooking her arm around his waist in an effort to calm him. "They want to bury the story, don't they?" she asked the agents.

"Is that true, Agent Gossner?" Senator Hutton said in an admonishing tone.

Giving away her nervousness, the female agent wiped her hands on her skirt. "The FBI feels it would be best if the American people weren't alerted to the nature of today's events."

"What's your opinion, Senator?" Rachel asked, angling her body toward him. "Do you believe the American people should be kept in the dark?"

The senator strode to stand next to her, his gaze on the agents and his eyes narrowed into slits. "Bioterrorism is the number-one threat to this country, and that's not going to change simply by pretending it doesn't exist. I understand your agency's inclination to sweep the embarrassment over your rogue agents under the rug, but I'm afraid I can't allow that to happen."

He'd delivered his statement in the same controlled yet forceful manner as he had delivered his speech during the filibuster of Senator Byron's bill. The man didn't have to shout to demonstrate his anger with the agency. His clipped tone and the fire in his eyes were enough.

Agent Gossner took a step forward. “Senator Hutton, with all due respect—”

The senator pointed at the door. “You tell your boss they’ll be hearing from me. Now get out of here.”

The two agents quickly exited, no doubt relieved to remove themselves from the room. Rachel couldn’t blame them. She’d hate to be on the other side of the senator’s wrath.

Once the door closed, Senator Hutton’s demeanor softened. “Ms. Dawson, Mr. Bradford, you saved my life. If there’s anything I can ever do for you, please don’t hesitate to contact me.”

Logan nodded curtly. “Thank you, sir, that’s—”

“I would love to do an exclusive interview with you about your thoughts on the afternoon’s events,” Rachel said.

The senator blinked rapidly. “Of course. Unfortunately, I’m due to return to Washington, DC, tomorrow night.”

Excited by her idea, she pressed on. “I could get a crew by this afternoon. We could even do the interview in the comfort of your hotel room.”

This interview would not only bolster her career, but would help to inform the American people about the crimes that had occurred at the hands of Evans and Fink. She needed to get the truth out there so that people wouldn’t continue to believe she and Logan had committed murder.

What better way than to interview the senator whose life she had saved? A senator who had gained recent notoriety for his filibustering.

The senator frowned, clearly unconvinced. She could tell he was about to turn her down.

She couldn't let the opportunity slip away. "The longer we wait to tell the story, Senator, the lesser the impact it will have on the American people. While I don't want to incite panic, I do believe our nation has the right to know that a biological terrorist attack was thwarted today. This story is just what you need to sway public opinion and get the votes you needed in the Senate to prevent the Homeland Security spending cuts."

"Yes, it is." A light shone in the senator's eyes as he mulled it over. He bobbed his head. "Very well, I think I could alter my schedule for the evening. I'm staying at a donor's home in Lake Las Vegas." He took out his wallet and produced a business card then handed it to her. "Call that number on the bottom and you'll reach my assistant. She'll coordinate it with you."

After the senator left, Rachel grabbed Logan's hand, adrenaline pumping through her veins. "Let's get out of here. I need to make dozens of phone calls for tonight."

He backed her into the door and nuzzled her neck. "Make your calls, but then plan on spending a couple hours in bed with me."

Heat spread throughout her lower belly. "So our original bargain has changed?" She raked her nails over her scalp. "Because I seem to recall we agreed I'd only submit to you until we cleared our names."

"Yeah, things changed and you know it," he said huskily. "This isn't about sex, although I plan on fucking you well and often. This is about me wanting to hold my wife in my arms at night and wake up with her beside me every morning."

She inhaled sharply. "You want to stay married? What if the chapel doesn't file our marriage license?"

He intertwined his fingers with hers. "I spoke my vows to you and you to me. Granted, they were on the short side," he said, laughing. "But I take them seriously. I don't care whether they file the license, because in my mind, in my heart, you already belong to me. If it's not legal, we'll make it legal." His eyes twinkled. "That is, if you want to be married to me."

She waited for the panic to set in, but all she felt was a sense of peace. The idea of falling in love had always frightened her. Until Danielle and Cole, she hadn't ever really spent time with a married couple other than those from her old church. Cole was a Dominant, the owner of a sex club, and yet Rachel never saw him try to control Danielle. Cole treated her like a queen and hung on every word she spoke as if it was Shakespeare. And from what Rachel understood, they were in a twenty-four/seven Master-slave relationship.

But unlike Danielle, Rachel wasn't certain she was submissive. Sure, she enjoyed Logan's domination of her in the bedroom, but that was all fun and games. She didn't need it like her friends.

Her inner voice called her a liar. If she didn't need the domination, why hadn't she ever had an orgasm during sex before? She hadn't even liked sex until Logan and his ropes. If she was honest with herself, it was his dominance that had attracted her in the first place. It was also the reason she had fought so hard not to fall for him. No one had ever challenged her the way Logan did. She couldn't manipulate him as she did the other men she'd been with in the past.

But he didn't try to control her.

He treated her as his equal.

"What do you think about my interviewing the senator?" she asked in lieu of answering his question.

He raised a brow. "I think the interview will get you all the accolades you deserve. It was a brilliant move convincing the senator to use it to promote his cause." He cupped her cheek. "I'm proud of you."

That was all she needed to hear.

She stroked her fingers up and down his chest. "I never wanted to get married. To me, marriage meant giving up your hopes and dreams and losing your identity." She fisted his shirt. "I can't allow marriage to change who I am. If my job entails putting myself in danger in order to get a story, I'm going to do it. Although, I promise you I'll use every available safeguard to limit the risk. Will you be able to accept that?"

He paused, his lips pressed together in a thin line, then blew out a breath. "Honestly? I'd like to say yes, but after worrying about you today, I don't know if I could go through that all the time. And it's not because I don't support your career. It's because I want you safe. I'd feel the same if you were a cop or fighting fires. I admire your strength and your tenacity, but I'm not sure how I'm going to react if I know you're in danger."

Her heart plummeted to her feet. She understood him wanting to keep her safe because she felt the same way about him. That's why she hadn't left him when he told her to leave at the port. But it still hurt to hear that he wasn't sure he'd be able to accept her career.

She swallowed the threatening tears. "It doesn't happen often, and most of the time you won't even know until the story airs. As much as I want you to accept it, I understand how you feel. But before we return home, you need to decide if you're willing to try to make our marriage work or whether we should go our own separate ways."

He plunged one hand in her hair and slipped the other around her back to press her against him. "I don't need time because I've already made my decision. I love you, Rachel Bradford, and I'm not letting you go."

"I love you too. And I love my new name, although you should know, I'm keeping my professional name, Rachel Dawson. But that wasn't the name my parents gave me. I chose it when I was eighteen after watching *Titanic*. Before that, I was Rachel Kaczynski."

His lips captured hers in a soft kiss. When he pulled his mouth away, he smiled. "You can call yourself whatever you want, so long as I can call you mine."

Chapter Twenty-Six

RACHEL RODE HIS cock, swiveling her hips then raising herself up on his hard length before slamming back down. Sweat slickened both their bodies from their hours of furious fucking. He'd already brought her to an orgasm both when he'd eaten her out and when he'd taken her ass while her pussy was full of an ice-cold glass dildo. He'd lubed up her chest and smashed her tits together, sliding his cock between them and bringing himself to an explosive climax, ropes of hot semen marking her breasts, neck, and chin.

Her nipples had turned a dark red from the sucking, licking, and biting he'd done to them, and she was pretty sure he'd left bruises on her inner thighs from the force of his thrusts. Her hair was a mess, she hadn't slept a wink yet, her interview was in two hours, and she never wanted to leave this bed.

After they'd returned to Paradise Lost from the FBI office, she'd quickly showered then made all the necessary phone calls to set up this afternoon's interview. Her boss had assured her he'd never believed all the reports accusing her of murder and that he'd been fielding phone calls from other networks and news outlets all week hoping for an interview with her. She was a hot commodity right now, and once today's interview aired with the senator, she might finally have made a big enough name for herself to catch New York's attention.

But now that the opportunity loomed, she wasn't sure she wanted New York anymore. While her job was important to her, it was no longer the only thing in her life. Over the past few days, she realized she'd used her career to keep herself from forming any meaningful relationships so that she wouldn't risk losing her heart. But she had formed relationships anyway. She had friends in Kate, Lisa, Danielle, and Gracie. And despite her best effort to avoid it, she had fallen in love. Her career fulfilled her, but it didn't make her happy. If she took a job in New York and moved away from those she loved, she'd be leaving a huge piece of her heart behind.

A hard smack on her ass tore her from her thoughts.

"Am I boring you?" Logan asked with a grin.

She flattened her palms on his chest. "No. I was just thinking how much I love you."

He reached up and tugged the ends of her hair. "I love you too. And I'm about to show you how much."

She squealed as he suddenly rolled them over so he was on top of her. He pushed her thighs farther apart and drove his cock back inside her, moving annoyingly slow.

"I've fucked my wife all afternoon. Now I want to make love to her."

"Missionary? Isn't that a little vanilla?"

His heated gaze snared hers. "There's nothing vanilla about my rock-solid dick inside your snug wet pussy. But sometimes, I want to slow things down, look into my wife's eyes, and breathe her in."

He kissed her, their lips and tongues coming together in a sensual mating. In a leisurely rhythm, their bodies joined again and again, every downward stroke of his cock bumping against her clit. Hot pleasure coursed through her pussy, driving her higher toward climax.

Pulling back from the kiss, they stared into each other's eyes, their breathing in sync as if passing their breaths back and forth between one another.

His cock twitched inside her, signaling her to his impending orgasm. The muscles around his eyes trembled as if he was about to lose control, but he didn't close his eyes or look away. She drowned in the love reflecting in his gaze.

His hand snaked down between their bodies and to her clit, where he pinched it between his fingers. Tears rolled down her cheeks from the intensity, but she forced herself to keep her eyes open as a climax crashed into her without warning, the muscles in her pussy clenching hard on his cock. As waves of contractions racked her pussy, she watched as Logan lost himself in his own orgasm. His face contorted and his body shook before he collapsed on her with a low moan.

A minute later, he rolled off her, shifting them so her head rested on his chest. His fingers played with her nipple, his half-hard cock thickening against her thigh. The man was insatiable, but she'd never complain. He took her lips, forcing them apart. She couldn't get enough of him, would never tire of his touch.

Knocking on their door broke their revelry. "Logan, we need to talk."

Logan groaned, catching the come dripping down her thigh with his fingers and pushing it back inside her pussy. He finger-fucked her, the sound of her wet tissues sucking those digits inside filling the room. "Not now, Sawyer. I need some alone time with my wife."

"You guys need to come to Tech Central," Sawyer said through the door. "We've got something you have to see."

His fingers stilled. "Fine. Give us five minutes." With a sigh, he pulled them out of her pussy and into her mouth. "Clean them off," he ordered.

Sometimes, she didn't mind his bossiness.

Sticky and sweaty, they took another quick shower before dressing and heading down the hall to meet the guys. Now that the sexual high was wearing off, she wondered what was so important that Sawyer felt the need to interrupt them.

Sawyer, Oz, Rowan, and Hunter stopped their conversation the minute she and Logan stepped into the room.

Oz grinned at them. "Congratulations on your marriage." He sniffed and pretended to dab his eyes. "It was a lovely ceremony. The only thing missing was your best man, Oz."

Hunter punched Oz in the arm. "What makes you think you would have been best man? Maybe Logan would've asked me."

Sawyer grinned widely. "Judging by the sounds coming from your room, it's too late to get the marriage annulled, so I'm guessing you've decided to stay married?"

She and Logan shared a glance. He looped his arm around her and tugged her into his side. "Why fight the inevitable?" He kissed her cheek before giving his friends a scowl. "Mind telling me what was so important you felt the need to interrupt our honeymoon?"

Rowan motioned to his computer. "I was able to trace the money given to Fink's mother. Whoever was behind everything really tried to keep it buried. There were several layers between the origination and the final destination. It came from a PAC Fund called A Better Tomorrow and was listed under an unclassifiable consulting expenditure."

Her neck prickled with heat while a chill passed through her. Political action committees were primarily formed to pool campaign contributions and to donate those funds to help elect chosen political candidates.

Rachel didn't believe in coincidences. "So how do we figure out who authorized the payment?" she asked, her mind spinning with the implication of this new information.

"I checked the recipients, and this PAC oddly donates money across party lines," Rowan said. "Guess the two senators who have received the largest contributions from this PAC."

"Hutton and Byron," Logan said through gritted teeth.

Rowan nodded. "Bingo."

Oz dropped into his chair in front of the computer and spun it from side to side. "Senator Hutton wouldn't have put himself at risk of contracting a deadly disease. It doesn't make sense. And what motive would either of them have to do it?"

"Hutton has introduced a bill to increase spending for the prevention of biological warfare," Logan told him. "Releasing a deadly disease like Leopold would support his position that additional funds are necessary."

Seemed to Rachel like a drastic way to earn money. "But he'd be crazy to expose himself to the virus." She'd met Hutton and had a hard time believing he could do such a thing. "What about Byron?"

Logan shook his head. "Why would he do it? Wouldn't it hurt his chances that his bill would pass?"

"Maybe he just wanted Hutton dead," Hunter said, perched on the edge of a desk.

"There are easier ways to do that," Rowan pointed out.

Suddenly somber, Oz stopped moving his chair. "You should also know that according to Byron's intern, Byron is also in Las Vegas."

Rachel perked up at that bit of news. What reason did Byron have for being here at the same time as his senatorial nemesis? Surely, that couldn't be a coincidence. She didn't want to believe that the man she'd met at the FBI office could be capable of such an act or that Logan and she had gone to such lengths to protect a man who had possibly been behind the whole plot to release Leopold on innocent people.

"I'll research the treasurer of the PAC as well as Byron to see if there's something we're missing, but let's just focus on Hutton right now," Rowan said with his usual logic. "What would we need to tie him to the Rinaldi or the agents?"

Logan squeezed her side in reassurance as if he sensed her distress over the recent revelation. "If we could hack into his computer, we could go through his files and emails. Maybe we'd find something there."

"How do we do that?" she asked, burrowing in closer to his side.

"I don't suppose he gave you his IP address," Oz quipped.

She laughed. "No, surprisingly, that wasn't on the card he gave me. Isn't there another way?"

Sawyer rested against the wall, his feet crossed in front of him. "If he brought his computer with him and if it were on, there are a couple of different ways we could access it." He looked at Rachel. "You can locate the IP address and give it to us. Then we could hack him remotely, but we'd only be able to do it so long as the computer was on. The other way is to hack it through the Wi-Fi. It's harder to trace that way, but we could download his files in a single swoop through an app on a cell phone."

Her heart started hammering from the surge of adrenaline racing through her. While she didn't have the computer skills on par with the guys, she had experience working undercover. She could help them access Senator Hutton's computer. "That's what we'll do," she said excitedly. "Give me a phone with the app on it, and I'll use it when I do the interview."

Logan grew rigid against her. "Guys, can you excuse us?"

The room went dead silent for a beat. Then shooting each other looks that spoke volumes, Sawyer and the others left the room. A sense of dread fell upon her, and she braced for the words that would slice her heart in half.

Logan's arm fell away from her waist and he moved to stand in front of her. "I don't want you to do it," he said quietly.

She inhaled a deep breath as if drawing strength into herself. "Why not?"

"If he is responsible for everything and you get caught, what do you think a monster like that would do to you? And if he's not responsible and you get caught, you'll have pissed off a powerful senator who will have you thrown behind bars. In both scenarios, you'll end up hurt."

She placed her palm on his chest. "How about the scenario where I don't get caught and nothing happens to me?"

It pained her when, shaking his head, Logan took a step back from her. "It's not worth the risk. We can take what we know and pass it on to the FBI." His tone gave her the impression that his decision was final.

She felt the hope of their marriage working slip through her fingers like sand. "Right, because they've been oh so helpful so far," she said, laughing bitterly. "They want to pretend like none of this ever happened. They'll give their official statement and that will be it. We need to find something that incriminates Hutton before we can go to the FBI."

He folded his arms across his chest. "We should wait until we have more intel before charging in and putting your life in danger."

Was this about control? Or a result of his time in the army when incomplete intelligence had cost the lives of his fellow soldiers and an innocent civilian? Regardless, his traumatic experience had obviously affected him strongly.

"How are we going to get that intel?" she asked.

"I don't know." Averting his eyes, he dipped his chin toward his chest and ran his fingers through his hair. "We'll figure it out."

Frustrated, she clenched her hands. "And by then our chance to hack his computer will have passed." Her voice came out louder than she'd intended, but he wasn't listening to reason.

He threw his hands in the air. "Then I'll do it. I'll come with you to the interview. Or I'll stop by his room another time and do it."

This had nothing to do with waiting for more intel. He just didn't want *her* to do it. And while part of her knew he did it out of concern for her, the other part realized her greatest fear had come true. She'd fallen in love with a man who wanted to control her.

"You'll do it. It's too dangerous for me, but it's okay for you? You're not even thinking rationally. If you get caught, he'll assume I'm in on it anyway." She waved her hand at him. "This is about you wanting to control everything. But you can't control me, and it scares you."

"I'm not trying to control you." He stalked forward and grabbed her shoulders, his fingers digging into her skin. "I'm only trying to keep you safe."

A war raged inside her. She knew he was telling the truth, but it didn't matter.

The result was the same.

She blinked back the tears. "This isn't going to work. I told you my job is dangerous sometimes, and you promised you'd try to accept that. But the first opportunity to test that promise, you're forbidding me from doing my job."

He took her face in his hands. "You haven't been out of danger for a day yet and already you're throwing yourself back to the wolves. I love you. My job as your husband is to protect you even if you don't want that protection."

Wetness stained her cheeks. This didn't feel like a marital argument. This felt like good-bye. "Your job as my husband is to support me and my decisions. This is why I never wanted to get married. I'm never going to obey you outside of the bedroom, Logan. I'm not submissive."

His throat worked over a swallow as he tenderly brushed her tears with his knuckles. "You say the word *submissive* like it means you're weak. You know that's not true. There's strength in submission."

She pushed him away. "The strength comes from handing over that power to another. I'm not giving it to you. You're trying to take it from me. I won't let you do it. You say you love me. Then let me take a risk. Let me be the same woman you fell in love with. The one who defied you in the dungeon and followed you outside at Benediction. The one who put herself in front of a dog to protect it the same way you put yourself in front of Evans's gun to protect me. That's who I am. I can't change for you. I won't."

His hands outstretched, Logan began to step toward her, but he stopped himself. "I can't change who I am either. I wish I could," he said, his voice cracking. "And I can't be a part of your plan tonight." His eyes held an ultimatum. "If you do this, you're going to have to do it without me."

Chapter Twenty-Seven

WITH MAKEUP ON, her hair curled and sprayed to perfection, and a smile on her face, no one would guess that Rachel was dying on the inside. After she and Logan had broken up for good, she'd held it together long enough to go over how to work the software that would hack into the senator's computer.

Sawyer had tried to get her to talk about what had happened between her and Logan, but she refused to discuss it. Taking comfort in the familiar, she regressed to the woman who focused solely on her job. Tonight was about more than the interview. It was about proving to Logan that she was her own woman. Just as with her other stories, it wasn't solely about her career. It was about exposing the truth. She'd thought after spending the week with her, Logan had accepted that, like him, she had a drive to protect people. But he hadn't and, as a result, she was nursing her first broken heart.

Rather than watch her take what he perceived as a risk, Logan had taken a commercial flight back to Michigan. Sawyer and the guys had installed the app on her new cell phone and shown her how to use it. The app would tap into the Wi-Fi and download the data from every computer on the network. The chances of Senator Hutton having his computer on were slim to none, but unless she could find a legitimate excuse to use it, they'd have to cross their fingers. If she didn't get access tonight, she'd have to find another time she could try again. But she wouldn't give up. She'd do what she had to do in order to uncover the truth, whatever that was.

She kept her purse behind her chair, the cell phone tucked away inside. As soon as she'd arrived at the Lake Las Vegas mansion where Hutton had been staying, she'd checked the available Wi-Fi networks, clicking on the one that matched the last name of the home's owner. Then, to bypass the required password, she'd opened the app and typed in the code that Sawyer had made her memorize before slipping the phone back into her purse. It was out of her hands at this point.

But she didn't plan on going easy on the senator. She had a list of questions that she needed answers to in order to assure herself he wasn't responsible for the hell she'd gone through this past week.

Working in conjunction with her station, the local news crew had arrived an hour earlier to set up. She'd kept herself busy, throwing herself into her job, making sure everything was ready before the senator came downstairs and joined them. Once the interview was completed, her station's producers would edit it for the eleven o'clock news. Her boss mentioned the possibility of it getting picked up by the national network, but she didn't want to get her hopes up. She'd already had her hopes dashed once today. She didn't need to go through it again.

Relaxing on the chair that had been set up for the interview, she stood when Senator Hutton entered the room. Dressed in a different suit than he'd worn in the FBI's office, he looked just as polished, no sign of the exhaustion that Rachel felt from having gone without sleep last night.

"Can I get you anything, Senator?" asked one of her crew. "Water?"

Senator Hutton waved him off. "I'm fine. Ready for my interview." He took Rachel's hand and shook it. "It's nice to see you again, Ms. Dawson."

She gave him a smile she wasn't feeling inside. "You too, Senator." They settled in their seats, the senator completely at ease under the lights and cameras. "Thank you again for agreeing to this interview."

"You saved my life and possibly millions more. There's very little I wouldn't do for you. In fact, if you ever decide to leave your career, I could always use a woman like you as my press secretary."

Her life was spent pursuing truth and justice. In her opinion, she'd find neither in politics. "Thank you for that kind offer, but I love my job, and there's nothing else I'd rather do."

Intentionally omitting a couple, she went over the topics they'd be discussing before she began the interview.

She angled her knees toward him. "You made headlines this week for your record-breaking eighteen-hour-long filibuster of Senator Byron's bill. Can you give the average American who knows nothing about politics the short reason you chose to do that?"

Relaxing, he leaned on the arm of his chair. "Despite my efforts to defeat Senator Byron's proposed legislation, the bill had made its way to the floor for a vote. I felt very strongly that decreased spending to Homeland Security would place our country in a vulnerable position. We need to spend more on protecting our borders rather than less. With a filibuster, I was able to delay the vote until the Senate returns from its break, using that time to sway the votes in my favor, so that the bill would be defeated."

She could understand how he'd been so successful in politics all these years. When he spoke, he captured everyone's attention with his deep, powerful voice. "You also have a bill up for consideration, is that true?"

"Yes, as the chairman of the Senate HELP Committee—the Health, Education, Labor, and Pension Senate Committee, which overseas public health and health insurance laws, including governmental agencies such as the Centers for Disease Control and Prevention and the National Food and Drug Administration—I've come across disturbing statistics regarding the probability of certain life-threatening viruses crossing into our borders both naturally and intentionally."

She cocked her head. "Intentionally? What do you mean by that?"

His expression grew somber. "I'm talking about biological warfare. Terrorists or even governments using viruses to kill our citizens and weaken our economy. Unfortunately, as you learned this week, Ms. Dawson, the probability has become a reality. Two agents in our Federal Bureau of Investigation conspired along with an alleged serial killer to smuggle the Leopold virus into our country from the Congo, in a gas canister meant to hold oxygen. It was only due to your bravery that our country is not facing one of its worst terrorist disasters since 9-11. Thousands of people may have lost their lives if the airborne virus had been spread into the Tuscany Casino. Which is why I'm proposing to increase our funding to Homeland Security and to both fast-track drugs through the National Food and Drug Administration and loosen restrictions in case of no alternatives."

She frowned. That was the first she'd heard of that portion of his proposed legislation. "I'm sorry. You lost me. No alternatives?"

The senator crossed his leg, reclining in his chair. "For example, there are diseases with treatments that may not cure but will lessen the severity of the symptoms or extend life expectancy. If a new drug is invented that will cure the disease in a percentage of those suffering, but will cause severe side effects for others up to and including death, it would never be approved for use in this country. But let's say there's a disease like the Leopold virus that has no treatment, an airborne virus where eighty percent of those infected will die within days of transmission. We must approve those drugs for use until an alternative is available."

Rachel continued questioning him for another hour until her throat had grown dry. Then she asked, "Senator Hutton, have you questioned why you were targeted by those seeking to release the virus?"

His eye twitched as he paused, a bit thrown off by her question, but he recovered quickly with a shake of his head. "I've thought about this all day, Ms. Dawson, and I've come to this conclusion: Infect the man who has been warning our country about the virus and send him back to Washington, DC, unaware of that infection. Within days, I could've spread Leopold to the entire Senate. I was selected as their nuclear bomb, unaware that I was programmed to go off. They chose me for both the irony and the opportunity."

She wasn't sure if she bought his explanation, but she'd wager most of those watching the interview would. "I've heard rumors that you plan to run for president of the United States in the next election," she said.

His shoulders dropped, the tension in his body gone from when he'd answered her previous question. "I love this country, Ms. Dawson. My father was president, my brother was president, and someday, if God graces me with the opportunity, I'll serve our country as president too."

She knew she was playing with fire, but she had to see if she could garner a reaction from him. "You're a national hero. Donations into your campaign must be pouring in faster than you can count them." She held his gaze. "Contributions from, say, A Better Tomorrow."

A muscle in his jaw jumped. "I don't know anything about contributions. I have people who do that for me."

She flashed him a smile. "Of course." She stood and offered her hand. "Thank you for the interview, Senator. It was absolutely enlightening."

He didn't move from his chair for a moment, and then suddenly he was right in front of her, a tad too close. "For me as well, Ms. Dawson," he said quietly, shaking her hand.

She saw the same anger in his eyes as before, when it had been directed at Agent Gossner. Only this time, his wrath was directed at her.

The urge to flee overwhelmed her.

She yanked back her hand and circled around the chair for her purse. "My crew will be out of your way in a few minutes, but I'll just get out of your way now."

With homicidal butterflies battling each other in her belly, she bent and retrieved her purse, but as she straightened, a few items spilled out onto the floor with a clatter. She kneeled down, her hands shaking as she picked up her compact mirror. "I'm such a klutz. Sorry about that." She stood and almost slammed into the senator.

He held her cell in his hand. "I believe you dropped this as well."

She grabbed it from him and jammed it back into her purse, but not before she saw the words *download complete* on the screen.

The senator tipped his head, a slight smile on his lips. "Until we meet again, Ms. Dawson."

Stumbling over her feet, she hurried out of the room and into the hallway, smashing into a familiar body.

His hands gripped her biceps, steadying her. "Easy now."

Her heart spread wings and hope filled her chest as she looked up at her husband. "Logan. You're here. I thought you left already."

"I couldn't." He let go of her, his eyes dimmed with regret. "Not until I knew you were safe." He blew out a breath, rubbing the back of his neck. "Great interview."

Her hope deflated like an old balloon. "Thank you."

She should tell him that the senator might be suspicious of her, but she didn't want to be Logan's obligation. He'd come only because he was worried about her. If he knew she could be in danger, he'd stand by her, if only to act as her bodyguard.

It was best to stay quiet about it for now. Even if the senator had seen the cell phone's screen, he wouldn't know what it meant. She'd be fine.

At least physically.

She'd taken care of herself for years.

But as she walked away from her husband for the last time, she knew she'd never fully recover from her broken heart.

Chapter Twenty-Eight

A DAY AFTER Rachel's interview with the senator had aired all over the country, she'd returned to her small house in Michigan and discovered she had eighty voice mail messages. Not only had she received calls for interviews, she'd gotten several job offers from prominent news stations across the globe. It should have been a dream come true.

Instead, it gave her a giant headache.

Even the offer from New York didn't excite her. Regardless of what had happened with Logan, Michigan was her home and her friends were her family. She didn't want to leave them.

Staring at the two empty wineglasses on her coffee table, she sat on her couch next to Lisa, twirling the wedding band she couldn't make herself remove. "I never thought I'd need a publicist to keep the media away from me."

Lisa had taken the situation into hand and was now fielding all her calls. She'd catalogued all eighty voice mail messages from most to least important. "You've got interest from all the major networks, but it's your call. Personally, I'd love to see Barbara Walters interview you. She can get anyone to cry."

She shook her head, a slight smile on her face. "I'd never cry on television." Before Logan, she'd never cried period. But once she'd opened the floodgates, the waterworks kept flowing. How embarrassed she'd been to return to Paradise Lost and have Logan's friends try but fail to console her.

But at least they were busy now digging through Hutton's files. The app had worked well—almost too well. Along with the senator's files, it had also downloaded the files from three other computers. Because of the way the program was designed, they couldn't tell which files belonged to whom until they opened them. And according to Sawyer, there were thousands.

"Exactly," Lisa said, adjusting her glasses. "Why not show your sensitive side?"

Curled into the corner of the couch, Rachel tucked her feet under her. "Because I don't want to be known as the tough reporter who cried. I want to be known as the tough reporter who kicked some ass and saved the world from one nasty virus." Rachel angled toward her friend. "I'm not granting any interviews. I'm not ready to talk about what happened. Besides, I'm a reporter. I have no desire to sit in the other chair, even if it's for Barbara Walters."

"Have you heard from Logan?" Lisa asked gently.

Earlier that day on the phone, Rachel had given Lisa a quick overview of what had transpired between her and Logan. She'd also filled her in on their suspicions about Senators Hutton and Byron, leaving Sawyer's name out since he didn't want anyone to know about his ties to Paradise Lost.

"No." She looked up at the ceiling, warding off the tears. "Guess there's a good reason they say what happens in Vegas, stays in Vegas."

"Fuck that," Lisa said, shocking the hell out of her with the profanity. "Listen to me. Both of you are just too stubborn to lay it out there. You love each other. That's the only thing that matters."

She'd almost believed that for a little while in Vegas, but now, the pessimist in her had returned. "Sometimes, love isn't enough. I thought he accepted me. All of me. But he wants a woman he can control. He wants a...submissive."

Lisa blew out an exasperated breath. "How do you know that's what he wants? Just because he's dominant in the bedroom and he likes his lovers to give up control to him doesn't mean he wants a submissive woman."

"What do you know about dominance and submission? You've never made a single comment about the lifestyle before."

Lisa played with the ends of her short brown hair. "Before I became a born-again virgin, I may have dabbled in kink."

"What the hell?" Rachel said a bit too loudly, knocking over a wineglass and Lisa's purse on the coffee table with her foot. "How have you been keeping this from me? Does Kate know?"

"No," Lisa said vehemently. "And you have to promise not to say anything."

"Why? Why would you keep that from us, especially from Kate when she's in the lifestyle? No one would judge you. In fact, I'm sure Danielle would give you a membership to Benediction at a reduced rate."

Lisa looked down at her lap. "It's a part of a past I've put behind me. Some people don't deserve pleasure or passion or love."

"I think I've come to know you pretty well over the last year or so. The woman who I call my friend deserves all that and more."

Sadness registered in Lisa's eyes. "That's just it, Rachel. You don't know me. You don't know me at all. No one does. But that doesn't mean I'm not your friend. I made a mistake five years ago that cost me the man I loved. Don't give up without a fight. You may be a submissive in the bedroom, but you're one hundred percent dominant outside of it, so don't wait for him to come after you. Decide what's most important to you, what will truly make you happy, and make it happen. Don't lose your chance like I did."

If only it were that simple.

"Thank you for revealing that part of your life to me," Rachel said, patting her friend on the leg. "I promise I won't tell anyone. Even Kate. But maybe you should take your own advice and stop punishing yourself so that you can go after your happiness. You never know. You may find love a second time."

Lisa bit her lip. "It's not in the cards for me." She rose from the couch and slipped her purse over her arm before giving Rachel a hug. "Call me if you need anything. And we missed you at Girls' Night last week. Make sure you come this Thursday or Gracie's going to march over here and harass you until you tell her everything."

Rachel walked Lisa out and shut the door. Back in the family room, she picked up the wineglasses and brought them into the kitchen to wash. The rest of the bottle sat on the counter by the cheese and crackers she'd forgotten about. Her appetite must have stayed with her husband because it hadn't come back with her from Vegas.

Rinsing the glasses in the sink, she was startled to hear the doorbell ring. She frowned as she turned off the faucet and wiped her hands dry on a kitchen towel. Lisa must have forgotten something. Rachel headed out of her kitchen and crossed her living room to the front door. "What did you forget this time, Lisa?" she asked, swinging her door open.

She didn't have time to process that the person behind the door wasn't her friend before it flew all the way open, hitting the wall with a crash, and Senator Hutton had barreled his way into her apartment, the force of him knocking her to the floor.

As she lay there in shock, her brain not caught up with the moment's events, Senator Hutton swung the door shut and locked it, the thunk of the lock turning causing her throat to spasm from fear. Clutching a gun in his hand, he loomed over her, his gaze glued to her as if he was the hunter and she was the prey.

With her in a heap on the ground and him standing right in front of her, blocking the door, there was no way to escape. He could shoot her at close range, here in her house, make it look as though a burglary had occurred, and no one would ever learn the truth.

Somehow, she managed to find her voice. "If you had wanted an invitation inside, you only had to ask, Senator." She didn't know what possessed her to speak to him like that, but she was shocked her voice had come out as calm as it had.

His gaze narrowed on her as he pointed the gun at her head. Attached to its barrel was a long cylinder extension. *A silencer.* So no one would hear the resounding boom when the gun went off. No one would even know she was dead.

Rather than cry or plead, her eyes dared him to shoot. She wouldn't give him the satisfaction of showing her fear. Even in death, she refused to be a victim.

"Get up," he said with a snarl.

He wasn't going to kill her? Her surprise must have shown on her face as she stood.

Keeping his gun away from her, he used his other hand to yank her up, holding her tightly under her armpit. Then he nudged her back with the butt of the gun, shoving her into the living room and propelling her onto the couch. "You and I are going to have a conversation. If you're a good girl, I won't make you suffer before I kill you. But if you're bad—there's a part of me that's hoping you are—I'll torture you first and make your death as excruciatingly painful as possible. And trust me. I've learned all the ways to hurt someone without killing them."

Since her only hope at this point was to keep him busy talking, she went for a basic conversation starter. "Why are you here?"

"Let's not play games, Ms. Dawson. You took something of mine, and I know you don't have the capability of doing anything with it on your own. I need to know who has that information and get it back."

"I don't know what you're talking about. I don't have—"

Her head snapped back from the force of his backhand against her cheekbone. "Don't lie to me. I wasn't bluffing when I told you I'd enjoy hurting you. There are spots on the body I can shoot that won't kill you right away, but will cause you misery beyond your darkest nightmares. Lie to me again and I'll prove it to you." He bent over her. "Who else has the information?"

"A friend of mine in Las Vegas. But he hasn't found anything yet."

He smiled, all teeth like a rabid dog. "His name. I want his name."

"Sawyer," she said, her voice cracking. "Sawyer Hayes."

He jerked. "Of Hayes Industries?"

She nodded slowly. "Yes."

She hated throwing him under the bus, but at least Sawyer had distance between him and the senator. Not to mention, Sawyer was at his hotel, and as he had mentioned, his name wasn't associated with it, making it difficult to find him for now.

She eyed the iPad sitting on her coffee table. Lisa had forgotten something after all. Would she come back for it tonight?

Panic shot through Rachel, making her heart race as if she was running a marathon. As much as she hoped for a miracle, she didn't want Lisa getting pulled into this mess. She prayed Lisa would stay far away from here.

"What were you looking for on my computer?" Senator Hutton asked, bringing her out of her thoughts.

She laced her fingers together to keep her hands from trembling. "Anything to connect you to Rinaldi or the release of the Leopold virus. Why risk your life by exposing yourself to the virus? With an eighty percent mortality rate, the odds were stacked against you surviving it."

He waved his gun at her. "With Exulanab, my odds were much better. I calculated the risk and decided it was worth it."

Thankful he hadn't shot her yet, she asked another question. "What is Exulanab?"

"During my interview, I spoke about fast-tracking drugs by loosening the restrictions in case of no alternatives. Exulanab is one such drug. Three years ago, the FDA rejected the application for the drug's approval for further studies due to the fact that thirty-five percent of those test animals that received the drug died within hours of the infusion from massive heart attacks. They were too shortsighted to see that while thirty-five percent might die, sixty-five percent would survive. That meant if one hundred thousand people were infected with the virus, sixty-five thousand people would live versus twenty thousand without it. Over forty-five thousand lives saved. Tell me, if you knew you had a greater chance of living if you took the drug, would you take that risk?"

She trembled. The man was certifiable if he was willing to expose himself to Leopold, which made him more dangerous than she could've ever imagined. "Probably. But it's an awful gamble."

He shrugged. "It's one I was willing to take. I believe in this drug, Ms. Dawson. Now that the American people have seen Leopold and Ebola are not restricted to African borders, they'll want reassurance that this country has taken every necessary precaution. What happens when the news leaks out that there are experimental drugs for these viruses but that they're not readily available? How many people who died in the latest African Ebola outbreak could have survived if only they'd received the drug?"

"So, what, you're doing this out of the goodness of your heart?"

"It's a cause I feel strongly about, but only because I see the future." He puffed out his chest as if he was giving a political speech. "Biological warfare is our biggest threat, and investment in our protection will benefit everyone, especially those with a financial interest in the pharmaceutical companies that manufacture the drugs. Just imagine how much money those companies will be worth when our country keeps stockpiles of the drugs available for its citizens."

"And let me guess. You own stock in the pharmaceutical company that manufactures Exulanab. This has all been about money?"

"Of course I didn't do it solely for the money. The money will help get me elected as president, but I'm doing this because I'm a patriot." He stepped closer to her. "I love this great country of ours, and I've made no secret that my ancestry can be traced all the way to George Washington. My blood runs blue, unlike so many who live in our country now. It's time to save this country and return it to its former glory. Reclaim the international respect it deserves."

She glanced at the iPad. "How will you do that?"

His lip curled in disgust. "Our country will have a biological weapon and its cure. Everyone will fear us. We'd have the ability to wipe out our enemy without ever losing one of our soldiers. Just think of it. We could rid this world of every minority."

She shuddered, disgusted by his evil. "And how were you going to do that with the virus? It's not as if it can pick and choose whom it sickens."

"No, but we can control who receives the cure," he said, tapping his chest with two of his fingers. "The worthy Americans will remain safe while those less desirables will succumb to death by virus."

Distracted by a scratching from outside on the porch, Hutton turned toward the noise. Trying not to think about being shot in the back, she dashed to the kitchen. With Hutton on her tail, she looked for a weapon and panicked, picking up the wine bottle from the counter. She swung it around, catching the senator on his temple. His body slammed to the floor, knocked out cold.

She didn't wait for him to recover. She ran through the kitchen to the front door and flung it open. A dark figure filled the entryway. Before she could cry for help, a fist to her chest sent her careening back into her house. The door slammed shut for a second time, and the man she recognized from television as Senator Byron stomped toward her, menace gleaming in his eyes.

They were working together?

"I don't understand," she said, every breath painful to take as she sat up. She crossed her arms over her middle, sure she had broken a rib.

Senator Hutton rounded the corner from the kitchen and handed Byron the gun. "Every good political fight needs a hero and a villain. We agreed that my chances of winning the White House were better than his, so I got to be the hero this time and fight for our nation's safety."

She almost laughed. A Democrat and Republican working together. "And Rinaldi? How did he get involved?"

Byron slid his hand up and down the barrel of the gun. "Communicating through Evans and Fink, Hutton and I negotiated to have all charges dropped against Rinaldi in exchange for his help. He never even knew who he was really dealing with. Rinaldi had an African mafia contact in Kinshasa, the capital of Congo, which was previously known as Leopoldville. The Leopold virus still sickens their monkeys from time to time. For a great deal of money, the virus was extracted from one such animal, and scientists on my payroll turned it into a gas form. Once Evans and Fink knew where and when to expect the shipment of the virus, Rinaldi's usefulness came to an end."

Hutton stepped closer. "Just like yours." He turned toward Byron. "She's already turned over the computer data to Sawyer Hayes. We'll have to eliminate him next."

Fear that she'd never known flooded her veins. "What are you going to do with me?"

Hutton smiled. "Remember when I said I enjoyed torture?" He gestured to Byron. "Meet my torturer. He knows more ways to make you scream than you could count."

Rachel knew enough to know there were worse things than death. She believed these men would have her begging them to kill her before they were finished with her. "Please don't hurt me. I promise I won't tell anyone," she said, her voice coming out as though her throat was filled with gravel.

Byron laughed sadistically. "That's what they always say." He kept the gun trained on her as he spoke to his partner. "Hutton, go to the kitchen and bring me a knife while I take her into the bedroom. Let's see if she can't take it hard up the ass like you can. Then we can carve us a pretty picture using her flesh as our canvas and blood as our paint."

Her tears and sweat dampened her T-shirt, and chills racked her body. She closed her eyes and imagined she was in Logan's arms, safe and warm underneath the blankets. If she concentrated hard enough, she could smell him around her, feel his touch on her skin, taste his kisses on her lips. No matter what happened, she'd hold him close to her and know that before she died, at least for a little while, she'd been loved. Although he wasn't there physically, she carried him in her heart and soul. He'd always be with her because she refused to let him go.

When Hutton went off to the kitchen, Byron yanked her off the floor and slapped her cheek, its sting waking her from the cocoon she'd created in her mind to protect herself. Clutching her nape, he pushed her through the house until he found her bedroom. Then he tossed her on the bed, facedown, and straddled her, his erection digging into her butt.

She wouldn't go down without fighting. She'd rather die than endure rape and torture. She flailed her arms and legs, trying to throw him off. "No! No! Leave me alone." His hands wrapped around her neck and tightened.

Her world went blurry around the edges and a buzzing sensation flooded her body.

"Get your hands off my wife."

Dazed, she fought to stay conscious. Was that muffled voice really Logan's or was she imagining him?

The hands around her loosened and she felt him shift on top of her. There was a loud blast that she heard even through the ringing in her ears from her lack of oxygen. The weight on top of her was gone, and then she heard the blast again, this time clearer as her lungs filled with air. Exhaustion didn't keep her from rolling over to see what had happened.

Eyes shining with unshed tears, Logan kneeled over her, a gun in his hands. "Byron's dead. He can't hurt you."

Forgetting about the pain in her ribs until she moved, she shot upright and looked on the floor beside the bed.

Byron's eyes were wide open, blood spreading across his chest in two different spots.

Logan didn't know the danger wasn't over. She grabbed him by the shoulders, her mouth moving but no words coming out. She swallowed, her throat bone-dry, and tried again. "Logan, Hutton's in the kitchen."

He held her to his chest and kissed the top of her head. "Shh. I've already taken care of him. He's dead. He can't hurt you anymore. No one will. I won't let them."

"How did you know?" she said, her throat sounding as if it had been scratched by sandpaper.

"Lisa. She drove by to get her iPad and saw a man hanging out on your porch. She called me first to see if it was me, and then once she realized it wasn't, she hung up and called the police. I got here quicker, but they're on their way."

She listened to his heart thumping under her ear and held him closer. "I'm sorry. You were right. Hutton got suspicious by my questions during the interview and saw the app on my phone. I shouldn't have put myself in danger."

He tipped up her chin. "No, don't blame yourself. You didn't do anything wrong. You were right. I was trying to control you. But you're the strongest, bravest woman I know, and those are only a couple of the reasons I love you. And while it may kill me to know you're putting yourself in danger, I respect the hell out of you for it. Besides, it couldn't be any worse than living without you. I love you, Rachel Bradford. Tell me you forgive me."

She softly pressed her lips to his in a promise of more to come. "There's nothing to forgive. I love you too." She smiled. "But now, I've got a story to report."

Epilogue

Three months later…

"I NOW PRONOUNCE you husband and wife, Master and collared slave," the reverend said into the microphone. "You may now kiss and seal your vow to one another."

Underneath the clear blue sky, the two hundred wedding guests stood and clapped loudly. Hundreds of colorful butterflies were released into the air, their wings spread wide as they soared toward freedom. The orchestra played Vivaldi's "Summer" as the handsome groom yanked his wife closer by her sparkling diamond collar and kissed the hell out of her in a display of ownership. When he pulled away, he dropped to his knees and tenderly kissed her swollen belly, gazing up at the love of his life with wonder.

In the backyard of Cole and Danielle DeMarco's mansion, Rachel dabbed a tissue at her eyes. The gazebo had been a beautiful location for Cole and Danielle to repeat their marriage vows and for the performance of the collaring ceremony. It didn't matter that this was Cole and Danielle's second wedding, the last one done privately out of state. She was so happy for her friends, who were expecting the birth of their first child in two months.

"You're crying," Logan said, surprise in his voice. His arm snaked around her, pulling her to him, and he pressed his lips to the top of her head.

She sniffed. "I always cry at weddings."

He raised a brow. "You didn't cry at ours."

"That's because we had two crazed FBI agents on our tails."

As everyone followed the bride and groom away from the gazebo and headed toward the reception just a few feet away, Logan dipped his head down to speak softly into Rachel's ear. "So, do you think you might want to do it again, like Danielle and Cole, in front of our families and friends?"

It had shocked the hell out of them when they'd discovered Jane had actually filed their marriage license.

She thought of herself dressed in white, a veil in her hair, with Danielle, Kate, and Lisa beside her as the bridesmaids. That was someone else's dream. Not hers. Just because she'd learned to balance love and friendship with her career didn't mean she'd suddenly become a different person. She'd never wanted the traditional wedding. And that hadn't changed.

"Honestly?" She took his hand and squeezed it, bumping her shoulder into him. "Our wedding was perfect. There's no point in trying to top it."

A grin lit up his face. "How 'bout I top you right now?"

She winked. "Ah, you know just how to sweet-talk me."

Lisa had done a beautiful job at organizing this wedding for Danielle and Cole. Long tables were adorned by silver silk and tall vases of white flowers that had been dipped in silver sparkles. The orchestra continued to play, switching from classical to more modern love ballads. Lights had been strung above the tables and dance floor to illuminate the party when the sun set. And the heavenly scent of garlic and tomatoes from the Italian dinner menu made Rachel's mouth water.

Cole's parents chatted animatedly with Danielle's stepbrother, Roman, and Rachel's friend Gracie. Some guests had gone into Benediction to play before dinner, but most had remained outside to mingle with other guests and drink champagne. It was strange to witness the vanilla and the kink communities interact with one another as the two worlds collided here at the wedding.

"You've been working so hard on your story," Logan said, snatching a glass of champagne for her off a waiter's tray and handing it to her.

She took a sip of champagne. "I'll never complain about my family again. How could our country have been run by sociopaths as presidents?"

Along with the financial records that Hutton had kept on his computer, tying him and Byron to the PAC that had paid off Fink, Evans, and Rinaldi, Maxwell Hutton had kept journals that read like an autobiography, chronicling his rise to power. The entries told the tale of a boy trying to understand how a benevolent God could allow such horrors to be inflicted upon a child. Rachel had vomited more than once as she read the atrocities he'd endured from such a young age. He'd been raised by a family of real-life monsters whom the country lauded as modern-day royalty, believing themselves to be the only real blue-blooded Americans. There had been no wonder that his parents had created a new generation of monsters in his brother and him.

When Maxwell Hutton had become a grown man, he'd exchanged one set of monsters for another. Byron and he had begun their affair more than ten years earlier after Byron discovered Hutton's penchant for extreme pain and torture.

Senators Hutton and Byron believed that between them, they could take the White House for the next sixteen years and, during that time, eliminate every race but their own. It was white supremacy at its worst. The American people had been horrified to learn that the men they had believed were American heroes were actually the villains they needed protection from.

The journals contained details of how the Hutton family had blackmailed politicians, foreign officials, judges, and others for more than fifty years. Many of those who had broken the law for the Huttons were arrested, but in their interviews with Rachel, several had thanked her for ending the Huttons' reign of terror and for allowing those blackmailed to ease their guilty consciences.

Of course, not all were thrilled with having their dirty laundry aired to the public. Two of the men under investigation had killed themselves, and she'd received more than five death threats, all which the FBI had traced back to various individuals whom Rachel had exposed through her investigation.

Logan worried constantly, but he hadn't prevented her from doing her job.

It had all been worth it.

Logan squeezed her hand as they searched for their assigned table. "I don't think I say it enough. I'm very proud of you."

Since they'd decided to remain married and had moved in together, buying a small house together with a fenced-in yard for their new dog, Barbara, in a quiet suburb of Detroit, he'd supported her career 100 percent. They were still working on how to balance their lives, and they still battled for control sometimes, but as in any healthy relationship, they compromised.

"The story isn't done," she said, her mind running away with her. "I think if I dig deeper, I'll probably uncover some suicides and accidental deaths of prominent people were actually murders ordered by the Huttons."

He clinked his champagne glass against hers. "I'm sure you will, Tiger. But do you think you could take a couple weeks off before you jump back into your busy workdays? We never did get to take a honeymoon."

A honeymoon sounded wonderful. As an adult, she'd never taken a vacation. "Where were you thinking?"

"Uncle Joe invited us to his new house down in the Everglades."

Joe had spent a few days in FBI custody, but once she and Logan had been exonerated, the charges against Joe had been dropped. Discovering he'd never truly been living off the grid had come as a shock to him, but he admitted he was enjoying the ability to try out some of the online dating websites.

She walked her fingers down Logan's chest. "Maybe we could stop by and spend a couple days with him before we go on a trip to Italy? I hear Tuscany is beautiful this time of year."

"I think that could be arranged." He wrapped his hand around her nape and pulled her in for a kiss, his mouth tasting of champagne and her, that particular flavor lingering from earlier in the evening when Logan had decided to make an appetizer out of her pussy.

She smiled as their lips parted and looked around the party. "Have you heard from Sawyer yet? I thought he'd be here by now."

Logan glanced at his watch. "He was running late. I gave him directions and gave security a heads-up to allow him through the gate." He pointed at a man strolling toward them. "Speak of the devil—"

"Hey, man." Logan shook Sawyer's hand. "Glad you could make it."

Sawyer gave her a quick hug. "Sorry I missed the wedding." At the raise of her brow, he changed his tune. "Okay, sorry I'm not sorry. Weddings bore me. But as you know, I've been dying to check out Benediction, and since I had a meeting in Detroit, this seemed like the perfect night."

"I'm sure I could find a sub for you if you're looking to scene," Logan offered.

Sawyer scanned the party. "Oh, I'm looking for someone in particular." He froze for a moment before pointing at Lisa. "Her."

"Lisa? Do you want me to introduce you?" she asked, recalling he'd asked about her in Las Vegas.

"Man, I told you before, she's not into kink," Logan said, warning him. "She's only here at Benediction tonight because she put this whole shindig together, and she's friends with the bride."

A smile pulled at Rachel's lips. She'd kept her promise to Lisa. She hadn't told a soul, including Logan, about Lisa's past experience with kink.

Maybe Sawyer was just the man to break Lisa's dry spell.

Sawyer's eyes twinkled mischievously. "Oh, I remember what you told me. But something tells me you're wrong."

Logan chuckled. "Okay, but after I introduce you, you're on your own. Don't come crying when she shoots you down."

The three of them crossed the grass to where Lisa was holding a glass of red wine. "Lisa," Rachel called out, "I'd like to introduce you to Logan's friend, Sawyer Hayes. Sawyer, this is Lisa Smith."

All the color drained from Lisa's face and the wineglass fell from her hand.

"Hello," Sawyer said, standing much closer to Lisa than what was considered polite. "It's nice to see you again, Annaliese."

"You know each other," Rachel said, sensing a story.

"You could say that," Sawyer said, not taking his eyes off Lisa for a second. "She's my wife."

Sawyer and Lisa are married?

Are you dying to know the story behind their relationship?

If so, don't miss the next Benediction novel…

BLACK LISTED

Coming Spring 2016

About the Author

SHELLY BELL writes sensual romance and erotic thrillers with high emotional stakes for her alpha heroes and kick-ass heroines. She began writing upon the insistence of her husband, who dragged her to the store and bought her a laptop. When she's not practicing corporate law, taking care of her family, or writing, you'll find her reading the latest smutty romance.

Shelly is a member of Romance Writers of America and International Thriller Writers.

Visit her website at ShellyBellBooks.com.

Discover great authors, exclusive offers, and more at hc.com.

Give in to your Impulses . . .
Continue reading for excerpts from
our newest Avon Impulse books.
Available now wherever e-books are sold.

THE BRIDE WORE RED BOOTS

A Seven Brides for Seven Cowboys Novel

By Lizbeth Selvig

RESCUED BY THE RANGER

By Dixie Lee Brown

ONE SCANDALOUS KISS

An Accidental Heirs Novel

By Christy Carlyle

DIRTY TALK

A Mechanics of Love Novel

By Megan Erickson

An Excerpt from

THE BRIDE WORE RED BOOTS

A Seven Brides for Seven Cowboys Novel

by Lizbeth Selvig

Amelia Crockett's life was going exactly the way she had always planned—until one day, it wasn't.

When Mia's career plans are shattered, the always-in-control surgeon has no choice but to head home to Paradise Ranch and her five younger sisters, cowboy boots in tow, to figure out how to get her life back on track. The appearance of a frustrating, but oh-so-sexy, former soldier, however, turns into exactly the kind of distraction she can't afford.

He studied her as if assessing how blunt he could be. With a wry little lift of his lip, he closed his eyes and lay all the way back onto the blanket, hands behind his head. "Honestly? You were just so much fun to get a rise out of. You'd turn all hot under the collar, like you couldn't figure out how anyone could dare counter you—the big-city doc coming to Hicksville with the answers."

The teasing tone of his voice was clear, but the words stung nonetheless. Funny. They wouldn't have bothered her at all a week ago, she thought. Now it hurt that he would ever think of her that way. She hadn't been that awful—she'd only wanted to put order to the chaos and bring a little rationality to the haywire emotions after her mother and sister's awful accident.

"Hey." She turned at the sound of his voice to find him sitting upright beside her again. "Amelia, I know better now. I know you. I'm not judging you—then or now."

Pricks of miniscule teardrops stung her eyes, the result of extreme embarrassment—and profound relief. She had no idea what to make of the reaction. It was neither logical nor something she ever remembered experiencing.

"I know."

To her horror, the roughness of her emotions shone through her voice, and Gabriel peered at her, his face a study in surprise. "Are you crying? Amelia, I'm sorry—I was just giving you grief, I wasn't—"

"I'm not crying." Her insistence held no power even though it wasn't a lie. No water fell from her eyes; it just welled behind the lids. "I'm not upset. I'm . . . relieved. I . . . it was nice, what you . . . said." She clamped her mouth closed before something truly stupid emerged and looked down at the blanket, picking at a pill in the wool's plaid pile.

A touch beneath her chin drew her gaze back up. Gabriel's eyes were mere inches from hers, shining with that beautiful caramel brown that suddenly looked like it could liquefy into pure sweetness and sex. Every masculine pore of his skin caught her attention and made her fingers itch to stroke the texture of his cheek. The scent of wind-blown skin and chocolate tantalized her.

"Don't be anything but what and who you are, Amelia Crockett."

His kiss brushed her mouth with the weightlessness of a Monarch on a flower petal. Soft, ethereal, tender, it promised nothing but a taste of pleasure and asked for nothing in return. Yet, as subtle as it was, it drove a punch of desire deep into Mia's core and then set her stomach fluttering with anticipation.

He pulled back but his fingers remained on her chin. "I'm sorry. That was probably uncalled for."

When his fingers, too, began to slide from her skin, she reacted without thinking and grabbed his hand. "No. It's . . .

It was . . . Gah—" Frustrated by her constant, unfamiliar loss for words, she leaned forward rather than let mortification set in and pressed a kiss against his lips this time, foregoing light and airy for the chance to taste him fully. Beneath the pressure, his lips curved into a smile. She couldn't help it then, her mouth mimicked his and they clashed in a gentle tangle of lips, teeth, and soft, surprised chuckles.

"Crazy," he said in a whisper, as he encircled her shoulders and pulled her closer.

"Yeah," she agreed and opened her mouth to invite his tongue to meet hers.

First kisses in Mia's experience were usually fraught with uncertainty and awkwardness about what should come next, but not this one. Kissing Gabriel seemed as natural and pleasurable as walking along a stunning stream full of rapids and eddies and satisfying things to explore. She explored them all and let him taste and enjoy right back. When at last they let each other go, her head continued to spin with surprise, and every nerve ending sparkled with desire.

[illegible] Calla—" Empowered by her constancy and familiar [illegible] words, she leaned forward rather than let [illegible] [illegible] a [illegible] upon his lips that [illegible] tight and [illegible] the changes [illegible] him fully. Beneath the pressure, his lips curved in a smile. She couldn't help it when his mouth [illegible] and they clashed in a gentle [illegible] of his teeth, and [illegible] surprised chuckle.

"Stay," he said [illegible] and pulled her down.

"Yes," she agreed and opened her mouth to invite his tongue to meet hers.

Their kisses [illegible] uncertain and awkward [illegible] about what she should [illegible] but not this one. [illegible] seemed unnatural and [illegible] as walking [illegible] full [illegible] and satisfying things to explore. She explored them all under [illegible] When [illegible] each other [illegible] continued [illegible] with surprise, and [illegible] sparkled with tears.

An Excerpt from

RESCUED BY THE RANGER

by Dixie Lee Brown

Army Ranger Garrett Harding is new in town—but not necessarily welcome. The only thing Rachel Maguire wants is to send this muscled military man packing. But when the stalker who destroyed her life ten years ago reappears, Rachel hits the road hoping to lure danger away from those she loves. Garrett won't let this sexy spitfire face trouble alone. He'll do anything to protect her. Even if it means risking his life—and his heart.

Pressed tight to the wall, Garrett waited. As she burst from cover, looking over her right shoulder and away from him, he stepped toward her. Catching her around the middle, he swung her off her feet and up against his body, holding her tightly with both arms. "It's me, Rach. Take it easy. I just want to talk."

She stopped struggling, so he loosened his hold as he set her back on her feet. Mistake number one. She dug her fingernails into his forearm, scratching until she drew blood. As soon as he leaned over her shoulder to grab her hand, she whacked his jaw with the back of her head, hard enough to send him stumbling back a step. He shook his head to clear the stars in time to see her swing that black bag.

"Wait a minute, Rachel!" Garrett tried to duck, but her shorter height gave her the advantage. She caught him across the side of the head, and there was apparently something heavy and damn hard in her bag. He staggered, lost his balance, and went down.

She looked surprised for a second before determination steeled her expression. "I told you not to look for me. What didn't you understand about that?" Shifting her bag onto her shoulder, she turned, and started running down the alley.

"Well, shit." Garrett glanced at Cowboy and damned if it didn't look like he was laughing. "Okay, already. You were right. Saddle up, Cowboy."

The dog took off, his long strides closing the distance to Rachel's retreating back easily. Garrett stood, brushing the dirt off and taking a moment to stretch the ache from the wound in his back. Then he jogged after the girl and the dog. He'd seriously underestimated Rachel today. Cowboy had his instructions to stop her, but keeping her there would require a whole different set of commands—ones that Garrett would never utter where Rachel was concerned.

Ahead of him, the dog ran circles around her, making the circle smaller each time. When she finally stopped, keeping a wary eye on the animal, Cowboy dropped to a walk, his tail wagging as he angled toward her. Though she didn't move, her body, tense and ready, said she was on high alert. Garrett picked up his pace to reach them.

Rachel looked over her shoulder, obviously noted the diminishing distance between them, and grabbed for her satchel. The next thing he knew, the damn hard object she'd hit him with—a small revolver—was in her hand and she was pointing it at Cowboy.

"You need to stay where you are, Garrett, and call your dog or . . . I'll shoot him."

"Cowboy, chill." The dog dropped to the ground, watching Garrett carefully. "This is what it's come to then? You want to get away from me so bad you're willing to shoot my dog?"

She shook her head dejectedly. "That's not what I want, but I will if I have to."

"I don't believe you, Rach. That dog's just following orders. My orders. Shoot me if you want to hurt somebody." Garrett moved a few steps closer.

Rachel laughed scornfully. "Did you miss the part where I tried to leave without anybody getting hurt?"

"No. I get that you're worried about Peg, Jonathan, and the rest of the people at the lodge, but damn it, Rachel, they love you. They want to understand. They want to help if they can, because that's what people do when they love someone. They don't sneak off in the night, leaving their *family* to wonder what happened."

"I can't—" She lowered the weapon until her hand hung at her side. Her eyes closed for a second, then she sat abruptly amidst the grass that bordered the alley.

Garrett walked up to her and knelt down. Prying the gun from her fingers, he placed it back in her bag and zipped it up. "Yes, you can. I'll help you." He tilted her chin up so he could see the sheen of her expressive green eyes. "Give me a chance, Rachel. What have you got to lose?"

"I don't believe you, Rachel. That doesn't fit with your pattern. My guess: Shoot me if you want to hurt somebody." Garrett moved a few steps closer.

Rachel laughed scornfully. "Did you miss the part where I tried to leave without anybody getting hurt?"

"No. I get that you're worried about Roy, Jonathan, and the rest of the people at the lodge, but damn it, Rachel, they love you. They want to understand. They want to help you, because that's what people do when they love someone. They don't sneak off in the night, leaving their family to wonder what happened."

"I can't—" She lowered the weapon until her hand hung at her side, eyes closed for a second, then she sat abruptly amid the grass that bordered the alley.

Garrett walked up to her and knelt down. Prying the gun from her fingers, he placed it back in her bag and zipped it up. "Yes, you can. I'll help you." He lifted her chin up so he could see the sheen of her expressive green eyes. "Give me a chance, Rachel. What have you got to lose?"

An Excerpt from

ONE SCANDALOUS KISS

An Accidental Heirs Novel

by Christy Carlyle

When a desperate Jessamin Wright bursts into an aristocratic party and shocks the entire ton, she believes it's the only way to save her failing bookstore. The challenge sounded easy when issued, but the one thing she never expected was to enjoy the outrageous embrace she shares with a serious viscount.

For the hundredth time, Jess called herself a fool for agreeing to Kitty Adderly's ridiculous plan for revenge against Viscount Grimsby. Kissing a viscount for one hundred pounds sounded questionable at the time Kitty had suggested it. Now Jess thought perhaps the jilted heiress had put something in her tea.

Initially she made her way into the crowded art gallery unnoticed, but then a woman dripping in diamonds and green silk had questioned her. When the lady's round husband stepped in, it all turned to chaos before she'd even done what she'd come to do. The deed itself shouldn't take long. A quick peck on the mouth—Kitty had insisted that she kiss the man on the lips—and it would all be over. She'd already handed the money over to Mr. Briggs at the bank. Turning back now simply wasn't an option.

She recognized Lord Grimsby from the gossip rag Kitty had shown her. The newspaper etching hadn't done him justice. In it, he'd been portrayed as dark and forbidding, his mouth a sharp slash, his black brows so large they overtook his eyes, and his long Roman nose dominating an altogether unappealing face. But in the flesh every part of his appearance harmonized into a striking whole. He was the sort of man she would have noticed in a crowd, even if she hadn't been seeking him, intent on causing him scandal and taking unimaginable liberties with his person.

He was there at the end of the gallery, as far from the entrance as he could possibly be. Jess continued through the gamut and a man snatched at her arm. Unthinking, she stepped on his foot, and he spluttered and cursed but released her.

Lord Grimsby saw her now. She noticed his dark head—and far too many others—turned her way. He was tall and broad shouldered, towering over the man and woman beside him. And he did look grim, as cold and disagreeable as Kitty had described.

Jessamin turned her eyes down, avoiding his gaze. Helpfully, the crowd parted before her, as if the respectable ladies and gentleman were unwilling to remain near a woman behaving so unpredictably. Every time she raised her eyes, she glimpsed eyes gone wide, mouths agape, and women furiously fanning themselves.

Just a few more steps and Jess stood before him, only inches between them. She met his gaze and found him glaring down at her with shockingly clear blue eyes. Furrowed lines formed a vee between his brows as he frowned at her like a troublesome insect had just spoiled his meal.

She opened her mouth to speak, but what explanation could she offer?

Every thought scattered as she studied her objective—or more accurately, his lips. They were wide and well-shaped but firmly set. Not as firm as stone, as Kitty claimed, but unyielding. Unwelcoming. Not at all the sort of lips one dreamed of kissing. But Jess had given up on dreams. Her choices now were about money, the funds she needed to keep the bookshop afloat for as long as she could.

Taking a breath and praying for courage, Jess reached up and removed her spectacles, folded them carefully, and hooked them inside the high neckline of her gown.

His eyes followed the movement of her hands, and the lines between his brows deepened.

Behind her, a woman shouted, "How dare you!" A hand grasped her from behind, the force of the tug pulling Jessamin backward, nearly off her feet. Then a deep, angry male voice rang out and stopped all movement.

"Unhand the woman. Now, if you please." He'd spoken. The stone giant. Lord Grim. He glared past her, over her head. Whoever gripped her arm released their hold. Then Lord Grim's gaze drilled into hers, his eyes discerning, not cold and lifeless as she'd expected.

For several heartbeats he simply watched her, pinning her with his gaze, studying her. Jess reminded herself to breathe.

"Are we acquainted, madam?"

The rumble of his voice, even amid the din of chatter around them, echoed through her.

She moved closer, and his eyebrows shot up. Oh, she'd crossed the line now. Bursting uninvited into a room filled with the wealthy and titled was one thing. Ignoring a viscount's question could be forgiven. Pressing one's bosom into a strange man's chest was something else entirely.

A surge of surprise and gratitude gripped her when he didn't move away.

Assessing his height, Jess realized she'd have to lift onto her toes if the kiss was to be accomplished. She took a step toward him, stretched up tall, and swayed unsteadily. He reached an arm out, and she feared he'd push her away. Instead he gripped her arm just above her elbow and held her steady.

A woman said his name, a tone of chastisement lacing the word. "Lucius."

Then she did it. Placing one hand on his hard chest to balance herself, Jess eased up on the tips of her boots and touched her lips to his.

An Excerpt from

DIRTY TALK

A Mechanics of Love Novel

by Megan Erickson

Brent Payton has a reputation for wanting to have fun, all the time. It's well-earned after years of ribbing his brothers and flirting with every girl he meets, but he's more than just a good time, even though nobody takes the time to see it. When a new girl walks into his family's garage with big thoughtful eyes and legs for days, this mechanic wants something serious for the first time.

Ivy Dawn is done with men, all of them. She and her sister uprooted their lives for them too many times and she's not willing to do it again. Avoiding the opposite sex at all costs seems easy enough, until the sexy mechanic with the dirty mouth bursts into her life.

Brent was the middle brother, the joker, the comic relief. The irresponsible one.

Never mind that he'd been working at this shop since he was sixteen. Never mind that he could do every job, inside and out, and fast as fuck.

Never mind that he could be counted on, even though no one treated him like that.

A pain registered in his wrist and he glanced down at the veins and tendons straining against the skin in his arm where he had a death grip on a wrench.

He loosened his fist and dropped the tool on the bench.

This wallowing shit had to stop.

This was his life. He was happy (mostly) and free (no ball and chain, no way) and so what if everyone thought he was a joke? He was good at that role, so the type-casting fit.

"Why so glum, sugar plum?" Alex said from beside him as she peered up into his face.

He twisted his lips into a smirk and propped a hip on the counter, crossing his arms over his chest. "I knew you had a crush on me, sweet cheeks."

She narrowed her eyes, lips pursed to hide a smile. "Not even in your dreams."

He sighed dramatically. "You're just like all the ladies. Wanna piece of Brent. There's enough to go around, Alex, no need to butter me up with sweet nicknames—"

A throat cleared. And Brent looked over to see a woman standing beside them, one hand on her hip, the other dangling at her side holding a paper bag. Her dark eyebrows were raised, full red lips pursed.

And Brent blinked, hoping this wasn't a mirage.

Tory, Maryland, wasn't big, and he'd made it his mission to know every available female in the town limits, and about a ten mile radius outside of that.

This woman? He'd never seen her. He'd surely remembered if he had.

Gorgeous. Long hair so dark brown, it was almost black. Perfect face. It was September, and still warm, so she wore a tight striped sundress that ended mid-thigh. She was tiny, probably over a foot smaller than him. Fuck, the things that little body made him dream about. He wondered if she did yoga. Tiny and limber was his kryptonite.

Narrow waist, round hips, big tits.

No ring.

Bingo.

He smiled. Sure, she was probably a customer, but this wouldn't be the first time he'd managed to use the garage to his advantage. Usually he just had to toss around a tire or two, rev an engine, whatever, and they were more than eager to hand over a phone number and address. No one thought he was a consummate professional anyway, so why bother trying to be one?

He leaned his ass against the counter, crossing his arms over his chest. "Can I help you?"

She blinked, long lashes fluttering over her big blue eyes. "Can you help me?"

"Yeah, we're full service here." He resisted winking. That was kinda sleazy.

Her eyes widened for a fraction before they shifted to Alex at his side, then back to him. Her eyes darkened for a minute, her tongue peeked out between those red lips, then she straightened. "No, you can't help me."

He leaned forward. "Really? You sure?"

"Positive."

"Like, how positive?

"I'm one hundred percent positive that I do not need help from you, Brent Payton."

That made him pause. She knew his name. He knew he'd never met her so that could only mean that she heard about him somehow and by the look on her face, it was nothing good.

Well shit.

He opened his mouth, not sure what to say, but hoping it came to him when Alex began cracking up next to him, slapping her thighs and snorting.

Brent glared at her. "And what's your problem?"

Alex stepped forward, threw her arm around the shoulder of the woman in front of them and smiled ear to ear. "Brent, meet my sister, Ivy. Ivy, thanks for making me proud."

They were both smiling now, that same full-lipped, white-teethed smile. He surveyed Alex's face, then Ivy's, and holy fuck, how did he not notice this right away? They almost looked like twins.

And the sisters were looking at him now, wearing matching smug grins and wasn't that a total cock-block. He pointed at Alex. "What did you tell her about me?"

"That the day I interviewed, you asked me to recreate a Whitesnake music video on the hood of a car."

He threw up his hands. "Can you let that go? You weren't even my first choice. I wanted Cal's girlfriend to do it."

"Because that's more appropriate," Alex said drily.

"Excuse me for trying to liven it up around here."

Ivy turned to her sister, so he got a better glimpse of those thighs he might sell his soul to touch. She held up the paper bag. "I brought lunch, hope that's okay."

"Of course it is," Alex said. "Thanks a lot, since someone stole my breakfast." She narrowed her eyes at Brent. Ivy turned to him slowly in disbelief, like she couldn't believe he was that evil.

Brent had made a lot of bad first impressions in his life. A dad of one of his high school girlfriends had seen Brent's bare ass while Brent was laying on top of his daughter before the dad ever saw Brent's face. That had not gone over well. And yet this one might be even worse.

Because he didn't care about what that girl's dad thought of him. Not really.

And he didn't want to care about what Ivy thought of him, but dammit, he did. It bothered the hell out of him that she'd written him off before even meeting him. Did Alex tell her any of his good qualities? Like . . . Brent wracked his brain for good qualities.

By the time he thought of one, the girls had already disappeared to the back room for lunch.